DEADLOCK

DEADLOCK

Graham Ison

This first world edition published 2018
in Great Britain and the USA by
SEVERN HOUSE PUBLISHERS LTD of
Eardley House, 4 Uxbridge Street, London W8 7SY.
Trade paperback edition first published
in Great Britain and the USA 2018 by
SEVERN HOUSE PUBLISHERS LTD.

British Library Cataloguing in Publication Data
A CIP catalogue record for this title is available from the British Library.

ISBN-13: 978-0-7278-8799-3 (cased)
ISBN-13: 978-1-84751-925-2 (trade paper)
ISBN-13: 978-1-78010-981-7 (e-book)

All Severn House titles are printed on acid-free paper.

Severn House Publishers support the Forest Stewardship Council™ [FSC™],
the leading international forest certification organisation.
All our titles that are printed on FSC certified paper carry the FSC logo.

Typeset by Palimpsest Book Production Ltd.,
Falkirk, Stirlingshire, Scotland.
Printed and bound in Great Britain by
TJ International, Padstow, Cornwall.

ONE

I t was five minutes to nine on a Tuesday morning in June, the eleventh to be precise, and I was about to drink my second cup of coffee of the day. I knew that my Murder Investigation Team was next on the list for any homicide that occurred in our area, and I was the detective chief inspector leading that team. But London being the lawless city it is, I didn't have long to wait.

Detective Sergeant Colin Wilberforce, the incident room manager, came into my office clutching some sort of electronic gizmo in his large hands. 'We've got one, sir. Female found in Richmond Park,' he announced. A slight smile crossed his craggy features, and he tugged at his cauliflower ear, doubtless the result of many scrums while playing rugby for the Metropolitan Police.

'Whereabouts in Richmond Park, Colin?'

'The Isabella Plantation, sir.' Wilberforce handed me a sheet of paper. He knew that I only dealt in paper; computers, clever telephones and other related toys were another world as far as I was concerned, and one I did not wish to explore. 'DI Ebdon's assembling the team, and Dave Poole is ready and waiting with the engine ticking over. And by the way, sir,' he said, glancing back at his electronic device, 'John Appleby's replacement has just arrived. A suave-looking finger by the name of Harvey.'

'At last. We've only been waiting since last August. Tell Miss Ebdon to take him with her. Nothing like going in at the deep end.'

'He's supposed to report to the commander at ten o'clock, sir.'

'He's had a lucky escape, then. If the commander asks where Harvey is, tell him DI Ebdon's taken him out for some hands-on experience.'

'Really, sir?' Wilberforce grinned. He obviously read a double entendre into my comment where I had not intended one to exist. 'I wonder if the commander will know what that means,' he muttered, half to himself.

'Watch it, Sergeant Wilberforce!' I said sharply.

'Sorry, sir.'

I waited until he'd left the office before I laughed.

The Homicide and Major Crime Command is divided into three groups, each of which covers a specific area of the Metropolitan Police District. The wedge-shaped piece to which I belong, HMCC West, is responsible for all the major villainy committed from the hinterland that is Hillingdon right the way down to Westminster. And if you imagine that Westminster is relatively crime-free, think again. There is nowhere in London that is now free of murder and mayhem, despite what our politicians may believe. It's a fool's paradise to think that the passing of an Act of Parliament will eradicate wrongdoing. Nevertheless, poor, overworked retainers like us have to enforce the law, regardless of race, colour or creed, and without fear or favour. And these days without adequate resources, thanks to our political masters who reside in cloud cuckoo land.

The Isabella Plantation is a forty-acre area of woodland gardens in the middle of Richmond Park, but this usually tranquil spot was now alive with police activity. Or to be accurate, police inactivity.

An inspector, clutching the indispensable clipboard, waggled a pen in Dave's direction. 'You shouldn't park that car on the grass, you know.'

Having recognized the inspector as a product of the forcing process known as accelerated promotion, Dave made a pantomime of looking under the car.

'I don't think so, sir,' he said. 'I make a point of never running over a grass. That, of course, is CID language for an informant,' he added by way of explanation.

'I'm Detective Chief Inspector Harry Brock, HMCC West,' I said, intervening before Dave got himself into trouble. I was not in the best of moods, having left my second cup of coffee untouched on my desk. 'And my sergeant will park wherever I tell him to park, Inspector.'

'Very good, sir.' The inspector gave up on the matter of grass desecration and pointed his pen at Dave. 'And you are?'

'Colour Sergeant Poole, ditto, sah!' said Dave, affecting a Jamaican sing-song accent, rocking his head from side to side and trying to look like a recently emancipated slave.

The inspector, confronted by a black detective sergeant making racial jokes about himself, swallowed hard and wrote down Dave's name. He was clearly at a loss to know whether Dave's comment breached the sacred rules of diversity, and wisely remained tight-lipped.

I should explain that Dave Poole is of Caribbean origin although he was born in Bethnal Green, where his grandfather, a medical doctor, had set up in general practice on his arrival from Jamaica in the fifties. Dave's father is an accountant, but Dave, after obtaining a good English degree at London University, joined the Metropolitan Police in what he described as a moment of madness. He somewhat provocatively refers to himself as the black sheep of the family for having decided not to pursue a professional career, but claims that he redeemed himself by marrying Madeleine, a petite principal dancer with the Royal Ballet.

The diminutive, short-haired Detective Inspector Jane Mansfield, a member of the Homicide Assessment Team and known as a HAT DI, was standing just behind the blue and white tape now surrounding the murder scene.

'What's the SP, Jane?' I asked, borrowing a term familiar to the horseracing fraternity but used by CID officers as shorthand to find out what had happened so far.

'A woman walking her dog came across the body at about half past seven, guv'nor. It was just a yard or two inside the plantation. Initial examination indicates that she was strangled, but there are no overt signs of sexual assault.'

'Where is this witness?' I asked.

'She was pretty shaken up, so I sent her home with a woman officer. I've obtained a short statement, but it might be as well to leave her for an hour or two before you interview her.' Mansfield referred to her clipboard. *Another clipboard!* 'She's Annette Kowalska who lives just outside the Kingston Gate,' she said, and added the woman's full address and telephone number.

'Is she Polish, Jane?'

'I didn't ask. She spoke perfect English. She could be second generation Polish, or just married to a Pole. Or both.' The tone of Mansfield's reply implied that the woman's nationality didn't matter a damn at this stage of the investigation or, come to that, at any stage. And she was right, of course.

'Is the pathologist here yet?'

'Dr Mortlock arrived about ten minutes before you did. He's camping out over there.' Mansfield pointed at the canvas screens surrounding the body.

'I didn't see his car.' It was impossible to miss Henry Mortlock's Mercedes with its distinctive maroon livery.

'We had to send a car for him. He said he wasn't sure of the way, and didn't fancy driving here from Chelsea in the rush hour anyway.'

'He's just being his usual idle self,' commented Dave sarcastically. 'There doesn't seem to be much traffic around here, anyway.' He waved a hand in the air to take in the entire park.

'Probably because the uniforms have closed the park,' said Mansfield. 'Much to the annoyance of those commuters who drive through it to get to work. Incidentally,' she continued, turning to me, 'the park was open yesterday from seven in the morning until ten o'clock last night.'

'Thanks for that, Jane. I'd better have a look at the body, I suppose.'

'The CSM has placed stepping plates between those tapes, guv.' Mansfield pointed to two narrow white tapes leading from where we were standing to the canvas screen surrounding my next dead body. It was a comment that caused me to remind Mansfield that this was not the first murder I'd investigated. I suppose I shouldn't have snapped, but I resent people trying to tell me my job. Linda Mitchell, the crime-scene manager, better known as the CSM, was extremely good at her job, and the delineated pathway would have been the first part of the murder scene to have been examined.

Dave and I crossed the few yards to the canvas screens just as Henry Mortlock emerged.

'Ah, good morning, Harry. Decent of you to drop by,' said Mortlock sarcastically.

'And good morning to you, too, Henry.'

Mortlock is a rotund man about five foot seven inches tall, and has recently affected pince-nez in place of the wire-framed antique spectacles he previously wore. But like the first set of glasses, this new set looks as though it has been moulded to his face. At first sight, he appears to have all the characteristics of the amiable family doctor in whom one can confide, but this belies the sharp temper he displays when confronted by people who annoy him. And they consist of the few who fail to understand his brief summary of the cause of death or – and these are the worst offenders – those who question his professional assessment of the situation.

'My initial opinion is that she was manually strangled,' announced Mortlock tersely. 'There are thumb marks on the back of the neck and fingermarks each side of the laryngeal prominence and just below the jawline. When I open her up, I'll probably find damage to the thyroid cartilage. Furthermore, I think she was probably strangled from behind. There are no signs of sexual interference, unless you think that a missing brassiere comes into that category.'

'Perhaps she wasn't wearing a bra in the first place?' suggested Dave. 'Some women don't bother these days.'

'It comes as no surprise to me that you're an expert on ladies' underwear, Sergeant Poole,' commented Mortlock drily. 'And, in particular, the removal thereof.'

'Time of death, Henry?' I asked.

'All things considered, I'd say between twelve and fifteen hours ago.'

'Just before the park closed, then,' said Dave.

'All right to let the crime-scene experts loose, Henry?' I asked.

'Yes, I've finished here, Harry. I'll let you know further particulars once I've got her on the slab and carved her up. It's ruined my hopes of a round of golf this afternoon.'

'There's a golf course here in the park, Doctor. Why don't you pop in there for a quick round now? I'm sure they'd be happy to lend you some mallets to play with.' Dave was in one of his pathologist-baiting moods this morning.

'Good God, Sergeant Poole! Do you seriously think I would

play on a *public* course?' Mortlock was clearly outraged at that suggestion, *and* that he should play with someone else's clubs. 'I suppose my chauffeur's here somewhere,' he said, glancing around. He picked up his bag of ghoulish instruments and went on his way whistling some obscure operatic aria. At least, I presumed that's what it was.

'Good morning, sir.' Kate Ebdon, one of the DIs on my team, is a flame-haired Australian. She has an impressive record as a detective, having served most of her time in the East End of London before coming to HMCC via the Flying Squad. Most of the time she is attired in jeans and a white shirt, much to the consternation of our beloved commander, who thinks that promotion to inspector automatically makes her an officer and a lady, and that she should dress accordingly. That said, she can 'tart herself up', as she puts it, when occasion demands, such as appearances at the Old Bailey, where her shapely figure, attractively dressed, has been described by more than one defence counsel as affording the prosecution an unfair advantage.

'There's not much to do here, I'm afraid, Kate. According to Jane Mansfield, there were no witnesses that we know of.'

'Oh, well, that's it, then,' said Kate dismissively. 'If that's what Mansfield said, there's no point in looking for any.' I'd sensed on previous occasions that some sort of enmity existed between Ebdon and Mansfield, but I'd never discovered the reason, and didn't care enough to ask.

'There are no houses within sight of the scene, so there are no house-to-house enquiries to be made. Dave and I will speak to the woman who found the body, and once the crime-scene experts have finished we can wrap it up here.'

'Has the victim been identified yet?' asked Kate.

'Not yet. The forensic people have only just been let loose on the body.'

'By the way, I've got our new DC with me.' Kate turned and beckoned to a twenty-something man who was talking to Jane Mansfield, and what's more was making her laugh. Most unusual. 'Steve, come and meet the guv'nor.'

Steve Harvey was wearing a suit and a tie. His leather shoes were polished, and his hair was a decent length. Such an ensemble was most unusual by today's generally accepted standards of slovenliness.

'Pleased to meet you, guv.' Harvey held out his hand. 'I understand that John Appleby was a good copper and very popular.'

'Yes, on both counts,' I said.

Harvey nodded. 'I reckon I've got a lot to live up to.'

'Don't even try,' said Dave. 'Just do your own thing. I'm DS Dave Poole. Welcome to the madhouse.'

'Thanks, Dave.'

Dave Poole reacted sharply to that. 'I understand you've come from the Flying Squad.'

'Yeah, that's right.'

'I don't know what the procedure is there, Harvey, but in this elite outfit, constables call sergeants by their rank. *Capisce?*'

'Sorry, Sarge.'

'Stick with Miss Ebdon for the time being, Steve,' I said. 'She's a damned good investigator and you'll learn a lot about homicide from her.' After a pause, I added, 'And don't upset Sergeant Poole. He's the best sergeant I've ever worked with.'

'I seem to have got off on the wrong foot, sir,' said Harvey ruefully. 'Perhaps I'd better go out and come in again.'

'No need for that,' said Dave. 'You can buy me a drink.'

'We've got an ID for the victim, Harry.' Linda Mitchell emerged from the screens. As usual, she was attired in a mob cap and coveralls designed to prevent contamination of the scene, and didn't look old enough to be the grandmother of a young woman who had just become engaged. 'She's Rachel Steele, aged twenty-five, and her address is 25 Superior Drive, Camden Town.'

'Superior Drive in Camden Town, Linda? You've got to be kidding.'

'One of my team lives in that neck of the woods and knows the area well. Apparently it used to be called Asylum Road, but that's not considered quite the thing in these days of political correctness. Consequently, they changed it to Superior Drive, added to which it's been gentrified.'

'How did you identify her so quickly?' I asked.

'Her shoulder bag contained a wallet with a driving licence and credit cards. She also had about a hundred pounds in cash and a set of house keys.'

'Robbery wasn't the motive, then,' I mused aloud.

'That would appear to be the case, *sir*,' said Dave, emphasizing the honorific. He always called me 'sir' whenever I made a stupid comment.

'Anything else on her person?' I asked, ignoring Dave's sideswipe.

'A smartphone,' said Linda. 'We'll check her contact list and let you have details of the numbers, and any photographs there are on it. You never know, she might have taken a selfie with her killer.'

'That'd be a first,' said Dave.

'All right to have a look at the body?' I asked.

'Yes, we've done most of the close quarter stuff. I don't know if the pathologist mentioned it, Harry, but there are marks on her shoulders and her back that indicate she was wearing a bra when she was killed. No bra was found in the vicinity of the body, but it might somewhere else in the park, of course.'

'It looks as though the killer took it with him,' said Dave.

'You're assuming the killer was a man, then, *Sergeant*,' I said, determined to have a little tilt at Dave.

The body of Rachel Steele was lying on its back, in an attitude almost of repose. She had long brown hair and appeared to be about five foot seven or eight, but Mitchell would let me know the woman's exact dimensions in due course. Her left hand, palm down, displayed a wedding ring and a rather ostentatious engagement ring. The only jarring features about the whole scene were the livid fingermarks around the woman's throat that Mortlock had described. As far as I could see, her shirt had not been ripped off, but had been carefully undone so that it was off the shoulders and arms, leaving her naked breasts exposed, presumably to facilitate the removal of her bra. If it had been removed by her killer – and I couldn't think of anyone else who might have done so – it presented us with a disturbing possibility: that we could be looking for a trophy-hunting homicidal maniac.

'Any chance of fingerprints from those marks on her neck, Linda?'

'I'll do my best, Harry, but I'm not making any promises at this stage. He might've worn gloves.'

'What, this weather?' asked Dave.

Mitchell gave him the sort of sorrowful look that she reserved for non-scientists. 'Persons of a malevolent disposition have been known to wear gloves to avoid being identified, Dave,' she said, and then smiled.

'We'll have a word with the witness who found her now, Dave,' I said.

On our way back to the car, I stopped by the clipboard-wielding inspector.

'As a matter of interest, Inspector, have you questioned the police who were on duty yesterday? They might have seen something of significance.'

'They wouldn't have done, sir.'

'You seem very sure.'

The inspector lowered his voice and looked furtive. 'There was only one PC on duty in the park yesterday, sir, and he spent the day in the police post at Holly Lodge fielding daft enquiries.'

'One PC to cover two thousand five hundred acres?'

'I'm afraid so,' said the inspector, 'but don't blame me. Blame the budget cuts.'

A barking dog greeted our knock when we arrived at Annette Kowalska's house. Seconds later a woman opened the door, holding a struggling Jack Russell in her arms.

'Horris is quite safe,' said the woman. 'The worst that will happen is that he'll lick you to death.'

'Are you Ms Annette Kowalska?' I asked.

'Yes, I'm Mrs Kowalska.' She was in her late forties or early fifties, soberly dressed in a tweed skirt, a long-sleeved sweater and what my mother would've described as sensible walking shoes. It struck me that she was overdressed for the current warm weather, but maybe she was accustomed to a tropical climate and felt the cold of an English summer.

'I'm Detective Chief Inspector Harry Brock, Mrs Kowalska,

of the Murder Investigation Team, and this is Detective
Sergeant Poole.'

'You've come to see me about that poor woman, I suppose.
You'd better come in. Would you like some coffee? I've just
made some.' We followed her into her comfortable sitting
room, and she invited us to take a seat.

'Thank you,' I said. 'Coffee would be most welcome. Has
the police officer who brought you home gone now?'

'Oh, yes. It was very kind of her but quite unnecessary. I
must admit that I had a large whisky when I got home.' Annette
Kowalska afforded us a quick smile of guilt. 'I never drink
until the evening, and not always then, but it was such a terrible
shock, seeing that poor young woman, that I had a double the
minute I got in. I won't be a tick.'

She returned a few minutes later with a cafetière on a large
wooden tray, together with cream, sugar and cups and saucers,
and set it down on a coffee table between the sofa on which
Dave and I were seated and the armchair in which she settled.

'I understand that you were out walking your dog.'

'Yes, it's a morning ritual, winter and summer,' began Mrs
Kowalska as she poured the coffee.

'What time was this?' asked Dave, pocketbook at the ready.

'The park opens at seven o'clock, by which time Horris is
sitting by the front door, letting me know it's time for his
walk. Unless it's raining. He doesn't like going out in the
rain. He's a very intelligent dog and loves the television,
particularly country life programmes. He'll sit quietly and
watch everything. Most mornings,' she continued, hardly
pausing for breath, 'I drive up to the car park by Broomfield
Hill Wood, just inside the park gates, and leave the car there.
It was quite by chance that I went into the Isabella Plantation
this morning; I don't always go that way. We like to vary our
morning walk. In fact, Horris usually dictates which way we
go.' Mrs Kowalska leaned down to fondle the dog's ears.
'Don't you, Horris?'

'As a matter of interest, what did you do when you found
the dead woman?' From what the inspector had said about
understaffing, I knew that she wouldn't have accosted a passing
copper; there wasn't one to accost.

'I called the police, of course.' Mrs Kowalska adopted a surprised expression that implied that as a police officer I should have known that. 'On my mobile phone.'

'How long did it take you to walk from the car to where you found the body, Mrs Kowalska?' asked Dave, as he busily wrote down the woman's answers.

'I did tell all this to that young lady detective in the park,' protested Mrs Kowalska mildly. 'A Miss Mansfield, it was.'

'I appreciate that,' I said, 'but this is a murder inquiry and we have to make sure that everything is as accurate as we can possibly make it.'

'Yes, I suppose so.'

'Does Mr Kowalski ever take the dog for a walk?' asked Dave innocently. It was an oblique attempt to discover if Mrs Kowalska was married, it being in a detective's nature to collect apparently useless information.

'There is no Mr Kowalski,' said Mrs Kowalska tartly, and left it at that. And so did we.

'What time would it have been when you actually found this young woman, Mrs Kowalska?' I asked.

She considered the question before answering. 'It would have been about half past seven, or maybe a quarter to eight, I suppose. I didn't think to look at my watch. I was so distressed at finding her. I'd never seen a dead body before.'

It didn't matter; the time of her emergency call would have been recorded by the police operator.

'Did you touch her at all?' I asked. And before the inevitable protest, I added, 'We have to be sure, just in case the body had been moved, even in the slightest way. It could make a difference to our investigation, you see.'

'Oh, good heavens, no!' Mrs Kowalska shuddered slightly at the thought. 'I couldn't.'

'I don't think there's anything else,' I said, as Dave and I stood up. 'If there is, we have your telephone number. And thank you for the coffee.'

'Have you found out who she is?' Mrs Kowalska asked as she conducted us to the front door.

'Not yet, no.' We knew the identity of the victim, of course, but these days the first thought anybody seems to have is how much a newspaper would pay them for the story. Even ostensibly respectable ladies like Mrs Kowalska may be tempted by chequebook journalism.

'Well, that didn't tell us much, guv,' said Dave, as we got into the car. 'What now?'

'Superior Drive, Camden Town, Dave.' I rang the incident room and told them where we were going.

TWO

After grabbing a quick lunch, Dave and I made our way to Camden Town. Considering the state of London traffic these days, we reached there in a remarkably short time.

The house at 25 Superior Drive was a terraced dwelling and the gentrification that had taken place appeared to be superficial, but we had yet to see the inside. The white-framed double glazing had plastic strips inserted between the sheets of PVC to create what is known as the cottage effect. The house number was white on a small enamel plate in French blue, a design popular in France and much loved by the chattering classes, who liked to give the impression of being much-travelled Francophiles. Alongside the house number was a wind chime which probably so infuriated the neighbours that it must be overdue for vandalization.

I rang the bell with little hope that I'd find anyone at home at this time on a Tuesday afternoon. But I was surprised.

The man who came to the door was tall, thirtyish and would probably have been described by some women as good looking. He wore khaki shorts, a T-shirt and glasses with heavy black frames. There was a crumpled copy of the *Guardian* held loosely in one hand, and a fierce expression on his face. Perhaps he was expecting itinerant salesmen and was prepared to repel boarders.

'Mr Steele?'

'Yes, I'm Daniel Steele. What is it?'

'We're police officers, Mr Steele. May we come in?'

My statement evinced no surprise. In my experience, the reaction to such a visit was often fear that some wrongdoing had been discovered and an arrest was about to take place, or concern that such a visit heralded bad news. But in Steele's case nothing, and that made me immediately suspicious.

'I am rather busy,' said Steele. 'Will it take long?'

'It's about Mrs Rachel Steele,' I said. 'I take it she's your wife.'

'She is at the moment.' Steele adopted a hunted look and glanced past me as though expecting someone else. 'You'd better come in,' he said, hurriedly pulling open the door. It seemed that even in Superior Drive the neighbours were not above earwigging. He showed us into the small front room of the house and invited us to sit down. The room was not very well furnished, at least not by my standards. On the bare floorboards were two weirdly shaped wooden armchairs which appeared too weak to support a human; a metal-framed sofa which looked distinctly uncomfortable – and proved to be so; a metal shelving unit holding a number of 'coffee table' books, doubtless displayed to impress visitors; and a television set. It looked more like a furniture warehouse than a living room. Needless to say, there were one or two abstract pictures on the walls that looked like the daubings of a five-year-old. Perhaps they were.

'You said Mrs Steele was your wife *at the moment*, Mr Steele,' I began, after I had introduced ourselves. 'What exactly did you mean by that?'

'We're going through a rather messy divorce, Chief Inspector. It seems to be dragging on and on, mainly because of a dispute about the division of the spoils.' Then, somewhat belatedly, Steele asked, 'But why are you asking questions about Rachel?'

There seemed to be no point in breaking the news gently – in fact, there's never a gentle way – but in this case, I got the impression that the death of Rachel was not going to burden him with grief. 'Your wife was found dead this morning in Richmond Park, Mr Steele. She'd been murdered.'

'Good Lord!' As I'd anticipated, Steele's face displayed no signs of shock or distress at the news of his wife's death. Perhaps he was trying desperately to avoid looking pleased that he would now keep all his own possessions, as well as inheriting his late wife's assets. Unless *he* had murdered her, of course. If that were the case, he would get nothing but a lengthy prison sentence. 'What on earth was she doing in Richmond Park?'

'We have to ask where you were yesterday, Mr Steele,' said Dave, countering Steele's question with one of his own.

'I was at work, all day.'

'Where is work?'

'I work for a firm of financial traders in the City, and I was there from seven yesterday morning until about nine last night.' Steele ferreted about in the back pocket of his shorts and eventually handed Dave a dog-eared business card. I wondered why he carried business cards in his shorts, but policemen are naturally curious creatures.

'And after that?' Dave was like a dog with a bone once he started asking questions.

'I took a girl out to dinner.'

'We'll need her name.'

'Why on earth should you want that?' demanded Steele, staring at Dave. 'There's nothing underhand about it. My wife and I have had an open marriage for several years now.'

'We're not marriage guidance counsellors, Mr Steele,' I said. 'Your wife has been murdered and it's our job to find out who was responsible. Unless I can satisfy myself that you have an alibi for the period in question, I'm afraid we'll have to continue this interview at Kentish Town police station.'

'Are you arresting me?' The expression on Steele's face betrayed a mixture of amusement and apprehension.

'Not unless I have to.'

'Her name's Stephanie Payne,' he said with apparent reluctance. 'She sits at the next workstation to mine. We've been dating for about a year now.'

'What time did you and she part company last night?'

'She stayed the night, and we parted company at about six o'clock this morning.' Steele's face assumed a lascivious smirk, presumably at the memory.

'I take it your wife no longer lives here, then,' I suggested.

'Oh, but she does. We have a Doodle on our smartphones, you see.'

As far as I was aware a doodle was an absent-minded scribble, but before I had a chance to make a fool of myself Dave stepped in with one of his cynical observations. 'I suppose it saves making embarrassing double-bookings. And did your wife say that she would be out yesterday, or more particularly yesterday evening?'

'I'd reserved last night on the Doodle, so Rachel knew I'd be making full use of the bedroom here,' Steele said with a superior lift of his chin. 'Anyway, she was probably shacked up with her current squeeze. We don't enquire into each other's relationships.'

'Have you any idea who the man was that she was seeing?' I asked.

'No idea at all, I'm afraid, although his name might be on her smartphone,' said Steele, as though he didn't give a damn. 'As I said earlier, we've been living separate lives for some time now. I don't ask who she's screwing and she doesn't ask me. It's a very civilized agreement.'

'Do you know the names of *any* of the men she's been seeing?' I was beginning to become a little exasperated with the supercilious Steele who, together with his late wife, appeared to have been in a marriage governed entirely by modern technology.

'No, I'm sorry.'

'As a matter of interest, why aren't you at work today?' asked Dave.

'I'm having a break for a few days. Catching up on things, you know.'

'We'll probably need to see you again, Mr Steele,' I said, as Dave and I eased ourselves out of his uncomfortable sofa.

'One other point, Mr Steele,' said Dave. 'Did you and Rachel Steele enter into a prenup agreement before you married?'

There was a short pause before Steele answered Dave's question. 'Er, no,' he said, and moved swiftly on. 'I suppose I'll have to arrange the funeral.' He looked thoroughly fed up at the prospect. 'I'll have to contact her parents as well. They live in Guildford.' He sighed, probably at the disruption this would cause to his cosy little closeted world.

'You won't be able to do anything until the coroner author-izes the release of the body,' said Dave, 'but in the meantime you can give me the name and address of Rachel's parents.'

Afterwards we walked out to the car. Suddenly the air seemed fresher, even for Camden Town.

'What d'you think, Dave?'

'He could be guilty, the callous, snooty bastard,' muttered Dave. 'How many toppings have we investigated where the husband turns out to be the killer, guv'nor?'

'I've lost count, but if that's the case with Steele, surely he'd try to put on a show of being devastated?'

'Perhaps it's a double bluff,' said Dave, as he started the engine. 'Anyway, we'll be able to check his alibi with Stephanie Payne.'

'He's probably on the phone to her right now, fixing up a story.'

'Yeah, probably.' Dave laughed; he knew how to deal with that sort of collusion.

'No time like the present to speak to the aforesaid Ms Stephanie Payne, Dave. Drive on.'

We entered the underground car park of the tower block where Steele's firm had its offices and rode up to the ground floor. A security guard directed us to a bank of lifts and told us which floor we needed.

We were confronted by another security guard at the entrance to the firm of traders where Steele worked. His officious attitude turned rapidly to one of sycophancy the moment we identified ourselves and told him who we wished to see. He promptly directed us to the office of someone he described as the *grand fromage*.

The woman into whose office we were shown seemed remarkably young to be holding down such a responsible post but Charlie Flynn, the former Fraud Squad officer on my team, once told me that people in this sort of business are burned out by the time they're forty.

'I'm Detective Chief Inspector Harry Brock, and this is Detective Sergeant Poole. We're attached to a Murder Investigation Team at Scotland Yard.'

'I'm Jessica.' Unfazed by my awesome announcement, the woman shook hands with a strong grasp. 'Please sit down.' I presumed that financial trading was the sort of business where first names were considered sufficient of an introduction. 'Who's been murdered?' There was a smile on her face, as though we were all taking part in one of those murder mystery evenings where the feckless and bored like to pretend they're detectives but without getting their hands dirty.

'Daniel Steele's wife,' I said. That wiped the smile from her face.

'Good grief! That's why he didn't show up for work this morning.'

'Didn't he ring to tell you about his wife, Jessica?' asked Dave innocently. It was a trick question designed to see if Daniel Steele had known of his wife's death before we told him, thereby displaying guilty knowledge.

'No. He just didn't show.' Jessica looked quite distressed at the news.

'How well do you know Daniel?' I asked. I wondered if there was anything more than a work-related relationship between the two of them.

'Not very well at all. He's just a work colleague,' said Jessica. If there had been more, she obviously wasn't going to admit to it.

'I understand that Stephanie Payne was one of Mr Steele's colleagues, Jessica. Would it be possible to have a word with her?'

Jessica looked puzzled. 'I've never heard of her. Stephanie Payne, did you say?' She gazed briefly out of the window of her goldfish bowl of an office at the vast sea of computer-operating traders, doubtless busily amassing fortunes, either for themselves or for their clients. 'No, sorry, the name doesn't mean a thing.'

'We interviewed Mr Steele earlier today, and he told us that she occupied the workstation next to his.' I decided to abandon any concern for Steele's reputation. 'But he also told us that he slept with her last night, so she's a bit more than a work colleague.' That wasn't exactly what he'd said, but an indisputable inference could be drawn from his actual words.

'Did he indeed?' Jessica managed to inject an element of pique into those three words, and I wondered if her denial of a close relationship with Steele really was the truth. 'Well, I can assure you, Chief Inspector, that I've never heard of a Stephanie Payne. I've been here for four-and-a-half years and no one of that name has worked in this office during that time.' She stood up and walked to the window. 'If you look down the second row from the left, Chief Inspector, you'll see a guy with red braces. The space next to him is where Daniel sits, and the girl on the other side of Daniel's vacant chair is called Emma, not Stephanie Payne.' She returned to her seat. 'Would you like me to phone you when Daniel returns?'

'That would be helpful, although I have a suspicion it may be some time before you see him again.' I gave Jessica my card with the phone number of the incident room.

'What would Mr Steele be worth?' asked Dave. 'Financially, I mean.'

Jessica weighed up the question for a moment or two, and I wondered if she would refuse to answer. Or maybe she didn't know.

'It'll be well over a million by now, I should think,' she said eventually. 'Could be more, but it's always difficult to estimate in this game. He's certainly received very good bonuses in recent years, and he's been here longer than I have. I think he's been with this firm for about eight years.'

That casual reply made me wonder how much Jessica was worth. 'Thanks for your help,' I said, as we prepared to leave.

'D'you know when Rachel's funeral will take place?' Jessica asked, a concerned expression on her face.

'We've no idea,' said Dave, and explained about the coroner having to release the body.

I found it odd that Jessica knew Steele's wife's name, since she'd said she didn't know Daniel Steele at all well. Perhaps there was more to her – and him – than was at first apparent. On the other hand, perhaps the firm kept records of next of kin of its staff. Even so, I wouldn't have expected Jessica to have the name at her fingertips.

'Interesting that Steele's said to be worth over a million at least, and that he and his wife didn't have a prenup,' said Dave as we made our way back to the car park. 'Sounds awfully like a motive for murder. However, what now, guv'nor?'

'Back to Camden Town.' I rang the incident room and brought Kate Ebdon up to speed on the progress we had made so far, which wasn't a great deal. 'Just in case Steele's done a runner, Kate, would you get a search warrant for twenty-five Superior Drive as quickly as possible, and meet us at the address.' Kate was pretty good at sweet-talking district judges, and I was sure she wouldn't waste any time.

It was seven o'clock by the time Kate arrived at Superior Drive, but she had the warrant and the house keys that had been taken from Rachel Steele's shoulder bag. I rang the bell but, as I'd anticipated, there was no answer and we let ourselves in.

The search was rather disappointing. There were no signs of a hurried departure, and no open wardrobes as though packing had taken place in a tearing hurry. There was, however, an unmade bed and all the rooms were in a state of untidiness. But perhaps this was the way he lived all the time. And that made me wonder whether Rachel really did still live here, albeit on and off, as Steele had said.

Kate went through all the usual checks: the fridge was fully stocked, there were no messages on the answering machine and no note left out for the milkman. But perhaps people don't have milk deliveries any more. I certainly don't, for the very simple reason that I never know whether I'll be there to take it in.

'I had a look in the bathroom cabinet and on the dressing table, guv,' said Kate. 'Perfume, make-up and all the usual things that are vital to a woman were there, and it's expensive stuff. Not that that really tells us anything, except . . .'

'Except what, Kate?'

'When we examined the body of Rachel Steele in Richmond Park she was wearing Estée Lauder Private Collection, but the perfume in the bathroom cabinet is Joy by Jean Patou.'

'I'm sorry, Kate, but you've lost me.'

'I don't think that Rachel Steele lived here at all. I think that Daniel Steele is shacked up with another woman, because Rachel would never wear Joy if she usually wore Estée Lauder. They're entirely different.'

All of which demonstrated how useful it was to have a woman detective on the team. And the matter of the perfume perhaps made Daniel Steele a stronger suspect for his wife's murder. It now became imperative to interview him again, and this time under caution. I was about to abandon the search of the house when the door chimes played a pretentious little tune.

'See who that is, Dave,' I said, following him to the front door. 'It might be Stephanie Payne.'

'We should be so lucky,' said Dave.

The woman who stood on the step was in her late twenties, I guessed, and appeared a little alarmed that a large black man had opened the door. Nevertheless, she immediately recovered.

'What are you people doing in Dan's house?' she demanded, hands on hips. This was clearly one feisty woman.

'We're police officers,' said Dave.

'Oh yeah?'

Dave produced his warrant card. 'Detective Sergeant Poole, Murder Investigation Team.'

'*Oh my God!* Who's been murdered? Not Dan, surely.'

'Who are you?' asked Dave.

'Natasha Stephens. I live next door.'

'Come in,' I said, from behind Dave. 'I'm Detective Chief Inspector Brock, and this is Detective Inspector Ebdon.'

The woman stepped into the small hall and I ushered her into the living room – the only tidy room in the house – and invited her to take a seat.

'You told my sergeant that your name is Natasha Stephens. Is that *Mrs* Stephens?'

'Yes, it is, but please call me Tash. Everyone does.'

'Who did you think we were,' I asked, 'when you knocked at the door?'

'I thought you might be burglars. I'm the Neighbourhood Watch coordinator.'

'Good grief!' exclaimed Kate. 'A little unwise of you to confront a gang of burglars, Tash. You should've called the police.'

'You're right, of course. I didn't think; silly me,' said Tash. 'But why are you here? You mentioned murder just now.'

'We're investigating the murder of Daniel Steele's wife,' I said.

'Rachel's dead?' Tash Stephens was clearly distressed by

that news, and paled slightly. 'But what on earth happened to her? They were such a lovely couple.'

'Lovely couple or not,' I continued, 'they were on the point of divorce.'

'Divorce!' Tash laughed scornfully. 'Who on earth told you that?'

'Daniel Steele told us,' said Dave.

Tash Stephens shook her head in disbelief. 'But neither of them said anything to me about getting divorced. They seemed devoted to each other. In fact, they often came to us for dinner, and we came here.'

'How long ago was the last time you and your husband teamed up with Daniel and Rachel?'

'About three weeks ago, I suppose, but I spoke to her on the phone this afternoon.'

'And you're sure it was Rachel Steele?'

'Absolutely.' Natasha Stephens paused. 'Well, it sounded like her. Yes, of course it was her.'

'What did she ring you about?'

'To tell me that she and Dan were going on holiday. She said they were jetting off to the Seychelles. I suppose it must've been a last-minute thing, but they often decided to push off like that. She said they'd be away for about three weeks and asked me if I'd keep an eye on the house.'

'Did she give you a key?'

'She gave me one some time ago, just in case anything happened. I was a bit reluctant at first because I was afraid I might lose it. I'm a bit of a scatterbrain, you see.' Tash made a circling motion with a forefinger at the side of her head. 'But I gave in and took it.'

'Why didn't you use it to come in, then?' asked Dave.

'I couldn't find it. I told you, I'm a scatterbrain. I'd lose my head if it wasn't screwed on.' She gave an embarrassed little giggle.

'How long have you lived next door to the Steeles?' Dave asked.

'Just over a year now.'

'I'm going to take you into my confidence, Tash, in your capacity as the Neighbourhood Watch coordinator,' I said. 'But

I have to have your absolute assurance that you will keep this to yourself.'

'Absolutely. Mum's the word.' She made a zipping motion across her mouth.

'It is vitally essential that we speak to Daniel Steele, but he mustn't know we want to talk to him. I'll give you my card with my mobile number on it, and you can call me at any time if he comes back.'

The thought of assisting a Scotland Yard officer in the investigation of a murder obviously impressed Natasha Stephens, and I knew that we had her on our side. I didn't think for one moment that Steele would return, but now that I had wound up Tash and pointed her in the right direction, she would report anything at all that she thought might be useful to us. All right, so that would include a load of trivia, but there might just be a tiny piece of gold among the dross.

'Would you be able to give us a description of Rachel Steele, Tash?' asked Kate.

'Of course,' said Tash Stephens, without asking why. She must have known that we'd seen Rachel's dead body, but perhaps it hadn't crossed her mind. She was, after all, a self-confessed scatterbrain.

'Go ahead, Tash.' Dave opened his pocketbook.

'She was tall, nearly as tall as Dan, I suppose, and she had long blonde hair and an enviable figure. She must've spent hours in the gym, and she certainly swam a lot. In fact, she said her ambition was to swim the Channel. Oh, and she had very blue eyes, and what my husband described as provocative lips.'

The description Natasha Stephens had just given us was nothing like the Rachel Steele we'd seen lying dead in Richmond Park.

'Does the name Stephanie Payne mean anything to you, Tash?' I asked.

The woman shook her head without hesitation. 'Sorry, no. I've never heard of her. Does she live around here?'

'Right now, we've no idea where she lives,' I admitted, although I was coming rapidly to the conclusion that she lived right here. 'But we are anxious to interview her, and we are here because we wanted to talk to Mr Steele again.'

'Again? You've seen him already?'

'Early this afternoon.'

'That was lucky. You must've caught him just before he left.'

I didn't think it was luck. Our visit, coming so soon after Rachel Steele's death, had obviously alarmed him, and he'd lost no time in doing a runner.

'Did you see them leave?'

'I only saw Daniel. That was about three o'clock. As a matter of fact, he paused just as he was getting into his car. A lovely BMW, it is.' A dreamy expression briefly crossed Tash's face. 'He said he was picking up Rachel from the beauty parlour and they were going straight to the airport.'

'I think that's all for the time being, Tash,' I said. 'But I've no doubt we'll be speaking to you again soon.'

THREE

I t was close to half past ten by the time we returned to the incident room at Belgravia police station. While we'd been working, our beloved commander, a strict ten-to-six man, had arrived and departed.

I was by no means certain that Steele and the woman, whoever she was, would have gone to Heathrow, the obvious airport. Consequently, I instructed Gavin Creasey, the night-duty incident room manager, to send messages to *all* airports asking them to check for any details of Steele's departure and possible return, which should be sent to me as a matter of urgency. I also made a formal request to all airports and seaports for his arrest, on suspicion of murder, together with the woman claiming to be his wife, but added that they were not to be questioned. Not that I had much hope of tracking him down that easily.

That done, I told Creasey to ask the police at Heathrow, Gatwick, Stansted and City airports to arrange a check of the car parks to see if Steele's BMW was there. Tash Stephens, who proved to be more than just a pretty face, had made a note of all the index marks of cars belonging to the residents of Superior Drive in case one of them was ever stolen. She thought that half the people living there didn't know the numbers of their cars, and it was part of the duties of the Neighbourhood Watch coordinator, she told Kate Ebdon, to make sure these were logged. Kate wasn't particularly impressed.

Finally, as a belt-and-braces precaution, I had Daniel Steele flagged up on the Police National Computer as a person of interest, in case he came to the notice of police in any other way – like speeding, for instance. I held out little hope, however, that Steele and his partner would return in the fore-seeable future. If we were obliged to move into the murky waters of extradition, we would require more evidence than

we had amassed so far. Apart from which, I would need to
know that the couple really had gone to the Seychelles and
not somewhere else in the world.

It was the end of a very long day, and I sent the team home.
An hour later, I went home myself.

I could describe Gladys Gurney as my cleaning lady, but that
would be very wide of the mark; she does much more
than that. She appears, rarely seen by me, in my humble
Surbiton flat and cleans it to such a high standard that I'm
sure even a Grenadier Guards sergeant major would have
difficulty finding fault.

Today was no different. The flat was sparkling clean and
immaculately tidy, my few items of crockery washed up and
put away; it seemed an unnecessary expense to buy a dish-
washer. The bed had been made, my shirts gathered up from
where I'd hung them on the floor of the bedroom and washed
and ironed. And for good measure, she'd rooted out a couple
of shirts I'd forgotten I owned and pressed them. Finally, there
was one of her charming little notes.

Dear Mr Brock,
   I haven't not found any of your lady friend's underwear
lying about in the bedroom/bathroom not for some time
now. I hope she's all right and that she hasn't not run
away with someone else. Give her my best when you sees
her next time.
                          Yours faithfully,
                       Gladys Gurney (Mrs)

Alas, Gladys, I soliloquized, Gail Sutton has left me for the
bright lights of Tinseltown and shows no signs of wanting to
return to dull old Britain from Los Angeles. I used to nurture
hopes that she might one day come back, but knew that those
hopes were most likely in vain.

As for my new girlfriend, Lydia Maxwell, I doubt if she
is the sort to leave intimate items of underwear lying around
on bedroom floors, apart from which she has yet to visit
my flat.

It was a telephone call from Bill Hunter at the beginning of last November, inviting me to dinner, that had put me in touch with Lydia Maxwell again. She'd lived in the apartment next to the murder victim who had been the subject of my last investigation, and for a time had herself been regarded as a suspect in the murder.

Although the affluent, widowed thirty-eight-year-old Mrs Maxwell had said that she intended to move out of her apartment and into a house, preferably one with its own swimming pool, I'd no idea where she'd gone. And to be perfectly honest, I wasn't much interested. In the course of a murder investigation you meet a lot of people, and once the trial's over you tend to forget all about them, usually because you're dealing with another murder and another set of people. Unfortunately, the last investigation was memorable for resulting in the murder of our own Detective Constable John Appleby.

Bill and his wife Charlotte Hunter, an actress, had been friends of Gail Sutton and I'd met them through her, before Gail had been unable to resist the offer of a mouth-watering fee for a part in an American soap.

Knowing what the Hunters' hospitality was like, I had not driven there. I'd taken a taxi to Esher, but was half an hour late arriving because taxis at Surbiton railway station had suddenly been in demand, added to which the driver didn't know Esher that well. The clocks had gone back the previous weekend, the night was chilly and it was spitting with rain. All in all, the weather promised a dark and rather wretched evening.

The Hunters' palatial residence in Esher is one of half a dozen situated on a gated estate. It boasts six bedrooms, each with an en-suite bathroom, a huge dining room and a spacious drawing room, and probably a host of other rooms I'd never seen. An extensive garden sports a swimming pool at one end, housed in a cedarwood chalet. Did I mention that the Hunters were filthy rich?

Bill Hunter, whose sweater must have cost more than my suit, opened the door and almost dragged me inside.

'Thank God you're here, Harry. I had a nasty feeling that you'd been called out at the last minute. I know these things happen in your line of business, but if something crops up to ruin one of Charlie's dinner parties she's apt to vibrate gently until steam comes out of her ears. And the air turns deep blue when actresses start swearing – but you'd know all about that.'

'Sorry, Bill, but I couldn't get a cab. I should have phoned. Believe me, I wouldn't miss one of Charlie's dinners if I could possibly avoid it.'

'You're here, Harry, that's the main thing. Come on through to the drawing room and let me fill you up with Scotch. Incidentally, Charlie has arranged a surprise guest for you – our new neighbour.'

Lydia Maxwell was seated in an armchair at one side of the Yorkstone fireplace. 'How lovely to see you again, Harry.' The sexy, husky voice evoked memories of the first time we'd met, albeit in different circumstances from these. Putting her champagne flute on a table, she stood up and kissed me lightly on the cheek. 'I'd have phoned, but I misplaced the card you gave me with your number on it.'

Gail Sutton had once said that the famous little black dress was a lazy woman's party frock and didn't require any forethought. But that comment didn't apply to Lydia Maxwell.

Her LBD outfit was classically simple, and her discreet gold jewellery completed the picture of an elegant woman. I noticed that her engagement ring and wedding band were again missing.

'What a dreadful thing, that young policeman being murdered, Harry. I was tempted to stay for the whole trial after I'd given my evidence at the Old Bailey, but I eventually decided it would be too harrowing an experience listening to all the gory details. Was Mr Appleby married?'

'I'm afraid so,' I said, as I accepted a large Scotch from Bill.

'How awful for his poor widow. It takes a long time to get over the sudden death of one's husband. Even if you didn't get on,' she added rather bitterly. 'Did they have any children?'

'No, they didn't, which is something to be grateful for, I suppose.'

I feared the conversation was about to become increasingly

mournful, and Bill, silently nursing a whisky, wasn't helping, but fortunately our hostess interrupted.

'Harry, it was good of you to come.' Charlie Hunter swept in from the kitchen attired in a scarlet silk sheath that must have cost a fortune. Her blonde hair was perfectly coiffed and she'd managed to preserve her usual serenity despite being immersed in preparing one of her masterclass meals. But she did have a cook to help her. 'I just popped in to say hello, so you'll have to excuse me, both of you, while I put the finishing touches to the first course.' She took my arm and steered me towards the door that led to the kitchen. 'If you're thinking of buying perfume for anyone in the near future, Harry,' she whispered, 'Lydia's wearing Yves Saint Laurent Black Opium.'

'You're incorrigible, Charlie,' I said.

'What, me, Harry? Perish the thought,' said Charlie, and poked her tongue at me before addressing her husband, now chatting animatedly to Lydia. 'Dinner in five minutes, honey.'

The Hunters are charming and generous hosts, but on this occasion Charlie was clearly matchmaking: the dining room was lit solely by a battery of candelabra. The meal was a gourmet's delight, particularly for a man like me who tended to live on ready meals from the supermarket, and the wines were superb. And I'm sure that Charlie had read somewhere that avocados are supposed to possess aphrodisiac qualities. The conversation sparkled and Lydia seemed quite at ease, chatting away as if she'd known the three of us for years. But I had to remind myself that she was probably as wealthy as Bill Hunter, who spent his working day juggling stocks and shares and effortlessly amassing large amounts of money in the process. And that sort of money gives the people who possess it a lot of confidence when it comes to the social graces. I just hoped that Bill wasn't about to suggest some risky scheme for Lydia to invest in.

Then I thought about what I'd just thought about; I was looking out for Lydia Maxwell's welfare already.

When the meal was over, Bill tossed down his napkin and stood up. 'Let me show you two the garden and the pool. I've put the lights on especially.'

'*Bill!*' Charlie spoke sharply and glared at her husband.

'Yes, darling?'

'Harry's seen the garden and the pool dozens of times, and I'm sure he's capable of showing Lydia around without getting lost. In any case, I need you to clear the table and make the coffee.'

I knew that the table would be left for the staff to clear in the morning and that the cook would have made the coffee. Nevertheless, I was aware of exactly what our hostess was up to, and I have to admit I was rather pleased to be able to spend a few minutes alone with Lydia now that questions about murder wouldn't dominate the conversation.

The threat of rain had disappeared and it was a pleasant if slightly cool evening. Lydia had draped a cashmere stole around her shoulders prior to leaving the house, and we strolled across the extensive and well-kept gardens, illuminated now by a dozen or more post lights, and into the wooden chalet that enclosed the swimming pool. 'It's got all mod cons: heaters, showers and changing cubicles,' I said, and pointed across the pool, 'and the sliding doors over there lead to the patio and a state of the art charcoal barbecue, and then there's a set of—'

My little spiel came to an abrupt stop as Lydia burst out laughing. 'You're beginning to sound like an estate agent, Harry,' she said. 'I know all that. I've been shown around the pool house and the garden before, and Bill and Charlie have told me I can use the pool any time I like – which I have done – until mine's ready. At the moment, mine is open air, which is not exactly conducive to swimming in this sort of weather, but I'm arranging to have it enclosed like this one.' As we left the chalet and began to stroll around the lawn, she suddenly changed the subject. 'I suppose you've worked out what Charlie Hunter's up to, haven't you, Harry?'

'Yes, Lydia, I have.' I knew exactly what she was talking about. 'The one thing I've learned about Charlie over the years that I've known her and Bill is that she's not the subtlest of women. When she has a plan in mind, she goes for it with frightening determination, and makes no attempt to disguise her motives.'

'You mean we've no chance of escaping?' Lydia glanced sideways at me and smiled.

'That about sums it up.'

'D'you mind awfully?'

'No, I don't, Lydia,' I said, perhaps a little too quickly.

'Good. Neither do I.' She linked her arm through mine as we turned towards the house. 'It's getting rather chilly out here. D'you mind if we go in?'

'Before we do, there's something I want to ask you.'

'Which is?' She stopped and turned to face me.

'That you'll have dinner with me one evening in the not-too-distant future.'

'Of course I will, Harry,' she said, and squeezed my arm as we carried on walking towards the house.

I had reservations about dating a wealthy widow. My salary, comparatively meagre when set against the money Lydia Maxwell was accustomed to, wouldn't run to the sort of restaurants which I'm sure she frequented. And I said as much.

'Oh, don't be so silly, Harry.' Once again, Lydia stopped and faced me. 'I'd settle for a sandwich on a park bench. It's the company that's important, my dear.'

It was then that I decided Gail Sutton was history. What was over was over.

But that was all last November. Now I had a murder to deal with.

On Wednesday morning, Dave and I journeyed to Henry Mortlock's carvery.

'Confirming what I told you at the venue, Harry, she died as a result of manual asphyxiation,' began Mortlock, 'and I'd think by a fairly strong man. She was definitely attacked by someone standing behind her, and as there were no defensive wounds I imagine the attack took her completely by surprise.'

'Could the assailant have been a woman?' I queried.

'I've just told you that in my opinion she was attacked by a fairly strong man,' snapped Mortlock, but then moderated his sudden temper. 'D'you have a reason for asking that?' He raised both of his bushy eyebrows.

I told him what we'd learned so far about the woman purporting to be Rachel Steele. 'According to the neighbour we spoke to, this mystery woman is about six foot tall, spends a lot of time at the gym and is a very strong swimmer. Of course, this is all hearsay.'

'It would be possible, I suppose,' said Mortlock, backtracking cautiously. 'Far be it from me to tell you your job, Harry, but is the dead woman likely to have been in the Isabella Plantation with another woman? Surely, it's more likely to have been a man.'

'Oh, come on, Henry! This is the twenty-first century. Women do have affairs with women these days. They even get married to each other.'

'Could the body have been moved from where she was killed, and dumped where Mrs Kowalska found it?' asked Dave, intervening just in time to prevent what promised to be a heated discussion about modern-day sexual mores.

Mortlock shook his head. 'The hypostasis indicates that she was killed where she was found, and as I said yesterday, I'm of the opinion that she'd been dead between twelve and fifteen hours.'

'Was she pregnant?' I asked. Unwanted pregnancies, particularly arising as the result of an extra-marital affair, were often a motive for murder.

'No. She wasn't pregnant and she wasn't a virgin, but she hadn't engaged in recent intercourse, by which I mean in the hours leading up to her death. The only other thing I can tell you is that she took the birth control pill. Oh, and one other thing – she had a termination some years ago.'

'Thank you, Henry.' I didn't ask how Mortlock had come to the latter conclusion, but who am I to query the findings of our learned pathologist. For all I know, he might've been guessing.

We were just leaving the mortuary when I got a phone call from Colin Wilberforce.

'Rachel Steele's credit card company came up with an address for her, sir. It's a luxury flat in Richmond.' Wilberforce reeled off the address.

'Thanks, Colin. Dave and I will have a look at it this afternoon.'

So much for that. We'd not added very much to what we'd learned yesterday.

*   *   *

We arrived back at the office at half past ten to be greeted by Linda Mitchell, the crime-scene manager.

'What have you got for me, Linda?' I asked, as she, Kate Ebdon and Dave settled in my office.

'Not very much, I'm afraid, Harry, but what we have got may prove useful in the long run.' Linda opened a folder and rested it on her knee. 'There was still a dew when we arrived at the scene, but once it had lifted we were able to carry out a close inspection of the ground. There were no discernible signs of a struggle, and although there were footmarks aplenty, we couldn't obtain a clear shoe print from any of them. Not that that means anything; thousands of people must roam around the Isabella Plantation in the course of a summer. We did, however, find a cigarette butt. There aren't so many people who smoke nowadays and—'

'You speak for yourself, Linda,' muttered Dave.

Linda laughed. 'You should try, Dave. It's easy to give up.'

'I know it's easy to give up,' said Dave. 'I've done it dozens of times. It's knowing how to stop starting again that I have trouble with.'

'What about this cigarette butt, Linda?' I said, steering the conversation back on course.

'I'm having it tested for DNA. But even if we're lucky, it could turn out to have been anybody's. And even if we find a match in the database it still won't prove that it belongs to the murderer.'

'But he'll have a few questions to answer, especially if he's on the sex offenders' register,' said Kate Ebdon, who relished interrogating sex offenders to the extent that I almost felt sorry for them. Almost, but not quite. Kate is very feminine, an image she likes to foster when it suits her, but heaven help any man who tries to take advantage. She has a black belt in judo and I once saw what happened to a fifteen-stone baggage handler from Heathrow Airport who tried it on with her. I'd swear she didn't move a muscle, but the next moment this guy was flat on his back moaning loudly and complaining of police brutality.

That little scene had an amusing corollary. When the 'victim' had finished dictating his complaint against Kate, the detective

superintendent dealing with it read through it and gave it to
the baggage-handler to sign. Taking back the statement, he'd
assumed a straight face. 'Let me get this right. The nub of
what you've just told me is that this slightly built young woman
officer threw you on the ground? And you're, what, about
fifteen stone? You realize, of course, that any disciplinary
proceedings will take place in public and be reported in the
media. When your baggage-handling mates hear about that,
they'll laugh themselves sick, I shouldn't wonder.' The baggage
handler swore, grabbed his statement and tore it up before
marching out.

'If you eventually find the murderer,' continued Linda, 'and
there is DNA from the cigarette butt which matches his,
you've got additional evidence. But, like the footmarks, it
could belong to anyone.'

'Anything else, Linda?' asked Kate. 'Like, for instance,
something that'll help us find this bastard?'

'We recovered some fibres from the victim's dress which
don't match anything she was wearing. We've not done a
complete analysis yet, but they could've come from the assailant's clothing or even from the cloth upholstery of a car, not
that many cars have cloth upholstery these days. None of this
gets you any further forward, of course, but everything we
amass is in the bank for when you arrest a suspect.'

'You did mention yesterday that you might be able to get
a fingerprint from the impressions on the woman's neck,
Linda,' suggested Dave hopefully. 'Did you have any luck?'

'No, I'm afraid it wasn't possible. It was a long shot anyway,
and as I said at the time, he might've worn gloves despite the
weather.'

'Any joy with the victim's smartphone?' I asked.

'Now, that could prove to be quite useful.' And by way of
a reply, Linda handed me a list of phone numbers. 'The ones
that have names against them were on her speed dial.'

'If her killer called her, I've no doubt he had a throwaway
mobile phone,' I said, injecting some pessimistic realism into
our murder inquiry. 'Any photographs?'

'I've had the photos developed, but there were some videos
on there, too, and I've had stills taken from those where the

victim features,' said Linda, handing over a sheaf of eight-by-ten prints. 'It's a selection of bucolic scenes as well as some indoor shots. There are quite a few which show either men or women – occasionally both; some are selfies and include the victim. What might help you is that the victim had the foresight to switch on location services.'

'What on earth is that?' I asked. Linda was moving into foreign territory, at least as far as I was concerned.

'It's an app that records where the photograph was taken, when it was taken and the time. It also links a photograph to any others taken nearby or close in time. The details are on each of those prints.'

'That'll be something for Harvey to get his teeth into,' said Dave, glancing at the prints over my shoulder. He was all for involving newcomers to the team as soon as possible.

'Take care of it, Dave,' I said, and handed him the phone list and the photographs.

'I'll let you know of anything we find as soon as we find it,' said Linda as she got up to leave.

Kate returned to her office and Dave and I went into the incident room.

Harvey had been sitting next to Colin Wilberforce, presumably finding out what he did, but leaped to his feet the moment I appeared.

'Sit down, Steve,' I said. 'We don't stand on ceremony here.' He was probably still conscious of the ticking-off he'd been given by Dave. 'Sergeant Poole's got something for you.'

'The guv'nor has just appointed you the official phone number and photograph investigating officer,' said Dave, and handed over Rachel Steele's phone list and the photographs that Linda Mitchell had prepared. 'I know you go in heavy-handed on the Squad, but here we like to do a bit of background before we go blundering in.' Dave had no high opinion of the Flying Squad, possibly because he'd never been selected to serve on it, and clearly didn't much care for Harvey, but that will probably soften. New arrivals on the team had to prove themselves in Dave's eyes before he accepted them.

Harvey gazed apprehensively at the document and photos. 'What am I supposed to do with these, skip?'

'Give them to me, Steve,' said Wilberforce. 'I'll show you what's what.'

'Colin, have you checked to see if there's any footage from cameras at the Richmond and Kingston gates to the park that might give us a few car numbers to work with?' I asked.

'There aren't any cameras, sir,' said Wilberforce, somewhat smugly, 'although I understand there has been talk of installing them.'

'You're such a comfort, Colin,' said Dave.

We had found a set of keys among the possessions that the killer had left with Rachel Steele's body, but as we'd discovered they were for her Camden Town address, that came as no surprise. There was, though, one other unexplained key on the ring. However, Colin Wilberforce had relentlessly pursued credit card companies until he had discovered where she was living at the time of her murder. It proved to be within walking distance of the Talavera wine bar in Richmond.

The giveaway, in terms of finding her latest address, was that she had transferred her balance from one credit card to another. But that newer credit card was not among the possessions found on her body.

The mystery key on the ring fitted the door of the apartment, and we let ourselves in.

Dave and I had brought Nicola Chance with us. Nicola had been with the team for a few years now. She managed to combine a very sharp brain with a demure disposition, but when occasionally she became sufficiently frustrated or annoyed enough to bring on an outburst, her obscene vocabulary would have made even a sergeant major blush. However, as I had found many times over, a woman will often spot things that a man might miss, and Nicola had proved her value in that regard on several occasions when we'd been searching accommodation.

The apartment was not particularly large, but well-furnished and adequate for a single person. As we moved around on a preliminary survey we came across an interesting piece of evidence. There were two bedrooms. This in itself is not unusual, but it was the second bedroom at the back of the apartment that interested us. The only furniture in it was a large bed and an umbrella stand. The bed had a tethering device at each corner, so that whoever was on the bed could be secured spread-eagled, and the umbrella stand contained a quantity of canes, similar to those used in schools many years ago, and a collection of dressage whips.

'She was a bloody tom,' said Dave, neatly summing up the situation.

'Bless my soul! I do believe you're right, skip,' said Nicola, with heavy sarcasm.

'There's no need to sound so pleased about the bloody obvious, Dave,' I said. 'You do realize what it means, I suppose. We've no idea how many clients she had, and any one of them could've murdered her.'

'Or none of them, guv,' said Dave.

'I'll have a look around, guv,' said Nicola. 'She might've kept a diary or an appointments book.'

'When you're looking, see if you can find this credit card that Colin Wilberforce was going on about, Nicola,' suggested Dave. 'That might tell us something.'

Nicola Chance laughed. 'Would you have paid by credit card for the sort of services Rachel Steele appeared to offer, skip?' It was the sort of classic put-down at which Nicola was very good.

A few minutes later, she opened a drawer in a ladder unit.

'A credit card, guv. And a bunch of statements.'

'What sort of statements?' I asked.

'Monthly credit card and bank statements.' Nicola whistled. 'This was one seriously rich lady,' she said. 'She's spent a fortune on clothes and perfume and cosmetics.' She handed me the bank statements. 'You'll see on there, guv, that she made a frequent number of irregular deposits, and they were large sums in each case.'

'Her business must've been booming,' I said.

'More like bruising,' said Dave, 'if what's in the umbrella stand is anything to go by.'

'I'll just have a look in the bathroom,' said Nicola. She emerged minutes later. 'If you wanted proof of how much Rachel's worth, this is fifty mill of Roja Enigma,' she said, displaying a small bottle, 'and it retails at about three hundred and eighty pounds.'

'We'd better seal this place until her estranged husband can be contacted to do something about it,' I said. 'Once we've had Linda Mitchell's team go over it for fingerprints.'

FOUR

'I've been checking out the photographs taken from Rachel Steele's mobile phone, guv.' Harvey came into my office holding some photographic prints.

'Are you going to tell me there's a shot of the murderer holding up a placard saying "I did it!"?'

'I didn't find one like that, guv,' said Harvey, without displaying a trace of humour. 'There were twenty-two photographs altogether, but most of them were of places without people in them, like places she'd been to. However, five of them were stills from videos taken at the Talavera wine bar in Richmond on separate occasions during the three weeks before she was found dead in Richmond Park. Each one was taken with a man. She looks as though she's having a good time.'

'She took a video with a *phone*?' I asked. 'How the hell did she do that?'

'Oh, I can do it, guv,' said Harvey, rather smugly. 'In fact, anyone can do it if they've got a smartphone.'

All this technical stuff was beyond my field of understanding. I gave up and went back to police work. 'Does the same man appear in any of them more than once?'

'No, sir.' Harvey laid five prints on my desk. 'As I said, she took videos, but these frames are the best ones for showing the face of the man who was with her. And each time it was a different man.'

'She obviously put herself about,' I said, 'but now we know she was a tom, that's not surprising. And the name of the wine bar's printed at the bottom of the photographs. How fortunate.' Yet another benefit of modern technology.

'So is the time, sir. Some were taken at midday – only one actually – but the others were taken in the evening, on either a Monday or a Friday.'

'You've done a good job, Steve.' To be honest, it was no

more than I expected of an experienced detective like Harvey; otherwise he wouldn't have been posted to us. But it does no harm to give the occasional word of praise to the guys working with you. 'Ask DI Ebdon to come in.'

'You wanted me, Harry?' Kate always used my first name when no one else was about, the result of a weekend of rather wine-soaked enquiries with my good friend Henri Deshayes of the *Police Judiciaire*.

'Have you seen what Harvey turned up, Kate?'

'Yes, I have. Are you and Dave going to make a trip to this Talavera wine bar in Richmond?'

'I think it would be better if you went and took Dave with you. A man and a woman will blend more easily than two men who look suspiciously like coppers. If you get there at about seven you might find some of the guys in these photos, but I'll leave it to you how you play it.' I gestured at the prints that Harvey had left on my desk. 'And you can take those with you.'

'I don't think so, Harry. We can hardly wander into a wine bar clutching a handful of large photographs and give the clientele a searching look. Bit obvious, don't you think?'

'Will you be able to memorize the faces, then, Kate?'

'I've got a brain like a sieve, Harry.' Kate laughed at the very idea. 'I'll get Dave to transfer the relevant photos and videos to his mobile phone. He's very good at that sort of thing. We can have a discreet look around, and we might even get lucky.'

Brain like a sieve, indeed! Kate had one of the sharpest brains going.

The Talavera was one of those twee wine bars where upcoming wannabees like to be seen. They walk in with a knowing nod to the barman, put their credit card behind the bar – where it will probably be cloned – and proceed to party. Or ignore everyone and spend the evening playing with their digital toys. In the old days there would have been a pall of tobacco smoke hanging beneath the ceiling, but not any more; not in a society worried sick about smoking, eating the right organic food, slavishly following the latest diet fad, counting calories, avoiding red meat and checking their cholesterol. High on this manic agenda comes jogging, thereby destroying their hips, knees and ankles in the process. And finally, signing up to a fashionable gymnasium.

It now looks as if the most likely cause of death in the near future will be worry.

The arrival of Kate Ebdon and Dave Poole was not greeted with suspicion; quite the contrary. The flame-haired Kate's figure immediately attracted the attention of almost every male on the premises. And that of two women. Whereas the hunk of a man that was Dave Poole received more than one admiring glance from the women, and from a couple of shaven-headed, musclebound men who were talking to each other in a corner of the bar.

'By the way, you can call me Kate,' said Kate. 'But that's a once only offer and expires the moment we leave here.'

'You do me great honour, Kate,' said Dave.

'I do you nothing of the sort, mate. But I once met an NYPD lieutenant who was over here on an exchange visit. He told me that he and a third-grade were looking for some lowlife in a Brooklyn bar when the third-grade addressed him rather loudly as "Loo-tenant". And that blew that discreet observation. So, watch it, Poole.'

'Knowing our luck, this'll be the one night none of them shows, Kate,' said Dave mournfully.

Kate bought a glass of inferior red wine and treated Dave to a non-alcoholic fruit drink of indeterminate content. They stood at one of the jutting shelves that were fixed at right angles from the wall and observed the scene.

The place was crowded with men and women, all of whom appeared to be in the mid-twenties to mid-forties age range. Most of the men were talking loudly, but above the general hubbub could be heard the occasional boast of how clever they were, the superior cars they drove and their enviable golf handicap. This inane chatter seemed to impress the girls, whose ambition in life was probably no more than to become a 'celebrity' and save the planet. Another group of four women were surveying the scene with expressions bordering on contempt while making snide remarks behind their hands

and giggling. A further couple were busy on their smartphones, which prompted Dave to suggest that they were
actually texting each other rather than engaging in a face-
to-face conversation.

In other words, it was a typical wine bar atmosphere and
similar to a hundred others in Greater London and beyond.

'That guy over there is one of those in the videos, Kate.
Follow my eyes,' said Dave, looking across the room
without actually pointing and then glancing at his smartphone
to make sure. 'Taken on the third of June, just over a week
before Rachel Steele's body was found.' He handed the
phone to Kate, and she nodded her agreement before handing
it back.

She glanced across the room. A couple were sitting sideways on and facing each other at the long counter against
the wall opposite the bar. Fortunately the man had been
looking towards Kate and Dave, and the woman had her
back to them. They were deep in conversation and appeared
oblivious to everyone else in the place. He was dressed in an
open-necked shirt and jeans, his blazer slung over the back
of his stool, and the woman was wearing a summer dress.
Her left hand was resting on the man's knee in such a way
that any onlooker could not fail to see the diamond ring
on the third finger of her left hand.

'She's very like Rachel Steele, Kate,' whispered Dave.
'Long brown hair, and I'd take a guess at her being about
five-eight. And she's not wearing a bra.'

'What's the significance of that?' asked Kate.

'The victim was wearing one, but we think the killer
nicked it.'

'What in hell's name are you jabbering about, Dave?'

'If the killer's a bra-collecting psychopath, Kate, he's not
going to pick up a woman who's not wearing one, is he?
Therefore that girl is unlikely to be his next victim.'

'Just come down to earth for a minute, Dave, and tell me
what we're going to do about the drongo you've just fingered.'
There were moments of frustration when Kate lapsed into an
almost theatrical Australian argot.

'I think he's just solved it for us,' said Dave.

The man had stood up and slung his blazer over his shoulder before holding the woman's hand to steady her as she got down from the high stool. Holding hands, they made for the exit, shouting '*Ciao*' to people they knew.

Kate and Dave followed the couple out into the street.

'Excuse me,' said Dave.

The man turned and, seeing that he had been accosted by a black giant accompanied by an attractive redhead in a white shirt and jeans, immediately stepped in front of his companion as if to guard her from attack.

'What d'you want?' The man had a hunted look. He'd read about the random stabbings that were occurring all over London practically every day.

'We're police officers,' said Kate, 'and we'd like a word with you.' Realizing that the man was still unconvinced, she and Dave produced their warrant cards.

The man relaxed and the woman moved to stand beside him. 'What's this about?' he demanded.

Dave produced his mobile phone and played the copy of the video he had transferred from Rachel Steele's smartphone. It showed the man standing as close as he could get to Rachel Steele. He had his arm around her waist, squeezing her tightly into his body, and she had an arm around his waist, her scarlet nail varnish very obvious against the white of his shirt. Her other hand held the camera so that she could video the two of them. And she had started the recording just before the man planted a kiss on her cheek, and they were both laughing.

'That began at seven thirty-five on the evening of Monday last week, the third of June,' said Dave, 'and lasted for ninety seconds in all.'

'But . . . er . . . that's not me,' stuttered the man unconvincingly.

The man's fiancée – for that was who she proved to be – had been holding his arm and watching closely as Dave was playing the video. 'It bloody well is, Max,' she said angrily and, moving slightly so that she was in front of him, slapped his face. Tearing the engagement ring from her finger, she threw it at him before storming off.

'Sophie, it's not what you think,' the man shouted desperately and dithered, unsure whether to run after the woman or attempt to find the diamond ring, which was somewhere in the gutter.

'Not so fast,' said Dave, laying a restraining hand on the man's arm. 'I said we wanted to talk to you.'

'Thanks a bundle,' snapped the man called Max. 'You've just destroyed a perfect relationship.'

'I think you did that, mate,' said Kate, her suddenly strong Australian accent seeming to surprise the man.

'What the hell is this about, anyway?' Max demanded. 'And why are you showing me that video?'

'I think it would be better if we continued this conversation at the local police station,' said Kate.

'Now just hold on a moment. Are you arresting me for something? Because if you're not, I'm not going anywhere.'

'You can either come voluntarily, or I *will* arrest you,' said Kate. 'On suspicion of murdering the woman in this photograph.'

'What on earth are you talking about?' asked Max desperately. 'I don't know anything about a murder. I don't even know who that woman was.'

'What's your name?'

'Max Roper.'

'Very well, Mr Roper,' said Kate. 'Get in the car, please.' She ushered Roper into the back seat of the car and slid in beside him.

It was a short run to Richmond police station on Kew Road. Once the necessary paperwork had been completed, Roper was taken into an interview room.

'I'm recording this interview as much for your protection as for mine,' Kate began. 'Present are Mr Max Roper, together with Detective Inspector Kate Ebdon and Detective Sergeant David Poole, both of the Murder Investigation Team at New Scotland Yard.'

Dave placed his phone on the table that separated him from Max and played the video once again. 'You said you didn't know this woman, Mr Roper, and yet you are clearly enjoying an intimate embrace with her.'

'There was a whole crowd of us in there that night,' said

Roper. 'Everyone was having fun and joking around. There was a lot of horseplay. Like that,' he said, gesturing at the phone. 'It was someone's birthday and they'd pushed the boat out, but none of us stayed for very long.'

'Long enough to be videoed with a strange woman, though,' said Kate. 'When did you last see her, Mr Roper?'

'That was the only time I saw her, at least to speak to.'

'But long enough to wrap yourself around her,' commented Kate. 'When you'd seen her previously, was it in the wine bar you were in this evening?'

'Yes, Inspector, but she was usually with someone.'

'Would that have been the same someone each time?'

'No, I'm pretty sure it was a different guy each time. Frankly, I think that she was prepared to go out with anyone, but to be honest I didn't pay much attention because on the other occasions I was with Sophie.'

'Prepared to go out with anyone? Is that a euphemism for having sexual intercourse with anyone?' asked Dave.

'Maybe.' Roper shrugged. 'She certainly seemed to enjoy the company of men.'

'The woman who was with you tonight – is she your fiancée?'

'Yes, but I'm not sure she's still my fiancée, thanks to you.' Roper paused. 'You said the woman in the photograph was murdered.'

'Yes. Her name's Rachel Steele. Mrs Rachel Steele.'

'Good God! She's the one who was found in Richmond Park yesterday morning. There was a bit on local TV about it, and a lot of comments on Twitter complaining about the park being closed to traffic.'

'Yes, that's her, Mr Roper.' Kate leaned on the table, linked her hands and moved closer. 'I don't think you realize that you are in something of a difficult situation here. You were photographed embracing this woman, a woman you say you don't know but who you had seen before, several times. That woman is now dead.'

'God! But I had nothing to do with this terrible business.' Roper sounded as though he was on the verge of panic. 'What can I do to prove that I had nothing to do with it?'

'For a start, you can give us a sample of your DNA,' said Dave.

'Sure, anything.' Roper was now desperate to assist the two detectives. 'How do I do that? Can you do it now?'

'Detective Sergeant Poole is leaving the room,' Dave announced, and went in search of a DNA swabbing kit. A few moments later he returned and took a sample of Roper's saliva. He spent a few minutes ensuring that the sample was sealed and correctly labelled. Failure to do so would guarantee at least twenty minutes of cross-examination by the defence counsel, designed to prove the police evidence invalid.

'Where were you on the night of the tenth of June, Mr Roper?' Kate asked.

'I'd had a row with my fiancée, and she flounced out of the flat. She said it was all over and she never wanted to see me again.'

'She seems to make a habit of that,' observed Kate. 'It's all very interesting, but what did *you* do?'

'I went down to the local pub and got pissed. The landlord's a mate of mine, you can ask him. Anyway, he threw me out at about eleven and I went home. To an empty flat.'

'Your fiancée didn't come home that night, then,' said Dave.

'No. I don't know where she went. I didn't see her again until I got home the following night and she was there, all full of contrition for having stormed out, I suppose.'

'Did you ask her where she'd been?'

'No, I just left it. I didn't want to reignite the previous night's row.'

'What was the row about?'

'Stupid really. Sophie wanted a church wedding with all the trimmings and a honeymoon in Barbados, but I said that would cost the earth and we'd be better off saving the money to put down on a house, but when I suggested a registry office wedding she went up like a can of petrol.'

'Show Mr Roper the photographs, Sergeant Poole,' said Kate.

'I am now showing Mr Roper the stills from the videos shot at the wine bar frequented by Rachel Steele. These were shot over a period of three weeks prior to her murder on or about the tenth of June this year,' said Dave for the benefit of the recorder and, placing the camera on the table, slowly displayed each of the stills in turn. 'Do you recognize any of these men, Mr Roper?'

'That one,' said Roper, as Dave reached the third print. 'I know him.'

'Mr Roper has indicated the still taken from the video on Friday the twenty-fourth of May,' Dave said, again for the benefit of the recorder. 'And who is he, Mr Roper?'

'His name's Tony Miles.'

'How d'you know him?'

'He's a good friend of mine. Actually, we work together.' Roper was now so anguished that he was prepared to point the finger at anyone he thought might redirect suspicion from himself. Even if it incriminated a friend.

'Doing what, Mr Roper?' asked Kate.

'We're in human resources. We work in central London, but we both live in this area.'

'Give my sergeant Mr Miles's home address, please, Mr Roper,' said Kate. 'And your own.'

For a moment Roper hesitated but, seeing the determined look on Kate's face, he relented and wrote down the addresses.

'Have you ever been in the Isabella Plantation in Richmond Park, Mr Roper?'

'Never,' said Roper unhesitatingly.

'One last question. What brand of cigarette d'you smoke?'

'I *don't* smoke,' said Roper piously, as though Kate had just made an improper suggestion to him.

'I'll now admit you to police bail to return to this police station in one month's time, unless you hear from me that you are not required.' Kate glanced at the clock. 'Interview terminated at twenty thirty hours. You're free to go, Mr Roper. But before you do, give Sergeant Poole your mobile phone number. Oh, and while you're at it, give him your fiancée's full name and phone number too.'

'Why d'you want that?' asked Roper suspiciously.

'To check what you've just told me is the truth,' said Kate.

Roper furnished Dave with the requisite information; his fiancée's name was Sophie Preston. 'But why are you releasing me on bail?' he asked, sounding mildly indignant. 'I've told you all I know.'

'So you say, Mr Roper, but we have certain scientific evidence that we have to check against your DNA.'

'Oh, I see. A formality.' Roper stood up and paused at the door of the interview room. 'I don't suppose you could have a word with Sophie, Inspector, and tell her that this business with the video was all quite innocent.'

'Goodnight, Mr Roper,' said Kate.

'We found one of the guys on Rachel's smartphone, Harry,' said Kate when she reported to me the following morning, and she gave me a rundown on the interview with Max Roper.

'What was your gut reaction?'

'I've got an open mind.' Kate's face assumed a wry expression. 'He was a bit arsy in front of his fiancée, who is probably his ex now, but when we took him to the nick he suddenly became desperate to prove his innocence. Anyhow, I've admitted him to bail for a month, and we'll see what the DNA has to say. He denied smoking, but he might be lying. If his DNA tallies with what we hope to find from the discarded cigarette, he'll have some serious questions to answer.'

'If he hasn't done a runner,' I commented gloomily. 'Pity we can't lock 'em up until we know for sure.'

'Talking of which, is there anything back from the airports about Daniel Steele's disappearance, Harry?'

'Not a word,' I said, 'but it's early days yet. These people never seem to realize that something like this is urgent. What really interests me is to discover if Stephanie Payne was travelling on her own passport or a bent one.'

'If Stephanie Payne really exists,' said Kate. 'For all we know, he might've made up the name to shield her real identity.'

'You have a point, Kate.' I phoned through to the incident room and asked Colin to get hold of Charlie Flynn.

'He's just come in, sir,' said Wilberforce. 'And the commander would like to see you.'

'Charlie,' I said when Detective Sergeant Flynn came into my office. 'I want you to go up to this place in the City.' I handed him the card that Daniel Steele had given me. 'Speak to a woman called Jessica who seems to be in charge of the trading floor. Daniel Steele, the victim's estranged husband, works there.' As a result of daily briefings, Flynn knew about Steele's hurried departure, and that he was accompanied by a woman the neighbours believed to be Rachel Steele. 'Have a word with Jessica, Charlie, see if any of their female traders disappeared on the same day as Steele and if they're still adrift. You could probably do it on the phone if you want to save time.'

'No, I'll go up there, guv,' said Flynn. 'I like to see their facial expressions when they lie to me.'

Once Flynn had departed I made my way to the commander's office, prepared to tell him as little as I could get away with.

'Ah, Mr Brock.' The commander closed the file in front of him with apparent reluctance. The commander adores paper, revels in it, and the more that passes across his desk the happier he is. From our point of view, it has the advantage of preventing him from wandering out to the incident room and interfering with police work. Consequently, the teams under his command have learned to snow him with paper, in addition to the unnecessary emails with which mischievous malcontents flood his computer.

'You wanted to see me, sir?'

'Tell me about the suspicious death of the woman found in the Isabella Plantation in Richmond Park on Tuesday, Mr Brock.'

Unlike so many of the governors I've worked for in the past, the commander would never use my first name, presumably in case I used his in return; he couldn't cope with that. He also irritated the real detectives by referring to a case that was palpably one of murder as a 'suspicious death' until it was proved beyond all reasonable doubt that it was a murder we were dealing with. But the commander was the beneficiary of what is known in the Job as a sideways promotion. The Uniform Branch having tired of him interfering in perfectly good traffic schemes and inventing new ways of dealing with football hooligans that usually resulted in more violence rather than less, he was eventually pushed across to the CID for what was supposed to be a purely administrative role. Unfortunately, he now believed he *was* a detective, and didn't hesitate to express his views about how we should go about an investigation. He even had a copy of Hans Gross's *Criminal Investigation* on his bookshelf. Perhaps he took it home for bedtime reading.

'Early days yet, sir. We are awaiting the results of various DNA tests on items of evidence found at the *locus in quo*.'

'Quite so, quite so,' said the commander, reaching hungrily for another file in his in-tray. 'Keep me informed, Mr Brock.'

I knew from the slight frown that flitted across his brow that he hadn't a clue that *locus in quo* meant 'the place in question'. And neither had I until Dave had told me what it meant.

It was later on that morning that DS Flynn returned from the City office where Steele worked.

'You were right, guv,' he said. 'There is a woman who's adrift. Her name's Sarah Parsons. She disappeared the same day as Steele and hasn't returned yet.'

'Same initials as Stephanie Payne, who I suspect is one and the same as Sarah Parsons.'

'Saves buying new handkerchiefs if you've got your initials on 'em,' commented Flynn.

'Did you get a description, Charlie?'

'Did better than that, guv.' Flynn took a photograph from his pocket and placed it on my desk. 'They keep photographs of everyone who works there for their security passes.'

I glanced at the photograph of a good-looking, long-haired blonde. But it was not a face I recognized. Yet. 'File it in the incident room, Charlie. We might need it one day,' I said. 'Did they have an address for this woman?'

Flynn referred to his pocketbook. 'Yes, it's in a block of upmarket apartments in Hampstead called Drover Court, which unsurprisingly is in Drover Street.'

'Good. Follow it up, Charlie, but somehow I doubt you'll find her there. On your way back, drop in on Mrs Natasha Stephens. She's the Steeles' next-door neighbour and the Neighbourhood Watch coordinator. Show her that photograph and ask her if that's the woman she knows as Rachel Steele.'

FIVE

By the time he was twenty-eight, Detective Sergeant Charles Flynn had been married and divorced, and was now in a relationship with a woman police officer stationed at Bishopsgate police station in the City of London. But even that was an on-off sort of affair because Flynn had an eye for the ladies, and they for him. He had, at various times, been described as raffish, cocky, debonair, and dismissed as an East End wide boy with all the finesse of a street-market trader. None of this, however, detracted from his ability as a police officer. In fact, it was what gave him his natural flair for sweet-talking reluctant female suspects or witnesses into telling him all he needed to know. His three years as a member of the Fraud Squad had honed an already keen brain to the point where it was capable of analysing facts in a comparatively short space of time.

When Flynn reached the modern apartment block at Drover Court in Hampstead, he rang for Apartment C on the first floor using the entry phone, but predictably there was no answer. He rang for Apartment D instead and was let in.

The woman who answered the door of the apartment was probably in her sixties, silver-haired and immaculately dressed. A pair of spectacles hung from a gold-coloured chain around her neck. She gazed at Flynn with a quizzical expression but said nothing.

'I'm a police officer, ma'am,' Flynn began, and produced his official identification. 'I'm terribly sorry to disturb you.'

'Oh, I hope there isn't any trouble,' said the woman, raising her spectacles so that she could read Flynn's warrant card.

'No, no, nothing like that,' Flynn said soothingly, 'but I wondered if you could help me.'

'Well, of course. Please come in. As a matter of fact, I was about to make a cup of tea, and I'm sure I could persuade you to try a slice of my homemade seed cake. I've never known a policeman yet who would refuse a piece of seed cake.'

'I adore seed cake,' said Flynn, who detested it, but was prepared to eat just about anything in the pursuit of information.

The woman showed him into her cosy sitting room and went into the kitchen. When she returned with a tea tray she put it down on the occasional table that Flynn had thoughtfully moved into place for her.

'Thank you. That's very kind of you,' said the woman, and smiled her gratitude. 'Are you from the local police station?'

'No, ma'am, I'm from Scotland Yard. Detective Sergeant Flynn.'

'Yes, I saw the name on your warrant card,' said the woman, proving that she was sharper than Flynn had at first thought. 'I'm Grace Booker.'

'Well, Mrs Booker . . .' Flynn paused. 'I'm sorry,' he said smoothly, 'I just assumed that—'

'No, I never married,' said Grace Booker, handing Flynn a cup of tea and a large slice of seed cake, 'although it wasn't for the want of offers,' she added coyly. 'My life was spent in the ballet, first as a dancer, then as a choreographer, but I retired last year. Now I just pop across to the school in Richmond Park and help out occasionally. But you're not here to listen to my life story. How can I help you, Mr Flynn?'

'Are you acquainted with the young lady who lives opposite you, Miss Booker?'

'Sarah, you mean? Sarah Parsons.'

'Yes, that's her.'

Grace Booker lowered her voice almost to a whisper, even though there was no one else in the apartment. 'She used to entertain a lot, you know.'

'Really?' Flynn leaned forward. 'Parties and that sort of thing, you mean?' he asked earnestly, as though Miss Booker had immediately grasped the reason for his visit.

'No,' said Grace. 'Men!'

'Good gracious!' exclaimed Flynn, giving the impression that such behaviour genuinely shocked him. 'Not different men, surely?'

'Oh, but they were. Until just about a year ago, when she told me she was moving out.'

'Are you saying she no longer lives there?' queried Flynn, wondering if he'd been wasting his time, to say nothing of having to eat seed cake.

'Not exactly,' said Grace Booker. 'That's the funny thing. She told me she wasn't giving up the apartment because she'd be back eventually. It was all very mysterious.'

'I must say it sounds very strange,' agreed Flynn with false gravity. 'So no one lives there at all at the moment?'

'That's right.' And then Miss Booker posed a question that she should have asked some time previously. 'As a matter of interest, why d'you want to speak to her, Mr Flynn?'

'We think she might be a material witness to a crime that we're investigating.' Flynn decided not to mention the murder of Rachel Steele. 'I can't say any more than that,' he continued, 'for legal reasons.' Apart from not wanting the story to be circulated all around the apartment block, and possibly among Miss Booker's ballet friends, it would take too long to explain.

'Oh, I quite understand.'

'Thank you very much for the tea, and for your delicious seed cake, Miss Booker. And I'm sorry to have disturbed you.' Flynn didn't bother asking her to phone the Yard if Sarah Parsons returned. He knew that she would anyway.

'Not at all, Mr Flynn. It's nice to have someone to chat to. It does get rather lonely here, you know, with all the neighbours being out to work.'

Flynn paused at the front door. 'Did Sarah Parsons have a job?' he asked.

'Oh, yes,' said Miss Booker. 'She had some high-powered job in the City of London. She was quite jubilant about it, but she said she'd had to break through a glass ceiling to get it. It sounded a very dangerous thing to have to do in order to get a good job. But the odd thing is that she didn't have any cuts or scars on her.'

It was half past four by the time Flynn reached Superior Drive in Camden Town.

'You must be Mrs Stephens?' said Flynn when the attractive young woman opened the door.

'That's me. Who are you?'

'Detective Sergeant Charlie Flynn, Mrs Stephens.'

'Please call me Tash. Are you one of Mr Brock's friends, Sergeant Flynn?'

'Yes, I am. But do call me Charlie.' Flynn decided that this was not the time to explain the rank structure of the Metropolitan Police, and that DCI Brock was his boss rather than a friend.

'Come through, Charlie,' said Tash, and led Flynn into the sitting room at the front of the house.

'Oh, what a charming room,' said Flynn, gazing around. 'Did you do it all yourself?' The tiny room had been decorated in Victorian style with brown velour drapes and net curtains and the sort of clutter with which parlours of the nineteenth century were filled. He thought it looked hideous.

'Yes, it's all my own work,' said Tash, with a gay laugh. 'I bought a lot of the stuff from charity shops, you know,' she added in matter-of-fact tones. 'Now, I suppose Mr Brock's got more questions about the Steeles.' She sat down opposite Flynn, ran her hands through her long hair and smiled.

'Mr Brock spoke very highly of you, Tash, and suggested I had a word with you as a reliable person. In fact, his exact words were, "Speak to Tash because she's got her finger on the pulse".'

'Oh, how nice of him,' said Tash, and ran her hands through her hair yet again. 'How can I help you, then, Charlie?' She giggled. 'To live up to my reputation.'

'I hope you realize that everything I say now will be in the strictest confidence,' said Flynn, adopting a serious expression, 'but as the Neighbourhood Watch coordinator, I know you can be trusted.'

'Of course,' said Tash. 'It happens all the time,' she added airily, as though she was about to be made privy to a top-secret dossier about weapons of mass destruction. 'Our local bobby often pops in for a chat and a cup of tea during the day.'

I'll bet he does, thought Flynn. 'I want you to look at this print, Tash, and tell me if it's anyone you know.' He produced a copy of the photograph he'd obtained from Jessica, the trading-floor manager at Steele's place of employment.

'That's Rachel Steele,' said Tash, without hesitation.

'Oh dear, oh dear!' said Flynn theatrically, and shook his head.

'Isn't it her, then?' Tash suddenly looked very interested, even conspiratorial.

'I'm afraid it's someone called Sarah Parsons, Tash, a work colleague of Dan Steele's.'

'D'you mean they aren't married, Charlie? How wonderfully decadent.'

'Not as far as I know.' There were so many unmarried couples living together these days that Flynn thought it hardly worth Tash's comment. 'But you will keep this to yourself, won't you?' he asked.

'Absolutely, Charlie. I know how to keep a secret,' said Tash.

Like hell you do, thought Flynn, as he stood up. *It'll be all down Superior Drive and halfway around Camden Town before I get back to the office.*

'Thanks very much for your help, Tash. I'll be sure to let Mr Brock know how helpful you've been.'

But Flynn hadn't finished yet. He crossed the road to the house immediately opposite the one owned by the Steeles.

The woman who came to the door was quite a bit older than Natasha Stephens and carried a bit more weight.

'Yes?' The woman sounded as though she'd been plagued by door-to-door salesmen and was now confronted by yet another one.

'I'm a police officer, madam,' said Flynn. 'I'm so sorry to interrupt your afternoon, but this is rather important.' He showed her his warrant card and, seeing the distressed expression that came over her face, quickly added, 'But it's nothing for you to worry about, Mrs . . . er . . .'

'Wilson, Helen Wilson,' said the woman. 'My husband cycles to work in the City every day, and one hears so much about cyclists being injured or even killed by those big lorries that I was scared you'd come to tell me he'd been in an accident.'

'I do understand, madam,' said Flynn sympathetically, 'but he's not been involved in an accident as far as I'm aware. However, that said, you might want to dissuade him from cycling. Get him to go on the bus or the Underground. The Northern Line should get him there.'

'He says he does it for the exercise,' said Mrs Wilson, 'but I keep telling him that it won't do him any good being the fittest man in the cemetery,' she added, making a statement that was, of itself, contradictory. Somewhat belatedly, she opened the door. 'You'd better come in, Officer. I'm sure you didn't come here to offer my husband advice about the dangers of cycling.'

'I shan't keep you a moment,' said Flynn, stepping into the small hallway, 'but I'd like you to look at a couple of photographs.' First he showed the woman the print of Sarah Parsons. 'Have you seen this woman before?'

'Oh yes, I most certainly have,' said Helen Wilson scornfully. 'She's the flibbertigibbet who lives with Daniel Steele. She moved in straight after his wife moved out. He didn't waste any time, you know, and she couldn't wait to get her claws into him.'

'Do you happen to know her name, Mrs Wilson?'

'It's Sarah something, I believe, although she tries to pass herself off as his wife. For all I know they might be married now. But to be honest, Sergeant, the Steeles weren't the sort of people we wanted to socialize with.'

'Is this the Rachel Steele you knew?' Flynn produced the post-mortem photograph of Daniel Steele's estranged wife.

'Yes, that's her,' Mrs Wilson said without hesitation. 'What's happened to her? Has she been in an accident?'

'I'm afraid she's dead, Mrs Wilson. Murdered. Her body was found in Richmond Park last Tuesday morning. I'm part of the team investigating her death.'

'Oh, my goodness!' exclaimed Mrs Wilson. 'The poor woman. How awful.'

'D'you happen to know how long ago it was that Rachel Steele left the marital home?' Flynn asked.

Helen Wilson assumed a pensive expression before saying, 'About a year ago, I suppose. Perhaps a little longer.'

'Have you any idea why they split up?'

'I did hear they'd gone their separate ways,' continued Helen Wilson almost enthusiastically. 'He thought nothing of having women in the house long before Rachel moved out permanently. But at the same time, she was not above taking strange men home. It was almost as if they had an arrangement not to tread on each other's toes, if you know what I mean.' Pausing briefly for breath, she added, 'Not that I'm a nosey neighbour, Sergeant, but you can't help noticing.'

'It's inevitable in a small community like this,' agreed Flynn airily, as though Camden Town was a village instead of an overcrowded area of London. 'Well, thank you for your assistance, Mrs Wilson. I'll not hold you up any longer.'

I was in the incident room when Charlie Flynn reported back to me at about six o'clock and confirmed what I'd thought all along: that the woman Natasha Stephens thought was Rachel Steele was actually Sarah Parsons, whom Daniel Steele was passing off to us as Stephanie Payne, and as Rachel Steele to anyone else who was prepared to believe him. And that he'd been lying about continuing to share the property with Rachel.

'Colin, we sent a warning to airports about Daniel Steele recently.'

'Yes, we did, sir.' Wilberforce turned and played a brief tattoo on his computer keyboard. 'Tuesday the eleventh of June, twenty-two forty hours, sir. No result as yet.'

'Send another message, Colin,' I said, quickly recovering after Wilberforce's lightning display of efficiency, 'amending the name of Steele's travelling companion to Sarah Parsons, date of birth unknown but probably about the same age as Steele. Charlie Flynn has a photograph of the woman that you can send.' I paused. 'I suppose you can do that on a computer.'

'Of course, sir,' said Wilberforce smugly, as though I had questioned his competence. I've no idea how these computer gadgets work, but he should know that by now.

I went into my office to find Detective Superintendent Patrick Dean seated in my armchair.

'There you are, Harry.' Dean was a small man with a bald head and spectacles, a combination that had deceived many a

villain until it was too late. He had started his CID career in
the East End, and like all the good detectives in the force
clawed his way slowly upwards and now found himself in
Homicide and Major Crime Command West, and my immediate boss. One thing was sure: he was no textbook detective.
It would be a foolish villain who tried to have Pat Dean
over. And the same went for any junior detective who tried
to pull the wool over his eyes.

'You don't often drop in for a chat, guv'nor,' I said, but
knew instinctively that wasn't why he was here.

'I'm sorry to put this on you, Harry,' Dean began, 'but
another woman has been found. This time on Ham Common.
I originally assigned it to Seb Mould, but the similarities
are such that it looks like the work of the guy who topped
Rachel Steele. Sorry to lumber you, Harry, but it's better if
you handle it. If you need any extra manpower, just give me
a bell. I'll leave you to liaise with Seb.' He paused at the door.
'By the way, Harry, there seems to be a grave shortage of
decent coffee in your part of HMCC.'

It was beginning to look as though we had a serial killer on
our hands, but Pat Dean was too experienced a detective
to say so. He would never make a rash judgement of that sort
until the evidence became irrefutable.

I walked down the corridor to Seb Mould's office. He was
a DCI who headed up another Murder Investigation Team
on HMCC West.

'Hello, Harry.' Mould was seated behind his desk, and was
eating a banana. I think he must've heard that I detested the
smell of bananas. 'I've got a dead body for you, old boy.'

'You're all heart, Seb,' I said, sitting down opposite him.
'Pat Dean's just dropped in to break the good news to me.
What's the SP?'

'Well, now, let's see.' Sebastian Mould spoke with what
my mother used to call a cut-glass accent. Apparently he'd
been commissioned into a hussar regiment and had the
longish hair to go with it, but after a few years, he'd tired
of the army and joined the police. He tugged briefly at his
luxuriant moustache and pulled a file across his desk. 'We
thought we had an unidentified female at first. She didn't

have any documents on her: no credit cards, no driving licence, nothing.'

'That's different from Rachel Steele, Seb. Her credit cards and driving licence were left in a shoulder bag by the body, together with a substantial amount of cash.'

'I don't think robbery was the motive here either, Harry,' said Mould. 'It was simply a case of her not owning credit cards or a driving licence in the first place. Apparently there are some people who manage without them.' He shook his head as though unable to comprehend life without such necessities of modern existence. 'In any case, she had about seventy-odd pounds in cash on her person, so I don't think it was a robbery gone wrong.'

'But from what you said just now, I take it you have identified her.'

'Yes, she had a few previous convictions for shoplifting and drugs, and we identified her from her fingerprints. In fact, she was a hoister in a big way – mainly from Oxford Street shops – to feed her drug habit. She eventually went down for a year in the nick before becoming a reformed character. But all that makes her a bad financial risk, which is probably why she hasn't any credit cards. Her name is Lisa Hastings, aged twenty-seven, five foot nine tall, with long brown hair.' He looked up. 'And significantly, she had been wearing a bra but it was missing when the body was found, and she'd been stripped to the waist, presumably so that her attacker could get the bra off. It wasn't found in the surrounding area. Our CSM is liaising with your Linda Mitchell and comparing notes, but it looks very much like the same killer.'

'Had she got any previous for prostitution, Seb?'

'Nothing on her file, Harry, but that doesn't mean that she wasn't on the game.'

'Where exactly was she found?'

'A few yards in from Ham Gate Avenue. It's quite dense there; I should think she was taken to the edge by car and then persuaded to walk into the undergrowth. She probably thought she was on a promise of a few quid to buy drugs.' Mould paused. 'But it seemed that she was unlucky, not realizing, of course, that her male companion had felonious intent.'

'It's really a part of Richmond Park,' I said, half to myself. 'What time was she found?'

'Half past eight this morning by a couple of schoolkids who were practising off-road rough-riding on their bikes on their way to school. They came across the body and rang the police immediately.'

'Where from? Where did they telephone from, Seb?'

Mould glanced at me with a despairing look. 'They each had a mobile phone, Harry,' he said, in a tone of voice a teacher might have used to explain something to an extra-ordinarily dim child. 'Kids do these days, you know. One of them rang the police and I've no doubt the other one was on his phone to a newspaper trying to negotiate a price for his story.'

'Have the boys been interviewed, Seb?'

'No. Once Pat Dean said he was handing it over to you, I left it. Didn't want to queer your pitch, old boy. I got my incident room skipper to send all the stuff he'd got on his computer to your chap. Should be there by now.'

'Thanks,' I said, and returned to my own incident room.

'I've got everything that Mr Mould's team have done so far on the Lisa Hastings job, sir,' said Wilberforce.

'Which I don't suppose amounts to very much, Colin.'

'I wouldn't dare offer an opinion, sir,' said Wilberforce, with a perfectly straight face.

'Not much! Where's Dave Poole?'

'He's getting the SP from Mr Mould's bag carrier, sir. The stuff that's not on the computer.'

'And the commander?'

'I understand he's gone across to the Yard to see the Assistant Commissioner, sir.'

'At half past six? Must be important,' I said. The commander was usually out of the office on the stroke of six like a rat up a drainpipe. 'What's that about, I wonder?'

Wilberforce, a master of tact and diplomacy, decided it was a rhetorical question and took a sudden interest in his computer. But I've no doubt he knew, and that meant that Dave would know, and Dave would tell me.

'Is Miss Ebdon about?'

'She's gone out to Richmond to interview Tony Miles, sir. One of the men identified in the wine bar at Richmond as having known Rachel Steele.'

'When did she go, Colin?'

Wilberforce glanced at the time shown in the corner of his computer monitor. 'About half an hour ago, sir. She took Steve Harvey with her.'

'And has the next team gone to the wine bar?'

Wilberforce swung back to his computer and scrolled down a page or two. 'Miss Ebdon detailed three teams, sir. She said that it wouldn't be a good idea for her to go again tonight, not after she took Max Roper to the nick.' He laughed. 'Particularly as one of the side effects was to break up Roper's engagement, is what she said.'

'Who has she sent, Colin?'

'She thought men and women pairings would be best, so she detailed Nicola Chance with Terry Gibbons, Mr Driscoll with Sheila Armitage and Liz Carpenter with Ray Furness.'

'Time you were off, isn't it, Colin?' I asked, glancing at the clock. Wilberforce should have been off-duty at six o'clock.

'Gavin Creasey asked me to do an extra hour for him. Apparently he's got something spoiling at his kid's school that Marion said he would only miss at his peril.' Wilberforce chuckled. 'I wouldn't want Gavin to get beaten up again.'

It was a standing joke on the team. Creasey always claimed that he was the personification of obedience because he was in fear of his wife, but everyone knew that he and Marion were blissfully happy. A rarity for a CID officer.

SIX

Tony Miles's flat formed part of a tastefully converted Victorian house in Weber Drive, Richmond, not far from the River Thames.

'I'm Detective Inspector Ebdon and this is Detective Constable Harvey. Mr Miles, is it?'

'Yeah, sure, I'm Tony Miles. Come on in.' Miles, a tall, well-built, perma-tanned man with a shock of blond hair and overpowering aftershave, was probably a year or two younger than Kate. His T-shirt was, Kate suspected, deliberately tight in order to show his upper body and arm muscles to advantage. She immediately recognized Miles as a man who had a very good conceit of himself. 'Max told me that a gorgeous lady detective would be coming to see me,' he said. 'And here you are.'

'Did he also tell you that I arrest people who don't cooperate, Mr Miles?' asked Kate, as she preceded Miles into his sitting room. She knew how to deal with men like him if the necessity arose.

Miles laughed. 'Take a seat and make yourself comfortable,' he said, as yet undeterred by Kate's frosty riposte. 'I'm sure I can persuade you to have a drink? You look like a G and T sort of girl to me.' He crossed to a cocktail cabinet and, taking out a bottle of gin, held it up and waggled it to emphasize his suggestion.

'No,' said Kate firmly.

'Oh, of course not. Sorry. Mustn't drink on duty, eh?' His laugh was almost a sneer.

'I don't mind drinking on duty, sport,' said Kate, deliberately hamming up her Australian accent, 'but I'm particular about the company I drink *with*.'

She signalled to Harvey to hand her the briefcase he'd brought with him. Taking out her own smartphone, she brought up the video taken from Rachel Steele's. She leaned across the coffee table that was between her and Miles and began to play the video.

'Once you've taken your eyes off my cleavage, mate, have a look at this,' said Kate. The video showed Miles tightly embracing Rachel Steele, his arm around her waist, and it was quite apparent that Rachel was not averse to the attention that Miles was giving her. At one point she leaned in much closer to Miles, put a hand firmly on his butt and began squeezing. It was clearly not a selfie. 'That is you, isn't it?' Kate asked, rather unnecessarily.

'Yes, it is.' Miles looked up, smiled and ran a hand through his hair.

'Who took that video?'

'Max Roper, the one who told me you'd be coming to see me. He's a workmate of mine.'

'How well did you know Rachel Steele?' asked Kate.

'Hardly at all, really. I'd only met her that night in the wine bar, and she immediately struck me as a good-time girl. Just my sort of woman, actually. A crowd of us get in there most nights when we come off the train, especially Fridays. It's a relaxation after a hard week's work.'

'I imagine that slaving away in human resources must be exhausting,' observed Kate drily. 'How many times have you seen this woman, before or since that video was shot?'

'Two or three times, I suppose, but she was usually in the company of another man.'

'The same man each time?' asked Harvey.

'No; as I implied just now, she was the sort of girl who liked a bit of variety.' Miles glanced at Harvey as if noticing him for the first time. 'Bit like me in that regard,' he said, switching his gaze back to Kate again and smiling. 'It was a different guy each time, and I think she went home with one or two of them.'

'When she went home with you that evening, I presume she stayed the night.' Kate had taken a chance on that having happened, not that it was much of one, but she made it sound as if she had already discovered it to be the case.

'Have you been having me followed, Inspector?' The question had taken Miles by surprise, and he was unable to disguise his shock at Kate's apparent omniscience. Suddenly the egotistical man-about-town pose vanished as he realized that, although this detective was an extremely attractive woman, she was not to be trifled with. Harvey was also taken aback by his DI's directness, but he managed to conceal his surprise. Being new to HMCC, he had a lot to learn about Kate Ebdon.

'I'd remind you that I'm investigating Rachel Steele's murder, Mr Miles,' Kate continued, 'so I'd advise you to stop playing to the gallery and answer my questions. And from now on, cut out the smart remarks. If you can manage that.'

'Phew! You get straight to the point, don't you, Inspector?'

'I don't have time to mess about, mate. What time did Rachel Steele leave you on the morning of Saturday the twenty-fifth of May?'

'How did you know the date? You *are* having me followed, aren't you?' Miles said accusingly.

'The date the video was shot is logged on the phone,' put in Harvey mildly. 'Therefore, if she stayed with you that night, she must've left the following morning. So perhaps you'd tell my inspector at what time she left.'

'About half past nine, I suppose. Being a Saturday, I didn't have to go to work.'

'Did Rachel have a job?' asked Harvey.

'I don't know, but I suppose she must've done.'

'How much did you pay her for your night of passion?' asked Kate, in matter-of-fact tones.

'Pay her? I didn't pay her,' protested Miles. 'In fact, I've never paid for it in my life.'

But Kate knew men, and knew that it would hurt the ego of a man like Miles to admit that he'd paid for sex. In any case, she was more inclined to think that Rachel had been a tom, something that was later proved to be the case. 'Where did she live?' persisted Kate.

'I don't know that either,' said Miles.

'Did you see her again, after the night she spent with you?' Kate asked.

'Only the once. It was a week later, I think. Yes, it was the following Friday.'

'And was that in the Talavera wine bar?'

'Yes.'

'And did she sleep with you that night as well?' Kate posed the question with unemotional candour, rather like a doctor discussing a sexually transmitted disease with a patient.

'No. As a matter of fact, she cut me dead,' said Miles ruefully, 'and went off with another guy. I never saw her again.'

'What did this other man look like?' Kate imagined that for Miles to have been superseded by another man must have injured his ego.

'He was about fortyish, I suppose, wearing a rugby shirt and a pair of jeans. Oh, and he had a moustache.'

Kate shuffled the prints and selected one. 'Is that him?'

'Yeah, that's the guy. What's his name?'

'I don't know,' admitted Kate. 'It was on the thirty-first of May, which tallies with what you just said. Have you ever seen this man in there again?'

'No, I haven't, but that doesn't mean he wasn't there. I usually go in on a Friday straight from work, as I said, but he might have been in on any other night of the week. I've never seen him getting off the train that Max and I are always on.'

'Are you and Max Roper good friends?'

'Sure. As I said just now, we work together and play together. We even went on holiday together. He brought his girlfriend, and I took my wife. When I had one,' he added, without any show of regret.

'When you say Max Roper took his girlfriend on holiday, would that have been Sophie Preston?'

'Good Lord, no. Sophie's only a recent acquisition, eight or nine weeks, I suppose. No, I think the girlfriend Max brought with him was called Maggie. Quite a stunner.'

'Where were you on Monday the tenth of June, Mr Miles?' asked Harvey suddenly.

'Er . . . the tenth? Hell, I can't remember what I was doing.'

'It was only last Monday,' said Harvey.

'Last Monday . . . oh, yes, I remember now. Well, I was at work all day. I got my usual train from Waterloo and arrived back at Richmond at about twenty past seven. I was supposed to play squash with a guy at about eight o'clock, but he cried off at the last minute. I went to the wine bar instead.'

'Did you speak to anyone at the wine bar?' Harvey was being thorough in discovering Miles's movements. 'Is there someone there who can confirm that you were there that night?'

'God, I don't know. I didn't stay long. Come to think of it, I don't think I saw anyone I knew. I only stayed for one, then came home and watched the telly.'

Given the ease with which most programmes can be recorded and played back, or even viewed an hour later on another channel or on catch-up, Harvey knew there was no point in asking what he'd watched. As alibis went, that was a non-starter.

'Who was this man you were supposed to play squash with?' asked Kate, taking up the questioning again.

'Just a guy I met in the wine bar.'

'What's his name?'

'Jason something.'

'You don't know his surname?'

'No, I'm afraid not.'

'Was he in the wine bar when you went there, instead of playing squash?' Kate sounded sceptical about Miles's story.

'No, but I wouldn't have expected him to be.'

'Have you seen him again since?'

'No.'

'I require you to give me a sample of your DNA, Mr Miles.' As the law stood, Kate had no legal right to take Miles's DNA at that stage, but she made it sound as though she did.

'Hey, now just a minute, Inspector. What are we getting into here? I think it's time I rang my solicitor.'

'Is he the solicitor dealing with your divorce?' Kate took another wild guess, but she was a good judge of character, especially when dealing with men like Miles.

'How the hell did you know that?' Miles was now thoroughly disconcerted. The woman he thought might be amenable to what he saw as his considerable charms was proving to be anything but.

'I would remind you again that I am investigating the murder of a woman you freely admit having slept with. You have a

very weak alibi for the evening of the tenth of June, the night
that Rachel was most likely murdered. Now, we can do this
one of several ways. You can provide me with a sample
of your saliva voluntarily, or I can arrest you on suspicion of
Rachel Steele's murder and obtain a superintendent's authority
to take a sample. It's up to you, really.'

Miles sighed loudly. 'You don't leave me much choice, do
you? OK, you win, Inspector. What d'you want me to do?'

By way of a reply, Steve Harvey took a DNA kit from his
briefcase. Taking an oral swab, he ran it around the inside of
Miles's mouth.

'Is that it?'

'That's it, Mr Miles.' Harvey put the swab into a phial,
bagged it, labelled it and signed it.

'We'll very likely have to see you again, Mr Miles.' Kate
stood and walked towards the door.

Miles rushed ahead of her to open it. 'I look forward to it,
very much,' he said, shaking hands and attempting to hold her
hand longer than necessary, but immediately relinquished it
when he realized that he was in danger of having several of
his fingers broken. 'Perhaps we could meet for a drink sometime. When you're on your own.'

'Wait in the car, Steve,' said Kate, and when Harvey was
out of earshot, she turned to face Miles. 'Now just you listen
to me, you half-baked, self-opinionated little upstart,' she began.
'You might think you're God's gift to women, but the last
mongrel who tried anything on with me finished up in a cell
at the nick.'

'I'll take that as a no, then,' said Miles.

'Everything all right, ma'am?' asked Harvey when Kate
joined him in the car.

'Why wouldn't it be?'

Kate Ebdon had decided to go straight to the Talavera wine
bar from Miles's flat, but she knew that DCs Nicola Chance
and Terry Gibbons would be there already. She rang Nicola's
mobile and told her about the man in the rugby shirt who
Miles said he'd seen hugging Rachel Steele.

'He's in one of the photos that you should have on your mobile,

Nicola. He's about fortyish with a moustache, and was wearing jeans and a rugby shirt in the video. See if you can identify him. If he's there, ring me back and we'll come in and deal with him without compromising you. We're right outside in our car.'

'Might even help us if you come in doing the coppering thing,' said Nicola. 'We can sympathize with the customers who think the Old Bill's being heavy-handed.'

'Just watch it, mate,' said Kate.

'Yes, ma'am,' said Nicola.

Five minutes later, Nicola rang Kate's phone. 'He's here, talking to a girl who looks young enough to be his daughter.'

'We're in luck, Steve,' said Kate. When she and Harvey entered the wine bar, one or two of the habitués nudged their partner and whispered a warning, having recognized Kate from the previous evening. Max Roper, Kate noted, was not there, but he was probably trying to patch up his faltering engagement to Sophie.

The man in whom Kate and Harvey were interested was wearing a colourful Hawaiian shirt and a pair of khaki combats, both of which seemed out of place in Richmond, or at least in this wine bar. As Nicola Chance had said, the girl he was talking to, and clearly trying to impress, appeared to be no older than twenty, but what had attracted the man was obvious.

'I reckon all her brains are in her boobs,' said Kate in a cutting aside to Harvey. 'Ah well, tough though it is, now's the time to break up their romantic tryst.' She crossed the floor of the bar and when she was next to the subject of her inquiry pulled out her mobile phone and stared at the picture of the man now sitting in front of her.

Kate's close proximity obviously annoyed the man. 'Can I help you?' he demanded.

'I hope so,' said Kate, turning the phone so that the man could see the photograph. 'Is that you? And before you come up with some smart answer, I'm a police officer. Detective Inspector Ebdon.'

The girl slid off the stool she was seated on and, with an apologetic smile, said, 'I'm just going to the ladies' room, Jason.'

'Yeah, right,' said the man, and turned back to Kate. 'Yes, that's me, and that's Rachel Steele with me in the photo.'

'How well did you know her?'

'Only casually. We slept together that night, and she stayed the weekend, but then I saw her cosying up to Max Roper. She was like that, though: she played the field. I heard she got murdered.'

This was not quite the reaction that Kate was expecting. 'When was the last time you actually saw her, Mr . . .?'

'Skinner. Jason Skinner. Like I said, it was the Sunday when she left. What was the date of that photograph?'

'The thirty-first of May, a Friday.'

'That'd be right, then. To make it absolutely clear, she stayed with me that night, and the Saturday and Sunday nights as well. It was the Monday that I saw her in here, wrapped around Max.'

'Why did you cry off a squash match with Tony Miles on Monday the tenth of June, Mr Skinner?' Kate took another wild guess purely on the basis that the man's name was Jason.

Skinner gave a derisive laugh that was more like a snort. 'He was the one who cried off. He said he had something spoiling, by which I assumed he had a bird lined up. No woman is safe since Miles's wife left him.' He suddenly realized what he'd said. 'Heavens, I didn't mean that literally, Inspector. I didn't mean he's the sort of guy who goes about murdering women.'

'I should hope not,' said Kate drily. 'Do you know where Rachel Steele was living, Mr Skinner?'

'No. I did ask her, in a casual sort of way, but she dodged the question. Perhaps it was a flop she wasn't proud of. She wouldn't tell me where she was working, either.'

'I take it you live locally.'

'Yes,' said Skinner, and after a moment's hesitation provided his address.

'D'you work in Richmond, Mr Skinner?' asked Harvey.

'I work all over the place. I'm a locksmith.'

'Yes, but I presume you must have business premises somewhere.'

Skinner laughed. 'That's yesterday's way of working. I advertise online – I've got a website – and all my equipment's in a van. I take my workshop with me.'

'You said just now that Tony Miles stood you up on Monday the tenth of June,' said Kate, taking up the questioning again. 'What did you do instead of playing squash?'

'I went for a workout. I belong to a health club.'

'Can anyone vouch for that?' asked Harvey.

'Dozens of people, I should think. Anyway, they log you in and out on their computer.' Skinner glanced around. 'Where's that girl got to, I wonder?'

'She just left,' said Harvey.

Skinner had been sitting with his back to the entrance of the wine bar, but Harvey, and indeed Ebdon, had seen the girl come out of the ladies' room and make a rapid exit.

'I don't think we need to trouble you further, Mr Skinner. We'll leave you to get on with your evening.'

'What's left of it,' muttered Skinner.

'I seem to have a habit of ruining people's evenings whenever I set foot in this place, Steve,' said Kate, completely ignoring Nicola Chance and Terry Gibbons, who were in conversation with a man in a white shirt and jeans.

'What now, ma'am?' asked Harvey.

Kate glanced at her watch. 'Half past eight. Time to visit Miles again, Steve, and find out why he's been lying to us.' She took her mobile phone from her shoulder bag in response to its distinctive ringtone. 'Ebdon.' And then, 'That's all we need, guv'nor. Yes, I will.'

'Problems, ma'am?' asked Harvey.

'Yes, for one thing stop calling me "ma'am" just because I'm a woman. It's "guv", same as for the men. Got it?'

'Yes, ma'am – er, guv,' said Harvey.

'As for the second thing, that was Mr Brock. The team has just got itself a second murder. Looks like the same MO as Rachel Steele. For a start, we'll find out where Miles was last night, and then we'll speak to Max Roper again. Damn, I don't think I brought his address with me.'

'I did, guv,' said Harvey. 'Sergeant Wilberforce gave it to me. He said we might need it.'

'Why am I not surprised?' said Kate.

*   *   *

'Have you come to take me up on my offer?' Tony Miles opened the door of his flat wide. It seemed that there was no way of suppressing the man's conceit about his perceived prowess with women. 'Oh, you've brought the same officer with you. Come in. I suppose it's no good offering you a drink?'

'Why did you lie to me, Mr Miles?' said Kate, as she led the way into his sitting room.

'What d'you mean?' Miles sounded disconcerted, first because Kate had completely ignored his childish attempt at an advance and second because he had a nasty suspicion that she knew something that he'd rather she didn't.

'You know damned well who Jason Skinner is.' Kate remained standing, forcing the pseudo-gallant Miles to stay upright too. 'You told me that he'd cried off a squash match, but it was you who opted out. Where were you? And you'd better tell me the truth this time because my patience is wearing extremely thin. You got that, mate?'

'Oh, God! Look, could I talk to you alone, Inspector?'

By way of reply, Kate turned to Harvey. 'Have you brought handcuffs with you?'

'Yes, guv,' said Harvey promptly. He hadn't, of course, but he knew the game that Kate was playing, and was prepared to play along with it.

'All right, all right.' Miles raised both of his hands in an attitude of surrender.

'Right, we'll start again,' said Kate. 'Where were you on the night of Monday the tenth of June?'

'I was with a girl. It was a last-minute thing, but I met her in the wine bar earlier that evening. She was drinking alone and she told me that she'd had a bust-up with her fiancé and walked out on him. I suggested that we brought a bottle of wine back here, so that I could console her.' Miles emitted a lascivious chuckle. 'And, well, one thing led to another.'

'The name of this woman?' demanded Kate.

'Oh, I say. It could cause no end of grief if the guy in her life found out.'

'Nothing like the grief you'll be in about ten minutes from

now.' Kate turned to Harvey once more. 'Ring Richmond nick and tell them we'll be coming in with a prisoner very shortly.'

'Well, if you must know,' said Miles hurriedly, 'it was Sophie Preston.'

Kate threw back her head and laughed. 'Don't tell me you were stupid enough to screw your best mate's girlfriend.'

For once, Miles was silent. He just nodded.

'Well, that's that out of the way. Now you can tell me where you were last night.'

'That's easy. I stayed in London and took a girl to the theatre to see *Motown* at the Shaftesbury Theatre. I've got the tickets.' Miles nearly tripped over in his rush to reach a bureau on the far side of his sitting room. After a few seconds' rummaging, he produced the tickets. 'There you are, Inspector.'

Kate glanced at the tickets. 'Who was the woman you went with, Mr Miles?'

'Oh, no! Do you have to?' But seeing the expression on Kate's face, he offered up the woman's name, address and phone number.

'Thank you. Good night, Mr Miles.' Kate turned when she reached Miles's front door. 'One other thing, Mr Miles. It's not a wise move to take me for a fool.'

For once, Miles made no attempt at a flirtatious riposte.

SEVEN

'**I**s that Sophie Preston?' asked Kate Ebdon when a female voice answered her call on the Friday morning following her interview with Tony Miles.

'Yes. Who's this?'

'The police. Detective Inspector Ebdon. I need to speak to you as soon as possible, Miss Preston. Where are you at the moment?'

'I'm at home.'

'And where's that?'

Sophie Preston gave Max Roper's address.

'Are you two reconciled, then?' asked Kate.

'On and off. But if you wanted to talk to him as well, he's not here. He's gone to work.'

'Don't you work, Miss Preston?' asked Kate.

'Yes, but not on a Friday. Anyway, what's this all about?'

'As I said, I need to talk to you. I'll be there in about an hour.'

Not having been in at the start of the investigation into the Lisa Hastings murder meant that I was at a disadvantage. Although Seb Mould had passed across everything he had, it was not the same as viewing the body *in situ*; that always seemed to me to be the logical place to start. Nevertheless, we had to do the best we could.

That said, it's a different technique entirely if you're dealing with a murder where there is no body, and there have been several convictions in such cases despite the lack of that fundamental and most useful piece of evidence. But we weren't dealing with a suspicious missing-person inquiry that finishes up as a murder.

The first stop on the Friday morning was at Henry Mortlock's post-mortem room.

'Just finished, Harry.' Mortlock took off his protective gloves and dropped them into a waste bin. 'Same as before, more or less,' he said, gesturing at the body of Lisa Hastings, which he had just finished roughly sewing up with sutures. 'Strangled from behind with marks on the neck similar to those I found on Rachel Steele. Again, there were no defensive wounds on the hands, and I imagine she was taken by surprise. When I examined the body at the scene yesterday morning, there were marks on her shoulders and back commensurate with having recently worn a brassiere.'

'Which was nowhere to be found, I suppose,' put in Dave.

'Ah, you've brought your lingerie expert with you, Harry,' Mortlock said sarcastically. 'But, Sergeant Poole, I only examined the cadaver. I didn't search the surrounding area for the lady's missing underwear. That, I seem to recall, is the job of the scientific people or, dare I say it, the police.'

'Oh dear! Did you lose at golf?' asked Dave mildly.

'Her physical appearance is strikingly similar to that of Rachel Steele,' continued Mortlock, completely ignoring Dave's banter. 'Roughly the same height and measurements, and she had long brown hair much like the other girl. And once again, she was not *virgo intacta*, but neither was she pregnant.'

'Any traces of recent sexual intercourse?' asked Dave hopefully.

'Sorry to disappoint you, Sergeant Poole, but there was no semen from which you could get a DNA sample. It seems that even murderers are heeding the advice to avoid having unprotected sexual intercourse.'

'Time of death, Henry?' I asked.

'About ten o'clock last night.'

It was obvious that Sophie Preston's days off were spent just slopping around. When she answered the door to Kate Ebdon and Steve Harvey she was attired in a pair of jeans and an old sweater, she wore no make-up and her hair was in disarray.

'It must be important for you to come all the way out to Richmond to talk to me,' said Sophie. 'Couldn't you have asked your questions on the phone?'

'No,' said Kate.

'Oh! Sounds serious.' Sophie and the two detectives took seats in the comfortably furnished living room. Kate could see that Sophie had influenced the décor. It was probably an untidy bachelor pad before she moved in with Roper following their engagement, or maybe before it. Assuming they were still engaged, that is.

Kate took out her pocketbook. 'Tony Miles claims that you spent the night of Monday the tenth of June in bed with him, Miss Preston. Is that true?'

Sophie blushed scarlet and looked around the room, a hunted expression on her face. 'Oh God!' she exclaimed. 'If Max finds out he'll kill me, and Tony as well, I wouldn't wonder.'

'Does Max make a habit of killing people?' asked Harvey mildly.

'No, of course not,' said Sophie scornfully. 'It's a figure of speech.' She leaned forward, elbows on knees, and ran the fingers of both hands through her hair. 'Does Max have to know about this?' she asked imploringly.

'Not unless you tell him.' Kate noticed for the first time that Sophie Preston wore a gold chain around her left ankle, and wondered who had given it to her.

'But why do I have to account for my movements that night? I don't understand. What d'you suspect me of having done?'

'It's not your movements I'm interested in,' said Kate. 'It's Tony Miles's.'

Linda Mitchell arrived in the office later that morning.

'I hope you've got more than Henry Mortlock was able to give me, Linda.'

'You probably already know that the victim's bra was missing, Harry.'

'Yeah, I heard.'

'Interestingly, another cigarette butt was found at the scene. It's the same make as the one we found in Richmond Park, and it's being tested for DNA. It was a common brand, though, Harry, and I don't want to get your hopes up, but it does seem a bit too much of a coincidence.'

'It's almost as if this guy wants to get caught,' I said, but realized immediately that pinning my hopes on two cigarette butts of the same make was hoping too much.

'Are you sure it's a man?' Linda raised a quizzical eyebrow. When we discovered the body of Rachel Steele I'd posed the same question, albeit as a sarcastic retort to one of Dave's comments.

'Why d'you ask?' I said. 'Is there any evidence to suggest it's a woman who killed these two?'

'Wouldn't be the first time a lesbian committed a murder, guv'nor,' remarked Dave. 'In fact, we arrested one for murder some time ago.'

'Yes, I remember the case, but from what we've learned so far about Rachel Steele's extra-marital activities, Dave, I don't somehow think she was a lesbian, and Henry Mortlock said that Lisa Hastings wasn't a virgin.'

'It was just a thought, Harry,' Linda said. 'I'll let you know as soon as we get anything more. Oh, by the way, we checked the DNA from the cigarette found at the Isabella Plantation against the database.'

'And?'

'And no trace. Sorry, Harry, but we'll see what the second butt reveals. If the DNA is the same as the first, you might start to get lucky.'

And that, it seemed, was the sum total of the scientific evidence thus far, but one of the things I learned early in my CID career is that forensic scientists don't always come up with the answers the detectives want. I had a nasty feeling that good old legwork, knocking on doors and talking to people, was going to be the way to solve this one.

'Rumour has it that the commander paid a visit to the assistant commissioner yesterday evening,' I said, once Linda had left us. I purposely didn't float the statement in the form of a question, but Dave knew damned well it was. And laughed.

'I've got a mate who swans about the Yard doing some obscure job that he won't tell anyone about, and informed opinion is that our commander had applied for a deputy chief constable's job somewhere in Wales.' Dave paused thoughtfully. 'Or did he say the Midlands?'

'Oh, really? Did he get it?' I asked carelessly, trying not to sound too hopeful.

'No, he fluffed it. The rumour mill suggests that the Police and Crime Commissioner for the relevant police force said he was too old to be considered.'

'Oh, what a disappointment,' I said. 'For the commander, naturally.'

'Naturally, sir,' said Dave, his face betraying not the slightest trace of a smile. 'What's next, guv?'

'A trip to Lisa Hastings's last known address, Dave, the one shown on her criminal record.'

'Be a bloody miracle if she went back there after she was released from the nick.'

'She did, Dave, but whether she's still there remains to be seen. Anyhow, we've got to start somewhere.'

The address shown on Lisa Hastings's criminal record at the time of her arrest was in Codsmere Road, Kingston upon Thames, less than three miles from Ham Common where her body was found. I'd asked Colin Wilberforce to speak to the local intelligence officer at Kingston police station to get the SP on the premises. The reply was not encouraging; drug squad officers had raided the house several times over the last year, the last occasion being four months ago, and several arrests had been made. The LIO knew of Lisa Hastings, and although she returned to that address immediately after her release from prison three months ago, he was not sure that she was still there. She'd not been placed on probation and was under no obligation to inform anyone if she decided to move. The resident landlord, he said, was Leroy Fitzgibbon.

'This address in Codsmere Road is where we'll start, Dave.'

'Sounds like fun,' said Dave gloomily. He'd read Wilberforce's report too.

'But we'll have a bite to eat first.'

The man who answered the door of the rundown Victorian three-storey house appeared reasonably clean. He had short hair – as opposed to matted locks that brushed the shoulders – and there were no tattoos on his bare arms. All of which should have indicated that he was close to being normal, except for the orange kaftan, the Moroccan-type sandals and the long string of chunky Mexican beads around his neck.

'We're police officers,' I said.

'I'm Dylan,' the man announced. 'I'm a poet and writer of metaphysical plays.'

'Good for you,' said Dave, whose English degree inclined him to regard such literary layabouts with scepticism, if not scathing contempt.

'There ain't no stuff here any more, man,' announced Dylan. 'We've cleaned it out ever since the fuzz was poking about.'

'That doesn't scan,' said Dave, in an aside that was completely lost on the Kingston bard.

'Does Lisa Hastings live here?' I asked, deciding not to reveal that she had been murdered. At least not yet.

'Yeah, sometimes.'

'What's that supposed to mean?'

'She lives here, but she spends a lot of time in her office, mostly evenings and sometimes all night if the price is right.'

'Two questions, Shakespeare,' said Dave. 'Is she here now? And secondly, where's her office?'

'No, and I don't know,' said Dylan.

'I think it might be a good idea,' said Dave, stepping a little closer to Dylan, 'if you were to search your brain, which shouldn't take too long, and tell my chief inspector where Lisa's *office* is to be found. This is in your own interest, Dylan, because my boss gets very angry when people don't tell him things, and he has this nasty habit of taking houses apart. From the inside out.'

'It's the last house on this side at the end of the road,' Dylan said hurriedly and, moving out to the doorstep, pointed down the street. 'That way.'

'And now you can show us to the room Lisa occupied in this grand hotel in which you live, Dylan.'

'Shouldn't you have her permission or a warrant, as she's not here?'

'Oh, but we do have her permission,' I said. 'Lead on.'

'When did you last see Lisa?' enquired Dave.

'Three mornings ago.' Dylan stopped halfway up the

stairs and turned. 'Why are you asking all these questions about her?'

'She's dead, Dylan. Murdered.'

'I knew it would happen sooner or later,' said Dylan philosophically. 'I told her.'

'Told her what?'

'Picking up men. I told her it would end in tragedy.' Dylan gave a great sigh. 'What's done cannot be undone,' he declaimed, throwing out his arms.

'Oh! You're familiar with the Scottish play, then,' commented Dave.

'Nah! That's from *Macbeth*, man,' replied Dylan.

Dave shook his head. 'Where did she go to pick up men?' he asked. 'And would you move up the stairs? I don't like talking to people halfway up a staircase. It gives me a crick in my neck.'

'Oh, yeah, right.' Dylan reached the top landing and stopped again. 'The nightclubs and pubs around Kingston are where she'd go to pick up a guy, and then she'd take him back to her office. But I think she got barred from most of those fun places, and she moved on to Richmond.'

'When?' I asked.

'About a couple of weeks ago, I suppose.'

'Good. Now which is her room?'

'This one.' Dylan pushed open a door and made to enter, but Dave stopped him. 'We'll take it from here. We'll speak to you again downstairs when we've finished.'

'Dave,' I said, once we were inside the room, 'was there a key found among her possessions?'

'No idea, guv. D'you want me to give Colin Wilberforce a bell?'

'No, there's no point now we're here, but I wondered if she'd been carrying a key to the room where she took her clients.'

'There might be a spare here,' said Dave. 'On the other hand, I daresay we could manage to gain entry.'

Lisa Hastings's room contained only the bare essentials. There was a bed, a cheap wardrobe containing one or two cheap dresses, a pair of jeans, a pair of shoes, and a chest of

drawers in which we found a few items of underwear. It was
the sort of place where I would expect to find a drug addicted
prostitute who'd reached rock bottom.

'Nothing here that'll tell us anything, Dave,' I said. 'And
no key to her office.'

We returned to the ground floor. Dylan was hovering in
the hall.

'D'you make enough money out of your artistic talent to
exist on, Dylan?' asked Dave conversationally.

'No, man, I'm waiting for the breakthrough. Meantime, I'm
on Jobseeker's Allowance.'

Dave nodded sympathetically. 'It must be difficult finding
a job as a poet or a metaphysical playwright. Not many vacan-
cies, I'd have thought. Now, Dylan, d'you know of anyone
Lisa was seeing regularly?'

Dylan shook his head. 'Nah!' He thought for a moment
or two. 'Apart from the landlord. She'd turn a trick for him
if she was a bit short of the readies to pay the rent. Sort of
like barter, really.'

From what we'd seen of Lisa's room, it was obvious to
me that the landlord wasn't too choosy. 'Where is the landlord?'
I asked.

By way of a reply, Dylan pointed silently at a door at
the end of the hall.

'What's his name?' I asked, seeking to confirm the
information I'd received from the LIO at Kingston nick.

'Leroy Fitzgibbon,' whispered Dylan.

'Is he in?'

'Yeah, man, he's always in.'

Dave pushed open the landlord's door, ensuring it crashed
noisily against a piece of furniture.

'What the hell?' Leroy Fitzgibbon was propped up on his
bed watching a programme on television, and started in alarm.
'Who the hell's you, man?' He was about the same skin shade
as Dave, and his ancestors probably originated from the same
part of the world.

'Police,' said Dave, picking up the remote control and
switching off the television.

'What's wrong? Are you da Vice Squad?'

'Now what makes you ask that, Leroy? Expecting the Vice Squad, were you?'

Fitzgibbon backtracked rapidly. 'No, man, I just thought, seeing as how there used to be junkies and hookers an' all that what was living here, that you might not be up to speed on the ongoing situation.'

'Unfortunate choice of phrase.' Dave tossed the remote control on to the bed.

'But we're all cleaned up now.' Fitzgibbon hadn't understood Dave's quip and therefore chose to ignore it.

'Is that a fact? By the way, you can cut out the Jamaican accent. You're not very good at it, and I know you were born in Poplar anyway,' said Dave. 'Tell me about Lisa.'

'She's a respectable young lady,' said Fitzgibbon, reverting to his native East London mode of speech, but it was obvious that he didn't expect to be believed.

Dave laughed. 'Of course she was. But to answer your question, we're not from the Vice Squad. We're from Scotland Yard and we're investigating a murder.'

'Murder?' Fitzgibbon swung his legs off the bed and stared at the detectives in alarm. 'Who's been murdered?'

'Lisa Hastings,' I said. 'The woman who used to pay her rent in kind. That is to say, pleasuring you in that pit you're sleeping in.'

Fitzgibbon looked shifty, but said nothing.

'Which means that you're guilty of living on immoral earnings,' said Dave, and turned to me. 'D'you think we should arrest him now, sir, or squeeze him a little bit more and see if any pips come out?'

'No, hang on, man. Wait a minute,' protested Fitzgibbon. 'You got that all wrong. She offered, like. Lisa was a very friendly girl, and she practically threw herself at me.'

'And you're so weak, you just couldn't resist,' suggested Dave. 'What d'you reckon, sir?' he asked, turning to me again.

'Rather depends on how much he's prepared to tell us, Sergeant. Of course, it's possible that it was him who murdered that *respectable* young lady called Lisa Hastings, and that would solve all our problems.'

That did it. Suddenly, Fitzgibbon was falling over himself to assist us.

'Look, man, I never knew what she was up to until I saw her going into this house down the end of the street with some guy. Well, then the penny dropped, like, and I told her she had to go, after all the troubles we had with the fuzz – er, I mean with the police, and she went.'

'When was this?'

'Three days ago. She said she'd come back for her stuff, and I told her she'd better make it soon or I'd take it down the tip. But she never come back. On my mother's grave, I never had nothing to do with her getting topped, man.'

'Your mother's still alive and living in Poplar, Leroy,' said Dave, taking a guess on the longevity of Fitzgibbon's mother, 'but that aside, what about this story that your poet friend downstairs told us about her paying the rent in kind?'

'Like I said just now, she come on to me, but she always paid her rent on time. Her getting all fruity, like, wasn't nothing to do with that.'

'I'll believe you, Leroy,' I said, 'but there's a thousand policemen who wouldn't.'

'A thousand and one,' muttered Dave. 'You said Lisa went three days ago. Where did she go?'

Fitzgibbon shrugged. 'Search me, man.'

'I'd rather not,' said Dave, and glanced at me. 'I think I know where she'll have gone, sir.'

'So do I,' I said. 'Did she have any particular men friends, Leroy? Men that she saw more than once, maybe?'

'She always kept her business affairs private,' said Fitzgibbon.

'Afraid of industrial espionage, I suppose,' commented Dave quietly.

'We'll be back if we don't get any satisfactory answers elsewhere,' I said.

'And next time we *will* bring the Vice Squad, Leroy,' said Dave, a comment that quite clearly discomfited Fitzgibbon ever further.

We went back into the hall to find a nervous Dylan hovering by the door to his room.

'Everything all right, man?' he enquired.

'Not yet,' I said.

'What's wrong?' asked Dylan desperately.

'I don't think Mr Fitzgibbon is very pleased with you, Dylan,' said Dave.

'He's not?' Dylan appeared very distressed at that comment. 'Did he say why?'

'He doesn't like your metaphysical plays.'

'But I haven't written any yet,' wailed Dylan.

The house at the end of Codsmere Road was similar in every particular to the one we'd just left.

'Yes?' The harridan who answered the door stared at us suspiciously, but she knew instinctively who we were. She must've been at least sixty-five. Either that or she was a forty-year-old who'd had a hard life.

'Police. We need to see the room that Lisa Hastings used for purposes of prostitution,' I said.

'Have you got a warrant?' The woman obviously had knowledge of such legal niceties, which wasn't surprising, but apparently not a very wide knowledge.

'We're about to,' said Dave, 'and it'll be for your arrest on charges of living on immoral earnings, being concerned in the management of a brothel and obstructing police in the execution of their duty.' After a suitable pause, he added, 'On the other hand . . .'

'Top of the stairs, first door on the right,' said the crone.

The room was furnished with basic prostitution equipment: an iron-framed bedstead, useful for tying up those customers who enjoyed that sort of thing; a washbasin in one corner; and a small tasselled rug that had probably been at its best in about 1950. But, unsurprisingly, there was nothing to indicate that anyone actually lived here. It was merely a sterile place of business used for a quick screw – pay up and get out. Next, please!

We returned to the ground floor. The crone was hovering at the foot of the stairs.

'Next time you see that Lisa you can tell her not to bother coming back, mister. I can do without trouble from your lot. I never knew what she was doing up there. She just used it to have a chat to old friends. Least, that's what she said.'

Dave laughed. 'As a matter of fact, we saw her this morning. In the mortuary. She'd been murdered.'

Apart from a shrug, that piece of news evinced no reaction.

'We'll talk in your room,' I said, fearing there might be ears listening.

It was a mistake. The woman's room was multifunctional: bedroom, kitchen and office. And it had the stale reek of decay.

'What's your name?' I asked, having declined to sit down on the motheaten settee.

'Agnes Hoskins. Mrs Hoskins.'

'And where's Mr Hoskins?'

'Don't know, don't care. He buggered off years ago.'

I couldn't help but have a secret admiration for the departed Mr Hoskins.

'Would I be right in thinking that Lisa was living here for the past three days, Mrs Hoskins?'

'No, it's not allowed. It's against the house rules.'

I nearly asked to see a copy of the house rules, but resisted the temptation.

'Was there one particular man who Lisa Hastings entertained here, Mrs Hoskins?' asked Dave.

'Might've been. I never saw who she was taking up to her room. It might've been the same man every time or it might've been a different one. We mind our own business here.'

'How much rent did you charge her?' I asked, and the suddenness of the question seemed momentarily to discomfit the woman.

'I don't see what that's got to do with anything.'

'Oh, but it has,' put in Dave. 'Her Majesty's Revenue and Customs takes a great interest in people who don't pay the correct amount of tax. Or who don't pay any at all.'

'There was one bloke who come more than once,' Agnes Hoskins volunteered hurriedly.

'What was his name?' I asked.

'Dunno.'

'What did he look like, then?'

'Bit shorter than him,' Agnes said, pointing at the six-foot-tall Dave Poole. 'White, of course, but ordinary like. Oh, and he had a suit on,' she added, raising her eyebrows in apparent amazement at such sartorial eccentricity.

'You say he came more than once. How often?' It was hard getting answers from this woman, but it was just possible that she may have the information we needed to find the Hastings girl's killer.

'Twice. Leastways, I only saw him twice. I just happened to come out of my room when he was going up the stairs.'

'How fortunate,' said Dave. 'And when did you last see Lisa Hastings?'

Agnes Hoskins screwed her face into its thoughtful mode. 'Yesterday,' she said eventually. 'About dinner time.'

'What time d'you call dinner time?' asked Dave, to whom dinner was an evening meal.

'One o'clock. Ain't that when everyone has dinner?'

'And that was the last time you saw her?'

'Yeah.'

'Was she going out?'

'Yeah.'

Dave emitted a loud sigh. 'And was she alone?'

'Yeah.'

'Thank you, Mrs Hoskins,' I said.

'You can let her room now,' said Dave, as we made towards the front door. 'But don't forget to tell the tax people. Before we do.'

'That description was worse than useless, Dave,' I said as we reached the car.

'I don't believe there was such a man, guv'nor,' Dave said. 'In fact, I didn't believe a word of anything she said.'

EIGHT

Dave and I got back to the office at about half past six to find that Detective Superintendent Dean had authorized the use of HOLMES, the Home Office Large Major Enquiry System, indication – as if I needed it – that I was now investigating a serial killer. Before settling down to dictate my statement about our visit to Codsmere Road, I checked with the incident room to see if there was anything fresh. There was.

'I've just received a call from Heathrow Airport, sir,' said Detective Sergeant Gavin Creasey, the night-duty incident room manager. 'Daniel Steele's been detained, along with a woman holding a passport in the name of Rachel Steele.'

'They didn't stay long,' I said. 'Today's Friday, and they only went on Tuesday. I wonder why.'

'Easily explained, sir.' Creasey chuckled. 'They were deported.'

'What for?' I sat down next to Creasey and glanced at his computer. The screen saver was a photograph of the original Scotland Yard, but there was nothing about knock-offs at Heathrow.

'It seems that the immigration guys on the Seychelles are pretty switched on,' said Creasey. 'Their computer showed that a Mrs Rachel Steele and her husband took a holiday there last year, but the passport presented on the previous occasion was still in date. The immigration officer asked the woman when that passport had been stolen and she told him it hadn't. At that point she became flustered and burst into tears.' Creasey grinned. 'With me so far, sir?'

'I think I'm ahead of you, Gavin. Bent passport?'

'More or less, sir. The Seychelles immigration officer did some digging and got their police to telephone the Yard. All this was on Tuesday when the Steeles landed, since when she's been locked up in the capital's police station in Victoria. Daniel

Steele was given restricted leave to land – reporting to police daily, and that sort of thing – and opted to stay at a nearby hotel. After a lot of email traffic back and forth, the Seychelles authorities finally received the photograph we'd forwarded to Heathrow. And bingo! That's when it was discovered that the current "Mrs Steele" was, in fact, Sarah Parsons. At that point she admitted having made a false statement to obtain the passport.'

'Did Daniel Steele get deported too, Gavin?'

'Yes, sir. After some internal debate the authorities out there decided that he must've been involved in the fraud and they were both put on the next plane back to the UK. She's in custody, but having checked the Police National Computer the arresting officer at Heathrow found that you had an interest in Daniel Steele as well, and detained him too. Heathrow police asked what you wanted done with them.'

'Arrange to have them sent back here under escort, Gavin,' I said. 'There's a convenient police station right here beneath our feet. That'll do for a start, and then we can hand the job over to the department at the Yard that deals with bent passports.' I was not best pleased. It meant that I'd have to await their arrival. I wasn't sure what an interview would elicit as I was certain now that Daniel Steele hadn't committed the second murder, even if he'd committed the first. Nevertheless, he still had to explain his sudden departure. Did he think I knew about the dodgy passport, or did he have something else to hide?

I returned to my office and telephoned Lydia Maxwell.

'Hello, stranger,' she said. 'How are you?'

'Snowed under, I'm afraid, Lydia. I had hoped to sneak away and take you to dinner, but as if two murders to deal with wasn't enough, I've now got a couple of suspects on their way from the airport. I'll have to interview them before I can get away. Maybe tomorrow?' I asked tentatively. So far, our short relationship had consisted mainly of two dinners and my frequent apologies for not keeping a date, but Lydia was a patient woman and, it seemed, happy to wait. But no woman will wait forever.

'Whenever you can make it, Harry. I know you can't control what you're doing.'

Oh, what a perceptive woman you are, I thought.

It was almost a quarter to eight before Creasey came into my office. 'They're downstairs in an interview room, sir. I've alerted Dave Poole and he said he'll meet you down there.'

Daniel Steele and Sarah Parsons both looked very tired after their brief sojourn in the Seychelles and the long flight back. Steele was in need of a shave and Sarah Parsons, devoid of make-up, looked drawn and haggard after her ordeal. I've never visited the Seychelles and I've no idea what the cells at their police stations look like, but I imagine that someone accustomed to the twee lifestyle of Superior Drive, Camden Town would have found incarceration something of a culture shock.

'D'you want this interview recorded, sir?' asked Dave.

'Not at the moment,' I said, and turned my attention to Daniel Steele. 'What made you rush off within hours of my interviewing you at your house, Mr Steele?'

'I needed a holiday.'

'And what about you, Miss Parsons?' I took a guess at her being single, but I've been known to make mistakes about women before.

'How did you know my name?' She didn't correct my assumption that she was unmarried.

'Your line manager, Jessica, gave us your name and provided us with a photograph of you,' I said.

'She'd no right to do that.'

'If she hadn't complied, we'd have arrested her for obstructing the police,' said Dave bluntly. 'We were investigating the murder of Rachel Steele – the real Rachel Steele – and we discovered that you were masquerading as her. That, together with your sudden departure with Mr Steele, led us to believe that either one of you, or both, were in some way connected to the murder.'

'But that's ridiculous,' said Daniel Steele.

'So is rushing out of the country with a woman who has obtained a passport by means of a false statement, immediately after being questioned by the police about the murder of your wife.' I let him ponder that for a moment or two, and then changed the subject. 'On another matter, have you spoken to Rachel's parents since I saw you last?'

'No, I haven't had the time,' said Steele lamely.

Edward and Gerda Jackson had already been told of their daughter's murder by Kate Ebdon, whom I'd sent there as soon as Steele had given us their address. Kate's visit was simply to inform them of Rachel's death, and she'd told them that I would be calling on them later.

The Jacksons lived in a small village on the outskirts of Guildford, a fairly easy drive from Belgravia. I decided that Dave and I would see them as soon as possible in the hope that they may be able to shed some light on their daughter's way of life. Right now, we didn't seem to be making much headway with either of the murders we were investigating. But first we had to interview the two lads who'd found Lisa Hastings's body.

'What will happen about the passport? They won't send me to prison, will they?' pleaded Sarah Parsons, suddenly starting to panic. 'I've already been locked up in a filthy cell for two days, and I haven't had a shower for ages.'

'The matter will be handed over to the appropriate department at New Scotland Yard,' I said. 'They will advise you when you are to be charged.'

'But what will happen?' Sarah Parsons was desperate now. 'Will I go to prison?' she asked again.

'I really have no idea.' I was unable to conjure up any sympathy for this woman, who appeared as self-serving as the man she'd been abroad with. 'As I explained, Miss Parsons, it's not my department. In the meantime, however, you will both be admitted to police bail to return to this police station one month from now. Once the necessary paperwork has been completed, you'll be free to go.'

'Why me?' asked Daniel Steele. 'What have I done that necessitates my being put on bail?'

'From the point of view of your wife's murder, Mr Steele, you're of no further interest to me unless more evidence comes to light. However, the Crown Prosecution Service may take the view that you were in some way guilty of conspiring with Miss Parsons to obtain her passport, and that's why you are being bailed. But the decision about prosecution is nothing to do with me.'

Once Dave had dealt with the matter of bail for our two 'persons of interest', we went back upstairs.

'Well, that was a waste of time, Dave.'

'But it does prove one thing, guv'nor. You don't have to be intelligent to make a fortune on the financial markets.'

My last task before going home was to telephone the parents of the two boys who had found Lisa Hastings's body on Thursday. Fortunately the two families lived next door to each other, and the twelve-year-old boys were firm friends. I arranged with the parents to interview the lads the next day, Saturday, at their respective homes.

Saturday was another blazing hot day, and my shirt was already damp by nine o'clock that morning when we arrived at the home of Tom Patel, one of the two boys who had found the body of Lisa Hastings. The boys and their families lived in a turning off Richmond Road, and the school they attended was only half a mile or so away. Ham Common was equidistant between the two on the route the lads normally took.

'You must be the detectives, sir,' said the man who answered the door. 'I am Ashok Patel.' He shook hands.

'Yes, we are, Mr Patel. Detective Chief Inspector Brock, and this is Detective Sergeant Poole.'

'What a terrible thing to have happened to that young woman.' Patel showed us into the sitting room and invited us to sit down. 'My wife has just made some lemonade. Would you care for a glass?'

'That's very good of you, thank you,' I said. It made a change from being offered tea, welcome though it always was.

'I have taken the liberty of asking Tom's friend Oliver to come in,' said Patel, once the lemonade had been served. 'I thought it might save you time if you saw the two of them together.' He laughed. 'They're practically inseparable anyway.'

'That's very helpful, Mr Patel.' I was satisfied that the question of collusion didn't arise. 'Are his parents happy with that?'

'I spoke to Peter and Naomi last night, after you phoned,

and they thought it was a sensible arrangement. But they'll come in if you think it necessary.'

'Not at all, Mr Patel. So long as we have an adult here while we're talking to them.'

'Excellent. I'll just drag the boys away from their computers. They're upstairs playing these mindless computer games. But I make a point of rationing Tom's time.' Patel glanced at his watch. 'And he's run out of today's allowance, anyway. If I don't keep an eye on him he won't get down to his books, and there's no way he can become a doctor if he doesn't study.'

The two twelve-year-olds were both clean cut and smart, given that they were attired in jeans and a T-shirt embellished with some inane slogan.

'This is my son Tom, Chief Inspector, and his friend Oliver Dawson.'

Dave and I shook hands with the boys, which seemed to come as a surprise to them. But I've always held the view that if you want youngsters to behave like adults you should treat them as such.

'Sit down, gentlemen,' I said, 'and tell me exactly what happened the day before yesterday when you found the body.'

The boys looked at one another, each with a guilty expression on his face, and it was immediately obvious that they had been forbidden by their parents to ride their bicycles across Ham Common.

'If you were doing something you weren't really supposed to be doing,' said Dave, 'my chief inspector will give you an official police pardon, which means that you can't get into trouble with your parents.'

It was another of Dave's strokes of genius, and I could only add my support to what he had just said, at the same time winking an eye at Ashok Patel.

'Well, sir,' began Tom Patel. 'Olly and I were on our way to school . . .' He paused and glanced at his father.

'You must always tell the truth, Tom,' said Ashok Patel, 'regardless of the consequences.'

'I know we shouldn't do it, but Olly and I were practising rough-riding across the common, and as we went through the trees we suddenly came across this lady lying on the grass. I thought to myself that's a funny place for a lie down, especially at that time of the morning.' Tom paused. 'What was even more strange was that her boobs weren't covered up.'

I sensed an admonition regarding slang was about to come from Tom Patel's father, and shook my head in his direction.

'Then I thought she might have been drunk,' said Oliver Dawson, 'and I moved closer. It was then that I saw that her eyes were wide open and staring. I called out to her, but she didn't answer. I didn't touch her in case I disturbed some vital evidence. I thought perhaps she'd been murdered, you see.'

'I touched her, sir,' said Tom Patel, taking up the story again, 'just to feel for her carotid artery, but there was no pulse.'

'Where did you learn all this, Tom?' asked Dave.

'On the telly.'

'It's a television set, not a telly,' put in Tom's father.

I held up a hand, gesturing him to remain silent. I didn't want any interruptions, and Ashok Patel acknowledged my signal with a nod of the head and a mouthed apology.

'Olly and I like watching American CSI programmes,' continued Tom. 'Anyway, we learned it in biology.'

'I got out my mobile phone and dialled nine-nine-nine,' said Oliver proudly, 'and called an ambulance and the police.'

'Why did you call an ambulance if you knew the woman was dead, Oliver?' Dave knew why, of course, but was interested in what the boys might say.

'Because Tom said we were not qualified to make that decision,' said Oliver.

'I'm not a doctor yet, you see, sir,' said Tom.

'Did you see anyone near the woman's body? Anyone running away, for instance, or a car pulling away as you rode on to the common?' There was no great point in asking that question. According to Henry Mortlock, Lisa Hastings had been dead for about ten hours when these two boys found her body. But I had to show interest. After all, one of them might want to become a policeman one day.

'No,' chorused the boys, and appeared genuinely sorry that they were unable to help.

'Well, you've both been of great assistance, gentlemen,' I

said, and we shook hands with the boys again as Dave and I stood up to leave. 'You're very observant young men.' They hadn't been much help at all, but there's no harm in encouraging youngsters who have willingly assisted the police. All too often these days people just walk away when they come across the scene of a crime, and even if they do stop to assist, the police can't be bothered to thank them.

'Remind me to send each of those lads a letter when we get back to the office, Dave,' I said as we were driving away from Ham on our way to Guildford.

Sally Croft was the woman Tony Miles claimed to have taken to the theatre on the twelfth of June. Kate Ebdon had telephoned her several times without success, but she had no intention of leaving a message on the answering machine, and it wasn't until Saturday morning that the Croft woman replied.

'I'm a police officer,' said Kate. 'I'd like to call on you, just to clear up one or two points.'

'Is it about Tony Miles?' The woman almost whispered the question.

'Yes, it is.'

'Could we meet at the coffee shop just around the corner from where I live?'

'Certainly,' said Kate, and ended the call. She turned to Steve Harvey. 'I've come to the conclusion that Richmond is a hotbed of adultery. It seems that everyone is at it, and I'll put money on Sally Croft being married.'

It was about ten o'clock when Kate and Harvey arrived at the coffee shop.

'That must be her,' said Kate, nodding in the direction of a woman sitting by herself at a table at the very back of the shop. 'Are you Mrs Croft?' she asked, as she sat down opposite a young woman with shoulder-length black hair, dressed in a crop-top and jeans.

'Yes, but how did you know I was married?'

'I've been a copper for quite a long time now,' said Kate, by way of a reply, 'and you get to know human nature fairly well in my job. When you asked if I wanted to talk to you about Tony Miles, you wanted to meet me in a coffee shop.

I knew straight away that you were married. To someone else. D'you want another coffee?' She nodded at Sally Croft's empty cup.

'Yes, please. No sugar.'

Kate turned to Harvey. 'Get the lady another coffee, Steve, there's a good bloke.'

'I didn't mean to finish up staying the night in London,' said Sally Croft, once Harvey had returned to the table. She spoke quickly and breathlessly, as though trying to purge herself of her indiscretion as quickly as possible. 'But the truth is that we went for a late supper after the show and then Tony said that the last train back here to Richmond had gone.' She shrugged. 'He said he'd book us into a hotel for the night, and, well . . .' She looked up as Harvey put a cup in front of her. 'Thank you.' She stirred the coffee absently. 'When we got to the hotel, I found that he'd booked it in advance.'

'How did you explain that away to your husband?' Kate asked. It was irrelevant to her enquiries, but she was always interested in the foibles of cheating wives and husbands. And she was amused that Sally Croft's innocence was such that she hadn't spotted precisely what Miles's intentions had been from the outset. The cost of the show was just the price he had to pay for a night in bed with the attractive woman sitting opposite her.

'He thought I was at the theatre with an old university girlfriend of mine,' said Sally. 'Anyway, why is any of this of interest to you?'

'We're investigating a murder that almost certainly took place that night,' said Harvey, 'and we need to be satisfied that Tony Miles was where he said he was.'

'Oh, he certainly was,' said Sally. 'We saw *Motown* at the Shaftesbury Theatre, followed by supper and a night in a hotel.' She looked down at her coffee, the expression on her face seeming to imply regret about the whole incident.

'Thanks.' Kate stood up. 'We'll not need to bother you again, Mrs Croft.'

'D'you think she's telling the truth, guv?' asked Harvey as they walked to where the car was parked.

'I don't know, Steve. Perhaps she's just saying what Miles

told her to say. And I'm sure that a lot of women would be that stupid,' she added cynically. 'For all we know *she* might have engineered this stay at a hotel with *him*, rather than the other way around. You never know, Mr Croft might be one of those terribly dull little men who has no interest in sex.'

'Further enquiries, then, guv?'

'In the fullness of time, Steve.'

It took Dave and me about an hour to get from Ham to the village outside Guildford where Rachel Steele's parents lived.

'Mrs Jackson?' I enquired of the woman who answered the door.

'Yes, I'm Gerda Jackson. I take it you are the policemen, come to talk to my husband and I about Rachel.' She was a tall woman and rather masculine in appearance. Physically, there was little similarity between her and Rachel.

'Detective Chief Inspector Brock and Detective Sergeant Poole, Mrs Jackson.' Although the woman spoke perfect English, I detected a German accent that I recognized. 'Are you from the Köln area by any chance?' I asked, as she showed us into her sitting room.

'Yes, I am. You know it?' The woman raised her eyebrows in surprise.

'I've been there a few times,' I said, without telling her that I was once married to a girl who came from the city. Helga had insisted on working as a hospital physiotherapist even after our son was born. The catalyst came when she left the four-year-old in the care of a neighbour and he fell into an ornamental pond and drowned. I could never forgive Helga for that, and what had started out as a happy and passionate marriage became increasingly acrimonious and, after sixteen years, resulted inevitably in divorce.

'I will fetch my husband. He is working in his study.'

'I hope we're not interrupting him,' I said.

'No, he knew you were coming, of course, but he's just catching up on a few things. He's in IT, you know.'

Edward Jackson was a slightly built man, and a good four inches shorter than his wife. He had a harassed look about him, a permanent frown and a toothbrush moustache.

'Mr Brock? We spoke on the phone yesterday.' Jackson shook hands with Dave and me and invited us to take a seat.

'I'm sorry about your daughter,' I said, shifting my gaze from one parent to the other.

'I'm not Rachel's mother,' said Gerda Jackson sharply.

'Oh, I'm sorry,' I said, 'but Daniel Steele didn't explain that.'

'We didn't know she was married until one of your lady detectives came here to tell us the news of her death,' said Gerda.

'I see. However, you'll appreciate that my job is to find out who murdered your daughter,' I said. 'Anything you can tell me about her, however trivial and seemingly unimportant, might help.'

Edward Jackson sniffed and stared at a mirror over a radiator before replying. 'She was a difficult girl,' he said eventually.

'In what way difficult?' asked Dave.

'Rachel was five when her mother died, and for the next thirteen years I was faced with bringing up the girl by myself, admittedly with occasional help from my mother, but then she died too. Believe me, Mr Brock,' continued Edward Jackson, shaking his head, 'those mid-teen years are when a girl needs a mother most, just to keep her in check.'

'I can imagine,' I said, even though I had no experience whatsoever of bringing up girls, but one or two of my friends had complained about the problems involved when their daughters became of an age to be interested in boys.

'Then I met Gerda when we were both working on a project, flying back and forth between London and Cologne. It was, I suppose, what you'd call a whirlwind romance, but at our ages it's best not to wait too long.'

I estimated that Gerda Jackson was at least fifty, and her husband a few years older.

'Did your stepdaughter get on with you, Mrs Jackson?'

'At first, yes, and I thought we would have a good relationship.'

'But it didn't work out?'

'No. Edward asked me to give Rachel advice about how she should dress and how she should conduct herself, but I'm afraid we always had a difference of opinion about such matters. She was quite rude at times and told me that I was not her mother and couldn't tell her what to do.'

'Then she became pregnant,' said Edward, with a deep sigh. 'Gerda arranged for her to have a termination, but it seems that was the last straw. She complained of Gerda's high-handedness, and after she'd recovered she walked out. We didn't know where she'd gone or where she was, and we've not seen her since.'

'How old was she when she left home?' asked Dave.

'Eighteen. That was seven years ago,' said Gerda, 'and as Edward said, we heard nothing more until your Inspector Ebdon told us she had been murdered.'

'To be perfectly honest, we thought she'd gone off with some boy, or was living in a squat somewhere,' said Edward. 'You hear such terrible things these days. We tried ringing her mobile, but she must've changed the number or got a new phone. Gerda and I contacted some of our colleagues and friends in IT to see if we could trace her that way, but we had no luck.'

We thanked the Jacksons and returned to London. It had been a wasted journey, and only served to confirm what we knew already: that Rachel Steele had been a wayward girl who'd developed into a woman who sought only her own pleasures and the company of men. Instead of which, she'd finished up dead in the Isabella Plantation in Richmond Park.

NINE

I t had been very much a wasted morning. The two boys who'd discovered the body of Lisa Hastings had done all the right things but in terms of moving the investigation forward weren't able to add anything. The Jacksons – outwardly anyway – had not appeared to be greatly disturbed by Rachel's murder, and had been unable to help at all in terms of pointing a finger at a possible killer. They did suggest that Rachel was promiscuous, but we'd already worked that out. I hated to admit it, but we seemed to have reached deadlock.

Dave and I had lunch at our favourite Italian and made our way back to the office.

'D'you want to do anything more about the last two men Rachel Steele called from her mobile, guv?' asked Dave. 'Roper, Miles and Skinner have already been interviewed, of course. DI Driscoll interviewed the other two and wrote them off as innocent parties. They'd met her at the wine bar, and after having had a few drinks exchanged phone numbers.'

'Anything in it?'

'Each of the men later got a call from Rachel inviting him to spend a night with her; at least, that was the implication. But having sobered up, they declined her offer – probably because they were married,' Dave added with a wry smile. 'DI Driscoll saw them again after the second murder and they denied any knowledge of Lisa Hastings. And they both had alibis to prove they were elsewhere at the time of her murder. The men's statements and DI Driscoll's covering report are with Colin Wilberforce.'

'Fine by me,' I said. Len Driscoll, who was the other detective inspector on my team, was thorough to a fault, and if he was satisfied with the outcome of those enquiries, so was I. Unfortunately, he was so good that we were going to lose him at any moment; he was next on the list for promotion to DCI.

'What about the other two outstanding selfies that were on Rachel's mobile? Any feedback on those?'

'Mr Driscoll and Sheila Armitage identified a guy called Dudley Fuller, and Liz Carpenter and Ray Furness fingered a Tim Harris. Fuller lives in the Richmond area, and Harris lives in Norbiton. Their phone numbers were on Rachel's phone.'

'Are those two teams still on duty, Dave?'

'Certain to be, guv. D'you want a word?'

'I'll just see Carpenter and Armitage, Dave.'

Moments later, they appeared in my office.

'These two guys you identified,' I began, and glanced down at my pad. 'Fuller and Harris. Have a word with them and see what they're made of, and find out if they'd ever met Lisa Hastings. Preferably tonight. Or earlier if you can find them.'

Given what we knew of the habitués of that particular wine bar, the chances of either of the two men being at home on a Saturday evening, comfortably dozing in front of their televisions, was remote. Neither officer looked happy about the assignment; they probably thought I'd sent for them to give them the rest of the day off. But that's police work for you. However, it turned out that Fuller and Harris didn't know each other and were married. More to the point, they were innocent of any connection with the death of Rachel, who they thought was a good-time girl. But by the time they'd sobered up, each of them had come to the conclusion that it hadn't been very clever to give her their phone number.

Given that rank hath its privileges, I decided that there was little else I could do before tomorrow, and seized the opportunity to ring Lydia.

'I've managed a few hours off this evening, Lydia. Would I be able to tempt you out to dinner?'

'No!'

'Oh, it was just that—' *She's going out with someone else,* I immediately thought. *I knew that sooner or later she'd get fed up with a copper letting her down time after time.*

'I've got a better idea, Harry.' Lydia paused and then laughed. 'I've never seen the inside of your flat. How about I come over there and prepare supper?'

'Er, well, I . . .' Police officers will face armed robbers, and although scared stiff will try to put on a brave face. But the thought of a newly acquired girlfriend wanting to enter one's flat and prepare a meal – or even inspect the accommodation – would throw even the stoutest of coppers into a panic. And it certainly did me. *Was it clean? Had the incomparable Gladys Gurney done everything? Yes, of course she had. Might Lydia want to view the bedroom? No, not yet anyway.* 'I don't think I've got anything in the fridge.' I was desperately trying to make up excuses.

'I didn't imagine you would have, Harry, my love,' she said. 'I'll bring what's needed with me, if you don't mind a simple meal. And don't rush around tidying up. I know what bachelor pads look like. I just hope that you've got some champagne in your fridge.'

'Yes, I have, and the fridge also contains white wine.' I wondered how many bachelor pads she had visited, and why. *No, don't go there; you're getting paranoid, Brock.* 'And I also have plenty of red wine.'

'I'm glad you've got your priorities right, Harry. About eight o'clock suit you?'

'Perfect.' Despite what Lydia had said, that would give me enough time to rush around and make sure the place was in reasonably good order for entertaining a lady, something I'd not done since Gail deserted me for the States.

Lydia arrived at precisely eight o'clock.

'You're very prompt,' I said, as she stepped into my small hall.

'More by good luck than good judgement,' Lydia said. 'I was able to get a cab straight away, and he found his way from Esher to your Surbiton apartment without any problems.' She handed me the cold bag she'd brought with her. 'Pop that in your kitchen, there's a dear.'

'Do I have to do anything with it? Put any of it in the fridge, or anything?'

'No, just leave it and I'll deal with it when the time comes. In the meantime, let's sit down and catch up.'

'What would you like to drink?' I showed her into the sitting room. 'Champagne or something stronger?'

'Champagne will be fine. Thank you.' Lydia took off her jacket and dropped it casually on the settee. Even wearing jeans and a denim shirt, she managed to look elegant. But she probably paid considerably more for her jeans than I paid for mine. 'The chalet is finished,' she announced, as she sat down in one of the armchairs.

'The chalet?' *What on earth is she talking about now?* I handed her a glass of Moët.

'Don't you remember? The night we had dinner with the Hunters I told you I was having the swimming pool covered in. Well, it was completed last week. You must come over and help me launch it.' She laughed. 'Though I'm not sure you can *launch* a swimming pool. Anyway, now tell me what you've been up to.'

'Oh, just investigating a couple of murders. The daily round, the common task, but nothing exciting. Until now,' I ventured.

Lydia laughed. 'You make it sound so commonplace, Harry.'

'It is. It's what I do.'

We chatted for about half an hour before she stood up. 'If you show me your kitchen, I'll get supper under way,' she said, and handed me her champagne flute. 'Be a dear and fill that up again.'

I watched her at work in the kitchen-diner, occasionally taking a sip of champagne as she moved about the confined space. She seemed to have no problem finding the necessary plates, cutlery and napkins, and within minutes had laid the table and served the starter.

'Smoked salmon on thin slices of walnut bread,' I said. 'It looks wonderful, and very cordon bleu.' My sole contribution had been to find wine glasses and uncork a bottle of Chablis.

'I'm afraid there's only a chicken Caesar salad to follow.'

'Only? I thought you said it was a simple supper.' I held up my glass of wine. 'Here's to us.'

'Here's to us,' she agreed. 'But don't get too carried away with what you seem to think is my culinary expertise, Harry. I couldn't manage to bring a pudding, so you'll have to go without.'

Despite Lydia's self-deprecation, the meal was really superb. 'That salad dressing was wonderful,' I said.

'It was nothing special, just something I put together myself.'

After supper we relaxed in the sitting room. It was still stiflingly hot and I opened the French doors that were a feature of my first-floor flat. There was no balcony, however, just an ornamental railing.

'Cognac, Lydia?'

'Just a small one, please.'

We talked about all manner of things, occasionally touching on the two murders at Cockcroft Lodge in North Sheen which had been instrumental in bringing us together. We talked also of our mutual friends Bill and Charlotte Hunter.

I glanced at my watch. It was almost eleven o'clock.

'Have you booked a taxi to take you back to Esher yet?' I asked.

'No, Harry, I haven't.'

'I'll see if I can get you one from the rank at Surbiton station, shall I?'

'I'm not in a hurry. Unless you're keen to throw me out.'

At twenty-two minutes past seven the following morning my mobile woke me with its loud, distinctive tone.

Moving Lydia's arm from across my chest, I reached over to the bedside table for the phone. She mumbled, turned over, but didn't wake up.

'Brock,' I said.

'Harry, it's Alan Cleaver.'

'Guv'nor?' I was wide awake in an instant. Cleaver was the detective chief superintendent in charge of Homicide and Major Crime Command, and he didn't ring up this early on a weekend without a damned good reason.

'Sorry to spring this on you early on a Sunday morning, Harry, but the body of another woman has been found.'

'When and where, guv?'

'Canbury Gardens, Kingston upon Thames, half an hour ago. Police from Kingston were called by a man whose dog ran into the trees there. The dog's owner followed and found the body. I know it's on HMCC South's patch, but the victim is similar in age and appearance to the other two you're investigating.'

'Who came to that conclusion, sir?'

'Jack Noble. He's at the scene and he's familiar with the other two toppings,' Cleaver continued, 'although he only attended the Ham Common one. But he reckons this latest victim was strangled in the same way as the other two. It makes sense for you to take this one as well. It looks like we've got a serial killer on our hands, Harry,' he said, confirming what I'd thought after the second murder. 'If you want any additional manpower or any more equipment, just give me a bell.'

'Thank you, sir. I'll get down there as soon as I can.' Jack Noble's opinion was worth listening to. As the HAT DI, he knew how to weigh up the situation accurately and rapidly.

'Good man, Harry.' Cleaver paused and chuckled. 'I hope I wasn't interrupting anything important,' he enquired airily.

'No, sir,' I said unconvincingly.

'Liar,' said Cleaver, and chuckled again. 'I've arranged for a traffic car to pick you up. In fact, it should be outside your place right now.'

'I'm on my way, guv'nor.'

Lydia was now wide awake. 'What's happening, Harry?'

'I'm sorry, but I've been called out. It's another murder.'

'Oh!' She pouted. 'Can't they send someone else?'

'It doesn't work like that, I'm afraid,' I said, as I rolled off the bed and gathered the various pieces of my clothing that had somehow finished up strewn across the bedroom floor. 'There should be a car outside as I speak.'

'Well, you're not going without a cup of tea.' Lydia threw back the duvet and stood up. Without bothering to put anything on, she walked through to the kitchen and filled the kettle.

'I do wish you wouldn't walk about like that when I've been called back to duty, Lydia.'

She just laughed.

By the time I'd dressed she'd made a pot of tea and put two slices of buttered toast on the worktop.

'I can't promise when I'm likely to be back,' I said. 'If you'd like to stay here, that is.'

'I'd love to stay, Harry love.' Lydia squeezed my arm. 'I'll go shopping, and if you ring me when you're leaving, I'll have a decent meal ready for you when you get in.' She smiled coyly as a sudden thought occurred to her. 'I'm not outstaying my welcome, am I? I wouldn't want you to think I'm pushing myself on you.' She sounded genuinely concerned.

'On the contrary, I think you're spoiling me.' I opened one of the kitchen drawers and handed her a key to the flat. 'You can put that on your keyring, and keep it there for as long as you like.'

She took the key and smiled, but said nothing.

As Cleaver had promised, there was indeed a car waiting outside.

'Morning, guv,' said the driver brightly. 'Lovely day for it.'

'Yes,' I said, somewhat tersely. Traffic Unit drivers were always sickeningly cheerful at any time of the day or night, but they were among the best drivers in the world. This one immediately set about proving it: it was about two miles from my flat to Canbury Gardens, and I arrived three hair-raising minutes after leaving home.

Four or five police cars and an ambulance were lined up in Lower Ham Road. Canbury Gardens, where the body was found, lay between there and the River Thames.

'We can't keep meeting like this, guv'nor,' said Jack Noble, the HAT DI, as I dismounted shakily from the traffic car. 'I gather that Alan Cleaver gave you the SP. In the circumstances I thought it wise to ring him direct, it being a Sunday morning and all that.'

'Yes, that's fine, Jack,' I said. 'Has she been identified?'

'Yes, she'd still got her handbag complete with cash, credit cards, passport, house keys and driver's licence.' Noble flipped over a page of his pocketbook. 'She's Denise Barton, aged twenty-five, with long brown hair and the same sort of neat figure as the other two. And she lived in Cobham.'

'Did she have a mobile phone with her, Jack?'

'No, she didn't. Unusual these days, and I wondered if the killer took it.' Noble paused, as though wary of putting forward an opinion. 'I know this isn't my case, but I wondered if he'd heard about the enquiries you'd been making about names and selfies on Rachel Steele's phone.' He shrugged. 'Only a thought, guv.'

'It's worth mentioning, Jack, thanks. Was this girl wearing a bra?'

'I don't know, but she's not wearing one now, and she'd been stripped to the waist.'

'How did you know she'd been strangled in the same way as the other two, then?' It wasn't a criticism, just curiosity.

'She's lying on her back and the fingermarks on the front of the neck are plainly visible, which seems to indicate strangulation from behind,' said Noble. 'Ah, here's the good doctor now. He should be in a joyful mood at this time on a Sunday morning.'

Dr Henry Mortlock proved to be the first of the murder technicians to arrive. He was followed quickly by Linda Mitchell and her evidence recovery team. A taxi pulled up and Kate Ebdon leaped out.

'Morning, Kate. How did you know about this?'

'You can blame me, guv,' said Noble. 'Once Alan Cleaver confirmed he was giving the job to you I phoned your incident room and gave them the heads up.'

'I told Dave Poole to meet us at the office, guv,' said Kate. 'There didn't seem much point in him coming down here from Kennington only to go all the way back to Belgravia, but as I live in New Malden it was no problem to get here. Don Keegan's the incident room manager, and he's assembling the rest of the team.'

'What did you tell him to do with them?'

'To hold them at Belgravia until you decide what you want done next.' She glanced around the area. 'There's a block of flats overlooking the gardens, so we might get lucky with house-to-house enquiries. Interesting, that, because with the other two toppings there weren't any places from which anyone could've seen anything.'

'I'll leave you to put that in hand, Kate. Now we'll wait to see what Henry's got to say about the body.'

The local police had already taped off the area, and Linda's people were laying stepping plates between the road and Denise Barton's body and erecting screens around the corpse.

'Paul Smith is the guy who found the body, and he's on a big white cabin cruiser just across from here. You can't miss it, it's the only one there,' said Noble. 'I got a brief rundown on what he saw and did, which wasn't much, and told him to go back to his boat and wait.'

'Thanks, Jack.' I turned to Kate. 'We'll have a word with Smith while Henry Mortlock's looking at the body.' We crossed Canbury Gardens to Paul Smith's cabin cruiser, ensuring we walked well wide of the crime scene.

'Mr Smith!' shouted Kate.

'Hello?' A suntanned man wearing just shorts appeared from a hatch in the stern cockpit.

'We're police officers,' I said. 'We'd like a word with you.'

'Come aboard.' Smith offered to help Kate, but she placed one hand on the narrow deck and vaulted aboard. 'You've done that before,' he said.

'A few times,' said Kate, as we followed Smith into the cabin.

'This is my wife, Trixie.' Paul Smith indicated a young blonde in a black swimsuit. Smith was about thirty, but I guessed that his wife was no more than twenty-two.

I introduced Kate and me, and accepted Smith's offer to sit down.

'I've just made a pot of coffee,' said Trixie. 'Would you like a cup?'

Once the coffee was served, we got down to the matter in hand.

'Tell me the order of things leading up to your finding the body, Mr Smith.'

'It was a bit of a shock, I can tell you,' said Smith. 'Our dog Tammy jumped ship, something he's always doing, I'm afraid. I went after him, but he shot across straight into the trees. I called him, and I heard him barking, which he only does when he's excited. When I found him, he was standing by this young woman's body. I could see she was dead, and so I rang the police. Within minutes several police cars and an ambulance arrived. One of the policemen told me to wait, and a little while later a detective inspector asked me a few questions and said I could go back to the boat. He said that someone would be along later to interview me. I suppose that's you.'

'Yes, Mr Smith, I'm the senior investigating officer. Have you been moored here all night?'

'Yes, we have. Actually, we've been across to Amsterdam for a fun week. It was fun, wasn't it, sweetie?' Smith smiled at his wife, and she laughed and nodded vigorously. 'And now we're on our way back home to Henley.'

'Did you hear anything unusual during the night?' asked Kate.

'Such as?' asked Trixie, and giggled.

'We're working on the theory that whoever murdered this woman killed her where she was found, and did so during the night.' Kate spoke in clear, concise tones, and her voice became a little sharper. She'd obviously dismissed Trixie Smith as an airhead.

'Murdered?' Trixie seemed shocked, and it confirmed my original assessment of her as a woman who'd married a wealthy man – if the size of the cabin cruiser was anything to go by – and who had never come up against the hard knocks of life.

'No,' said Paul Smith. 'We are both sound sleepers. I certainly didn't hear anything.' He glanced at Trixie. 'Did you hear anything, sweetie?'

'No.' Smith's wife shook her head.

'Was there anything at all that you noticed, Mr Smith?' I asked.

Smith considered the question for a moment or two. 'Only that the poor young lady wasn't wearing a bra. She'd been stripped to the waist, you see.'

'Yes, well, you would notice that,' said Trixie drily.

'If I can have your address, Mr Smith,' I said, 'we may have to contact you again, although I doubt it. And then you're free to go on your way to Henley.'

That done, and having learned nothing, we returned to the crime scene.

TEN

As Jack Noble had predicted, Dr Henry Mortlock was in a foul mood.

'How many more of these damned bodies are you going to find this early in the morning, Harry?'

'If you can tell me who the murderer is, my dear doctor,' I said, 'I'll pop out and nick him. Then, in future, I won't have to bother you before breakfast.'

Mortlock muttered something which though unintelligible sounded vaguely obscene, and stood up. 'The mixture as before, Harry. Manual strangulation, attacked from behind. And before you ask, yes, she had been wearing a brassiere but isn't wearing one now. Further and better particulars after I've carved her up. Satisfied?'

'Nearly. Time of death, Henry?'

Mortlock took off his pince-nez and, gazing unseeing at a tree, pursed his lips. 'I'd say around about ten o'clock last night, but with a leeway of an hour either side,' he said, realigning his gaze on me.

'All right to move the body?' asked Kate.

'Indeed, young lady, and be so good as to have it delivered to my usual address.' Mortlock packed the remainder of his ghoulish instruments into his bag and departed whistling a passage from Handel's *Dead March in Saul*, which seemed particularly apt, both for the occasion and the hour.

'We've almost finished the photography and video, Harry.' Linda Mitchell was outside the tent when Kate and I emerged. 'I'll get one of my team to take the victim's finger-prints, just in case. Jack Noble arranged for the uniforms to do a fingertip search of the area, but nothing evidential has been found so far.'

'No cigarette ends this time?'

'No, and no bra either, although Dr Mortlock said that she had been wearing one when she was killed or shortly before.'

'Yes, he mentioned that. I'll leave you to it, Linda.' I'd decided to send for Len Driscoll and a few members of the team to oversee the crime scene while Kate and I went to the address in Cobham that was on Denise Barton's driving licence.

Driscoll arrived just before eleven o'clock and I gave him a quick résumé of what had been done so far. He just nodded, almost giving the impression of being uninterested. But those who knew him – and it had taken me some time to get his measure – knew that he was complex of character, often irritable and always demanding. Tall, well dressed and well spoken, he possessed the superior attitude of a man who was efficient at his job and scathing about the inefficiency of anyone working for him. Or with him. I firmly believed that his suave, occasionally condescending, demeanour frightened even the commander.

By the time I'd briefed Driscoll it was midday, and Kate and I were able to get away from Canbury Gardens.

According to the address on her driving licence, Denise Barton had lived in a small cottage on the outskirts of the Surrey village of Cobham. Two identical Mini Cooper convertibles with sequential index marks were parked outside.

We'd brought the keys that had been found in her handbag, but I rang the bell in the hope that the owner of one of the two Minis lived there and was at home. He was.

'Yes?' The man who answered the door was probably in his late twenties or early thirties, tall and slender, and had the distracted, studious appearance of someone who could have been a teacher or a university lecturer.

'We're police officers,' I said, and Kate and I produced our warrant cards. 'I'm Detective Chief Inspector Brock and this is Detective Inspector Ebdon.'

The man put on a pair of glasses. 'What can I do for you?' he asked, apparently satisfied that we were who we said we were. Suddenly he realized that we weren't there on a Sunday afternoon for some trivial reason. 'Oh God! Something's happened to Denise.'

'I think it'd be better if we came in, Mr . . .?'

'Malcolm Warner. I'm Denise's fiancé.' He showed us into the small front room of the cottage and invited us to sit down. 'Now, for God's sake tell me what's happened. Has she been in an accident?'

'I'm sorry to have to tell you that Miss Barton is dead, Mr Warner,' I said.

'Dead? She can't be. I was talking to her only yesterday afternoon. What happened? A car accident? She was only twenty-five.'

Those were the sort of spontaneous comments often made by people in shock, and it certainly appeared that Warner had been severely shocked by what I'd just told him. Either that or he was skilfully disguising a fear that he was about to be arrested in connection with her death. But by the very nature of their profession policemen in general, and detectives in particular, are hard-bitten cynics.

'She was murdered, Mr Warner,' said Kate gently.

'Murdered? But who would want to murder Denise? She was a lovely girl. We were engaged. We were going to be married next month. Oh God! I'll have to tell her parents. And there are the bridesmaids, and all the guests. We've already sent out the invitations. And there are wedding presents to return. Oh hell, I'll have to deal with all of that.' The words tumbled out, jumbled and disconnected as various thoughts occurred to him. Suddenly, he stopped. 'Where did this happen?' he demanded almost accusingly, as though he thought we should have done something to prevent it occurring.

'Her body was found in Canbury Gardens,' said Kate.

'Where's that?'

'Beside the river between Kingston and Ham.'

'Had she been, you know . . .?'

'As far as we know so far, Mr Warner,' I said, 'she had not been assaulted sexually, but the post-mortem examination might tell us differently. Can you tell me where she was going last night?'

'Yes, to a wine bar in Richmond. The Talavera. She works there, you see.'

'She works at the Talavera?' asked Kate, thinking that we were at the beginning of a breakthrough. If Denise Barton had worked at the wine bar frequented by Rachel Steele and Lisa Hastings, it might confirm that the murderer was one of its regular clients.

'Good heavens, no.' Warner's reply was a scathing dismissal of the implication that he had been engaged to a barmaid. 'A year or two ago she and a friend set up an online business producing custom-designed greetings cards for businesses and charities. Their office was in Richmond. After they'd finished work she was going to the wine bar for a few drinks with this friend. I've always warned her against drink-driving and I told her to get a taxi home, for which I would pay.'

'Does she always work on a Saturday?' I asked.

'Yes. It's when they do most of their business, so she told me. Look, d'you have to keep asking all these questions?'

'If we're to find out who murdered your fiancée, Mr Warner, yes,' said Kate. 'You said that on this occasion you'd told her to get a taxi home. Does she normally go to work by car?'

'Yes, she does, but this time I drove her there. One of the Minis outside is hers; the other one is mine. His and hers, you might say.' Warner gave a bleak laugh. 'But not any more.'

'What time did you take her to Richmond?'

'I dropped her off at about half past eight, maybe a quarter to nine, yesterday morning.'

'Did you actually see her enter her business premises?'

'Yes. I wanted to make sure she was safe. You hear of so many random stabbings these days. But she said I worried too much, and it looks as though I had cause to,' Warner added sadly.

'What did you do when she didn't come home last night, Mr Warner?' asked Kate. 'Did you inform the police?'

'No, I wasn't here.'

'Oh, where were you?'

'I spent last evening playing chess with a friend of mine in Ripley.'

'What's his name and address?' I asked.

'Justin Lane,' said Warner, and gave us a Ripley address. 'I suppose you want to check up on me.'

'That's the general idea, Mr Warner,' said Kate, making a note of the friend's details. 'It's called a routine enquiry.' Like many detectives, Kate often resorted to that meaningless cliché rather than telling the questioner that he was a suspect until he'd been ruled out. 'What time did you get back here last night?'

'It must've been close to midnight.'

'And what did you do when you found that Denise still hadn't arrived home?'

'I just assumed that she'd stayed overnight with her friend – she does that sometimes – and that she'd come home this morning. In fact, I thought it was her when you rang the bell.'

'But she had her house keys with her,' commented Kate.

'Oh, yes. I'd forgotten that,' Warner replied vaguely.

'Didn't you think to ring your fiancée's friend and ask if she was there?'

'I didn't want her to think I was fussing too much.'

'We'll need her business partner's name and address, Mr Warner,' I said.

'Yes, of course. It's Abigail Robinson and she lives in Richmond.' Warner reeled off the address from memory.

'And perhaps you'd give us the address of Miss Barton's parents,' I said. 'We'll need to inform them, and ask them a few questions.'

'What about?' It sounded as though Warner didn't much like the idea of us speaking to Denise's parents.

'Just standard questions about her education and upbringing, that sort of thing,' said Kate. 'Building a profile of a victim often helps us to identify the killer.'

'They live in Tolworth,' said Warner and gave us the address, again from memory.

'How did you and Miss Barton meet, Mr Warner?'

'At a tennis club. We're both keen players. Only amateur standard, of course. Not in the Wimbledon class by any means. It was as much for the social side as anything. And then we found we had a mutual love of Gilbert and Sullivan operettas. We got engaged about a year ago.'

'And she's lived with you at this address since your engagement, has she?'

'There's nothing wrong with that, is there?' snapped Warner

defensively, as though we'd accused him of blatant immorality.
Or living in sin, as my mother used to call it.

'Nothing wrong with it at all,' said Kate mildly.

'Thank you, Mr Warner,' I said, 'and we're sorry to be the
bearers of such bad news. You have our condolences. We
can arrange for a family support officer from the Surrey
Constabulary to visit you, if you wish.'

'That won't be necessary, thank you,' said Warner curtly.
'When will I be able to fix up Denise's funeral?'

'Once the coroner has authorized release of Miss Barton's
body,' I said. 'We'll let you and Mr and Mrs Barton know.
And we'll probably need to see you again,' I added, 'but we'll
telephone beforehand. I take it you work during the week?'

'Yes, I'm a schoolteacher.'

We left Malcolm Warner to get on with whatever he was
doing. And to worry about cancelling the wedding plans and
returning the food processor and all the other things that people
give newlyweds.

'It's only about ten miles from here to Tolworth, Kate,' I
said as we drove away from Malcolm Warner's cottage.
'We'll speak to the Bartons on our way back to London.' I
paused. 'And while we're in the area we'll call in on this
Justin Lane, the friend Warner said he played chess with
last evening.'

'No worries,' said Kate.

'What was your take on Malcolm Warner?'

'Definitely someone to be looked at more deeply,' said Kate,
skilfully avoiding an idiot cyclist who seemed to think he was
entitled to ignore the rules of the road. 'He didn't seem at all
keen on us speaking to Denise's parents. I wonder what they've
got to tell us.'

'I got the impression that he couldn't have cared less about
his fiancée not coming home last night and not showing up
this morning.'

'That was a pretty lame excuse he made about her not
wanting him to fuss too much, Harry. He went on about seeing
her through the door but wasn't worried enough to find out
why she hadn't come home last night. Mind you, as Dave said

the other day, it wouldn't be the first time a boyfriend finished up in the dock for murdering his girlfriend.'

'Yes, but given the similarity between Denise Barton's murder and the two previous ones, could he have committed all three?'

'We could pull him in and ask him?' said Kate.

'Not yet, Kate,' I said. 'Let's wait and see what scientific evidence Linda can produce.'

'If there's any to produce,' said Kate gloomily.

It was five miles down the A3 from Cobham to Ripley, and we were knocking on Justin Lane's door within fifteen minutes of leaving Malcolm Warner.

'You can do the talking, Kate,' I said as I rang the bell.

'Hi!' The barefooted man who answered the door was wearing white shorts and a navy-blue shirt, and his sunglasses had been pushed up on top of his shaved head.

'Justin Lane?' asked Kate.

'Yes, indeed,' said Lane, smiling and affording Kate's figure an admiring glance.

'I'm Detective Inspector Kate Ebdon of the Murder Investigation Team at Scotland Yard, and this is my colleague, Detective Chief Inspector Brock.'

'Oh!' exclaimed Lane. Kate's awesome announcement had wiped the smile from his face, and presumably removed any lascivious thoughts he might have been harbouring. 'Are you sure it's me you want? There must be more than one Justin Lane in the world.'

'Has your friend Malcolm Warner phoned you recently?'

'How on earth did you . . .?' Lane stuttered to an abrupt stop, clearly impressed by the apparent omniscience of the police.

'Has he or hasn't he?' demanded Kate.

'Er, well, yes. A few minutes ago, as a matter of fact. But how did you know?' Lane opened the door fully. 'You'd better come in,' he said, 'although I don't know how I can possibly help you. I don't know anything about any murders. Was it local, here in Ripley?'

I didn't bother to explain that if that had been the case, the

Surrey Police would have been doing the investigating.
Interesting, I thought, *that he didn't mention Denise's murder.*

We were shown into a large room which appeared to be a
combination of sitting room and studio. There was an easel
bearing a canvas upon which was a half-finished painting of
what appeared vaguely to be a reclining nude. On the other
hand, it could have been an abstract, although it might just be
that whoever was painting it was a lousy artist.

A young woman holding a magazine was spread on a chaise
longue. She looked up briefly, stared blankly at us and returned
to her reading.

'My girlfriend,' said Lane by way of introduction, but didn't
tell us her name. 'Now, what's this all about?'

'Mr Warner told us that he was here all last evening, and
that the two of you played chess together. He said that he
left here in time to get back to Cobham at around midnight. Is
that true?'

'Oh yes. Absolutely,' began Lane, but got no further.

'He bloody well wasn't here,' said the girlfriend, without
looking up from her magazine. 'Justin was in bed with me.
We hit the sack at about eight last night and didn't get up
until ten o'clock this morning. Justin's bloody insatiable. Aren't
you, *darling*?' she added sarcastically. 'He spent most of the
night screwing the arse off me.'

'Ha!' snorted Lane. 'You've got some room to talk.'

'Can we get back to the point of this conversation, Mr Lane?'
snapped Kate. 'Was he here, or wasn't he?'

'Er . . . no!' Lane passed a hand over his hairless head,
inadvertently knocking off his sunglasses. 'He wasn't here,
but he has been on numerous occasions,' he admitted lamely.

'And that, presumably, is why he telephoned you a few
minutes ago, to arrange an alibi?'

'Yes, but why does he need an alibi? What's happened?'

'I hope you appreciate that it's a serious matter to lie to
police who are investigating a murder, Mr Lane,' said Kate
sternly, ignoring Lane's questions.

'Yes, I'm sorry. I thought it was to cover him for what he
was really doing.'

'And what was he *really* doing?' demanded Kate.

Before Lane had a chance to reply, the girlfriend looked up. 'Shafting his bit on the side most likely,' she said.

'What is your name, miss?' asked Kate.

'Amber Clark.'

'And what d'you do for a living?'

'I'm an artist's model.' She drew out the word so that it sounded more like 'muddle', and on reflection perhaps that's what she meant, if the painting on the easel was any indication.

'Do either of you know the name of this woman you call his "bit on the side"?' Kate switched her gaze from Amber to Lane.

'No,' they both said at once.

Kate turned her attention once more to Lane. 'How did you come to meet Mr Warner?'

'We're colleagues.'

'You're a teacher, then.'

'Yes, that's how we got to know each other,' said Lane. 'But why are Murder Squad detectives taking an interest in what Malcolm was doing last night?'

'Because Mr Warner's fiancée, Denise Barton, was murdered sometime yesterday evening,' said Kate in matter-of-fact tones.

'Good God!' Lane, who until now had been standing up, suddenly sank into a canvas structure that was supposed to be some sort of easy chair. 'Why on earth didn't he mention that on the phone?' he said, shaking his head and tugging briefly at his beard.

'Is this a bloody joke?' asked Amber Clark, at last closing her magazine.

'Shut up, Amber,' said Lane. 'What happened, Inspector?'

'Her body was found this morning in Canbury Gardens in Kingston.'

'Bloody hell! Poor old Malcolm. He won't know what on earth to do with himself. He doted on that girl.' Lane suddenly looked up. 'And he told you he was playing chess here with me last night?'

'He did,' said Kate, and left it at that to see what Lane would have to say.

'Ye Gods! And you think he murdered her?'

'We don't know who murdered her yet, Mr Lane, but we're interested to know why he lied to us.'

'Like I said just now, he was probably having it off with another woman,' said Amber. 'That's all you men ever think about.'

'Just wind your neck in, Amber, or—'

'Or what?' Amber swung her legs off the chaise longue and stood up, hands on hips. 'You'll throw me out? Where will you go for a quick fuck after that, eh, Picasso? Got a reserve lined up, have you?'

'I think that's all you can assist us with, Mr Lane,' said Kate, sensing that a 'domestic' was about to erupt, 'although we may need to talk to you again at some time in the future. But I must warn you that if you now speak to Malcolm Warner about this interview in an attempt to arrange another false alibi for him, it will be regarded very seriously. And we will find out, I can assure you. Perverting the course of justice carries a sentence of life imprisonment.'

'Yes, I understand,' said Lane, who paled quite significantly as the gravity of Kate's warning sank in.

'I reckon that any minute they'd have started to throw things at each other, Kate,' I said as we returned to the car. 'I think we just got out of there in time. That so-called model Amber seems a bit of a spitfire.'

'I know what she needs,' said Kate bluntly, but didn't elaborate.

'Right. Back to Cobham.'

'Oh, it's you again.' Malcolm Warner didn't seem at all surprised at our return so soon after leaving him.

'Why did you lie to us, Mr Warner?' demanded Kate, as he admitted us to his sitting room. 'And before you say anything, we have just spoken to Mr Lane, who told us that you didn't spend last evening with him playing chess. His live-in partner, who described herself as an artist's model, suggested that you were with someone else. Someone who was not your fiancée.'

'Well, I didn't think it would look good if I told you the real reason.'

'You're right about that,' said Kate who, over the years, had had a few run-ins with philandering males in her private life. 'So, now might be a good time to tell us exactly where you were last evening.'

'I spent the night with a colleague of mine.'

'A woman?' asked Kate, wishing to make absolutely certain.

'Of course it was a woman.' Warner sounded quite annoyed at the implication that he might be homosexual.

'You said she was a colleague. Does that mean she's a teacher too?'

'Yes.' Warner's voice had dropped almost to a whisper.

'In that case, we'd better have her name and address.' Kate made a big thing of taking out her pocketbook and pen.

'Oh God!' Warner ran a hand through his untidy blond hair. 'She's married.'

'Oh dear!' said Kate sarcastically. 'Name and address,' she repeated, more firmly this time.

'Shirley Manners. Mrs Shirley Manners.' Warner gave us an address in Effingham.' After a moment's pause, he added a mobile phone number. 'It'd be safer to call her on that number,' he said. 'If you must.'

'You've lied to us once, Mr Warner,' said Kate brutally. 'We just want to make sure you're not doing it again.'

ELEVEN

Denise Barton's parents lived in a modest end-of-terrace house in Tolworth.

'Mr Barton?'

'Yes, what is it?' The man who'd answered the door wore a pair of baggy cord trousers and, despite the warm weather, a green cardigan over a Paisley shirt. He was probably still in his fifties but his stooped posture, together with his ragged moustache, receding hairline and the grey-rimmed spectacles suspended from a cord around his neck, gave him the appearance of someone twenty years older.

'We're police officers, Mr Barton.'

'Whatever can you want at this time on a Sunday afternoon?' Barton's tone implied that people of his calibre should not be disturbed by police officers on Sunday afternoons. 'And how do I know you're the police?' He stared suspiciously at Kate, attired as usual in jeans and a white shirt.

'I can assure you we are, Mr Barton. I'm Detective Chief Inspector Brock and this is Detective Inspector Ebdon.'

'I'm sorry, but you can't be too careful these days,' said Barton grudgingly, once he'd examined our warrant cards. 'Please come in and tell me what you want.'

We followed him into a large sitting room where a grey-haired woman was watching a wildlife programme on television.

'Who was it, Mark?' she asked, without diverting her gaze from a pair of cavorting gibbons who seemed well aware that the camera was on them.

'The police are here, Patricia. They want to speak to us.'

Only then did the woman look up. 'Oh, I'm so sorry,' she said and, seizing the remote control, turned off the television.

'I'm afraid I have bad news,' I began, and introduced myself and Kate to Mrs Barton. There's never an easy way to deliver a death message, something I learned early in my police career. 'It's your daughter, Denise.'

'Is she hurt?' asked Patricia Barton. 'Was it an accident?' The questions were almost identical to those posed by Malcolm Warner. And a score of other people to whom, over the years, I'd delivered news of the death of a loved one.

'I'm afraid she's been killed, Mrs Barton.'

'Oh!' Denise's mother turned away and stared stoically at the blank television screen. 'Was it a car accident?' she asked again, turning to face me once more.

'I'm sorry to have to tell you she was murdered.' I went on to explain the circumstances surrounding the finding of her body.

'What a wicked, wicked world we live in,' exclaimed Mark Barton, suddenly sitting down in an armchair.

'What were the circumstances, Chief Inspector?' asked Patricia Barton. Apparently she had not taken in the details I had given her and her husband moments ago. Nevertheless, as is so often the case, it was the woman who retained her composure.

'Her body was found in Canbury Gardens in Kingston, Mrs Barton. She'd been strangled.'

'Have you caught whoever did this terrible thing?'

'Not yet,' said Kate. 'We have a number of leads we're working on – but my chief inspector is certain that we'll make an arrest shortly,' she added, nodding in my direction.

You're more confident than I am, Kate, I thought.

'Have you told Malcolm yet?'

'Yes, Mrs Barton. We left him not an hour ago.'

'Strange he didn't telephone,' commented Mark Barton.

'It's not strange at all,' said Patricia spiritedly. 'He never had any time for us. In fact, Mr Brock,' she continued, glancing at me, 'he treated us with contempt, just because Mark spent a lifetime as a clerk at a council office – a senior clerk, mind you.'

'What sort of girl was your daughter, Mrs Barton?' It was clear to me that I was going to get more sense out of Denise's mother than from her father.

'Very quiet and very studious. She went to university to study computer science. That's where she met Malcolm. They've been going out together for a few years now and they were supposed to be getting married next month, on the twentieth of July actually. They'd arranged their honeymoon in Corsica.' Finally, the dreadful realization that their daughter was dead hit home, and Patricia Barton dissolved into tears.

'Strange place to go,' commented Mark Barton, oblivious to his wife's distress. 'I don't know why people want to go abroad. I certainly don't. I haven't seen all of England yet.'

We made the usual offer of the services of a family support officer, which was refused, and left the Bartons to their grief, not much better informed about their daughter's lifestyle than when we'd arrived.

'There's one other thing we can do while we're in this neck of the woods, Kate,' I said as we left the grieving Bartons. I glanced at my watch. 'We'll have a word with Abigail Robinson, Denise Barton's business partner. It's not far from Tolworth to Richmond.'

'If she's at home,' said Kate. 'She might've gone away for the rest of the weekend.'

'I doubt she'd have gone away if Malcolm Warner has told her of Denise's murder,' I said. 'Anyway, Warner said the weekends are their busiest time, so I imagine she's still there.'

'D'you think he'll have bothered to ring her?' asked Kate. 'I got the impression he was too worried about returning wedding presents. Apart from anything else, I thought he was a bit of a cold fish.'

'Cold enough to have topped his fiancée, d'you mean, Kate?'

'I don't think he's got the bottle to do that, but a guy who has it off with another bird days before getting married ain't normal in my book. For all we know, Harry, he might be shafting this Abigail bird we're going to see as well as the Shirley Manners he mentioned as his alibi.'

'We'll soon find out.' I rang Abigail Robinson's mobile and she was at home.

'Yes, I heard. What a terrible shock,' she said as she admitted us to her flat. 'Malcolm telephoned me just after you'd left him. He said you'd probably be coming to see me.' With her long black hair drawn back into a severe ponytail and her heavy horn-rimmed spectacles, she looked every inch the successful, no-nonsense businesswoman.

Kate and I sat down in Abigail's comfortable, lived-in sitting room. 'I understand that you and Denise went for a drink after you'd finished work yesterday evening,' I said.

'That was the plan, but as we were about to leave the office I got a call from a charity we do business with, asking if we could do a rush order. We're not in a position to turn down business, and I told Denise to go on and I'd meet her at the wine bar once I'd dealt with our caller.'

'What happened then?' asked Kate.

'She wasn't there when I arrived, and I asked one or two people we both knew whether they'd seen her, but they said they hadn't. Not that that means she hadn't been in, of course.'

'Do you always go to the same wine bar?'

'Yes, always. It's the Talavera,' said Abigail, confirming what Warner had told us. 'But Denise had been complaining of a headache for some time before we split, and I assumed that she'd perhaps gone home. I rang her mobile but it went straight to voicemail. I knew that she was getting a taxi home that evening, so I waited long enough for her to have got back to Cobham and rang their landline, but there was no reply. I assumed that she'd felt better and she and Malcolm had gone out somewhere. Maybe to their tennis club.'

'Did you follow it up?' I asked.

'No, I didn't, although with hindsight I suppose I should've done. Not that it would have made any difference. I gather from what Malcolm said that she was murdered sometime last night.'

'Yes, that's what we believe,' I said.

'I know this is a delicate question, Miss Robinson,' said Kate, 'but is it possible that Denise was seeing someone else?'

'Not a chance,' said Abigail firmly. 'She was absolutely besotted with Malcolm.' She paused, as if wondering whether to offer an opinion. 'Not that I found him attractive. Too much the pedantic schoolteacher for my liking. Mind you, she knew one or two men at the wine bar on what you might call a nodding acquaintance, as did I. They're a friendly bunch that go in there.'

'Was there anyone in particular that Denise knew?' I asked.

Abigail shook her head. 'No one that I can think of.'

'Thank you for your time, Miss Robinson,' I said, as Kate and I rose to leave. 'We may need to see you again. On the other hand, if you think of anything that might assist us, perhaps you'd give me a ring.' I handed her one of my cards.

'I think we've done enough, Kate,' I said as we got into the car. It had been a long and largely fruitless day, and we'd both had enough. I asked Kate to drop me off at my flat, and suggested she take the police car home with her to New Malden.

During the journey I phoned Lydia and was delighted, and a little surprised, to find that she was still at my flat.

The moment I closed my front door, Lydia called out from the kitchen, 'There's a whisky on the table by your chair, Harry. Is that all right or would you prefer something else?'

'Perfect. Why don't you come and sit down for ten minutes?'

'If you don't mind dinner being a bit later,' she said, appearing in the doorway of the sitting room with a glass of red wine in her hand. A lock of hair had fallen on to her forehead, and she was perspiring.

'That's all right. Had you not been here I'd probably have called in at the pub and had a pie and a pint, which is what I had for lunch.'

'You shouldn't neglect yourself.' Lydia's tone was disapproving. 'Not doing the job you're doing.'

Hello, I thought. *I'm being taken over, and oddly enough I don't mind in the least.*

We chatted for ten minutes or so, although Lydia did most of the talking, mainly about the commonplace occurrences in her life which, for me, was a form of relaxation.

The comfortable way in which she had settled in reminded me of my mother's oft-uttered warning when I was approaching manhood. She told me that I should be wary of women who were keen to get their feet under my table. At that tender age I didn't have a table, and I wasn't sure what she'd meant. In later years I decided it was the sort of mother's cautionary tale that had been handed down from generation to generation without ever being queried. But now I thought I was old enough to know what I was doing, and to have a caring woman put her feet under my table was rather appealing. And there was no doubt that Lydia was caring.

Looking across at her, very much at home in one of my armchairs, I was still amazed that I'd been attracted to someone who was so different from Gail Sutton, my former girlfriend. Gail was a tall, svelte, blonde actress, whereas Lydia was an attractively buxom woman of thirty-eight with short brown hair. Her late husband, who had been 'something in the City' and a keen yachtsman, had died in a car crash some eighteen months ago, and his huge fortune had been left to Lydia. She was, therefore, very wealthy, and certainly had nothing to gain from a relationship with me. For my part, I had nothing much to offer her except perhaps companionship, unreliable working hours and frequent cancellations of social engagements at the very last minute. But she'd already discovered that, and the unreliable course of our short acquaintanceship had confirmed it. I couldn't work out what there was about me that she found attractive.

'We'd better eat now, Harry.' She stood up. 'The first course is already on the table.'

I stood up too, and held her by the shoulders. 'It's wonderful having you here, Lydia.' I pulled her close to me, kissed her and ran a finger down her spine.

'Not so fast, lover.' Laughing, she eased herself away from my embrace. 'Dinner first.'

She had prepared bruschetta and tomatoes to start, followed by duck cooked to a perfect pink, with new potatoes and peas. After raspberries and cream she produced a whole Camembert that was genuinely French, rather than an English imitation. And she didn't utter a word about cholesterol. This sumptuous meal was accompanied by a Beaujolais Juliénas that certainly hadn't come from my meagre stock.

'You're really spoiling me, Lydia.' It seemed an inadequate way to thank her for yet another superb meal. But she had managed to produce it with little apparent effort. 'Brandy?'

'Mm, yes please.' She paused. 'And then . . .?'

*   *   *

On Monday morning I settled in my office with a cup of coffee, intent on going over the evidence we'd amassed so far. Oddly enough, our revered commander had not bothered me of late. Either he had been warned off by the deputy assistant commissioner, of whom he was terrified, or he'd decided that a killer who'd probably been responsible for three murders was beyond even his self-perceived detective powers.

But I'd been reading statements no longer than twenty minutes when the aforementioned DAC, a cup of coffee in his hand, appeared in my office.

'Good morning, sir,' I said, struggling to my feet.

'Morning, Harry.' With a nonchalant wave of a hand, the DAC signalled me to sit down again, before sitting down himself. 'I was on my way to the Yard and thought I'd drop in to see how you were getting on.'

As succinctly as possible, I brought him up to speed. He gave me one or two pointers – always worth listening to – on how to proceed from now on, and once more offered me any additional manpower and resources I needed.

'Are you happy dealing with it, Harry? If you want someone with a bit more clout in day-to-day charge just say the word, but I wouldn't want you to think I hadn't got faith in you to finish the job.'

'Thank you, sir, but I'm coping all right. I've got a good team, and between us we'll crack this one.' Putting one hand beneath the desk, I crossed my fingers.

'I looked into the incident room just now and cadged a cup of coffee. They seem to be right on top of the job in there. That sergeant of yours, Wilberforce, gave me a thumbnail sketch of the whole inquiry. Very impressive.' The DAC leaned forward and put his cup and saucer on the desk. 'While I'm on the subject of your team, Harry, I'm afraid you're going to lose Len Driscoll next Monday. But I'll keep him here if you feel you need the continuity, although that would mean holding back his promotion to DCI and his transfer to division.'

'I wouldn't want to do that, guv'nor,' I said, pleased to hear the DAC still referring to it as 'division' rather than the cumbersome 'operational command unit', another creation of the boy superintendents at Scotland Yard, known to us at the sharp end as 'the funny names and total confusion squad'. 'Who am I getting in his place?'

'You've got a choice, Harry, and you know one of them. Jane Mansfield is a DI on the assessment team, but the other possibility is Brad Naylor of the Flying Squad who fancies a change from the muck and bullets of dealing with ordinary villains, as he puts it.'

'I know Naylor, too, sir. We got involved in a job some years ago. The murder of Spotter Gould.'

'It's for you to choose, Harry. They're both good detectives, but as you've got a woman DI already . . .'

'It wouldn't worry me to have two women DIs, guv'nor, but there's some sort of personality clash between Kate Ebdon and Jane Mansfield. I don't know what it is, but I'd guess it's because Ebdon is a brash Australian, not afraid to speak her mind, whereas Mansfield tends to be a little more sophisticated in her approach. But she's no shrinking violet, and I don't doubt she's tough enough to do the job.'

'Fair enough, Harry, but we can do without catfights. I'll send Brad Naylor to you today and he can spend a few days shadowing Len Driscoll before he takes over his slot.' The DAC stood up. 'And now, I've just about got time to put the commander in the picture about the transfers.'

'The commander's not here at the moment, sir.' I glanced at my watch: it was just nine o'clock.

'Where is he? Not off sick, is he? Dental appointment, perhaps?'

'He doesn't normally come in until ten o'clock, sir.'

'Oh, really? I'll have to speak to him at some other time, then.' Naturally enough the DAC didn't criticize the commander directly, but his expression indicated quite clearly that he wasn't happy about what he probably saw as the commander's cavalier approach to his duties. 'And don't forget, Harry. Anything you need, just give me a bell.'

I had things to do and didn't need to leave the office until later in the day. Consequently I waited for the commander to arrive, which he did on the stroke of ten.

I tapped lightly on the great man's office door, and entered.

'Ah, Mr Brock. Was there something you wanted to ask me?' he enquired airily, as if he were the fount of all CID knowledge.

'No, sir, but I thought you'd like to know that the DAC was asking for you. I think he wanted a word.'

'D'you mean he telephoned *you*?' suggested the commander, in a voice that made it clear that he couldn't understand a DAC speaking to a mere DCI. With feigned nonchalance, he reached across the desk for one of his beloved files.

'Oh, he didn't phone, sir. He was here in person.' I relished making that statement with what the law calls malice afore-thought. 'At a quarter past eight.'

'He was *here*?' The commander stood up suddenly, as if he'd just received an electric shock from the seat of his chair.

'Yes, sir. He decided to call in and inspect the incident room, and have a general look around. He wanted to see for himself how my triple murder inquiry was progressing. He stopped for a cup of coffee and a chinwag before going on to the Yard.'

'Did he appear, er, satisfied, Mr Brock?' enquired the boss carelessly, but I could sense that he was worried sick.

'Always difficult to tell with the DAC, sir,' I said. 'But I must say he didn't seem too happy,' I added, determined to put the boot in.

'I'd better call him, then.' The commander paused, his hand on the telephone. 'No, on second thoughts, I'll go across to the Yard and speak to him in person. There might be a confidential matter of some urgency he wants to discuss.'

'Very likely, sir.'

The commander almost pushed me over in his hurry to get out of the office.

Detective Inspector Brad Naylor, just as snappily dressed as the last time we met, arrived at midday. 'I'm supposed to report to the commander, guv'nor,' he said as we shook hands, 'but he's not in his office.'

'I've just sent out a search party, Brad,' I said. 'He disap-peared in the general direction of Commissioner's Office seeking the DAC at a quarter past ten this morning, since when we've seen no sign of him. It falls to me, therefore, to welcome you to HMCC West.'

'Thank you, kind sir,' said Naylor, and half bowed. 'I haven't seen Len Driscoll anywhere so far. Is he about?'

'There's a block of flats at Canbury Gardens opposite the murder scene. He's probably still doing house-to-house enquiries there, Brad. The DAC suggested you shadow him for a while, but do you need to?'

'Not really. I spent the last hour getting briefed by the incident room skipper.'

'Colin Wilberforce.'

'That's the bloke. He filled me in with all I need to know. He's on top of his job, that one. I'm surprised he hasn't gone for promotion.'

'Just be thankful he hasn't,' I said. 'I reckon the place would fall apart if he went.'

'So, we've got a triple murder to deal with. It looks as though I've jumped straight in at the deep end.'

TWELVE

'There's an outstanding action that you said you wanted to do yourself, sir,' said Colin Wilberforce.

'Remind me, Colin.'

'Malcolm Warner's alibi for the night that his fiancée was murdered, sir.'

'Thanks, Colin. I'll get on to it straight away.'

Warner had claimed, albeit reluctantly, that he'd spent the night with a Mrs Shirley Manners and, with even greater reluctance, had given me her address and mobile phone number. I didn't think he'd lied; it was, after all, too easy to check, but unless every minor point is covered in the report that goes to the Crown Prosecution Service, some functionary low down in the pecking order will make a song and dance about it.

I made the call at twenty-five minutes to one for no better reason than that I thought Mrs Manners would out of class for the lunch break by then. Warner had told us that, like him, Shirley Manners was a schoolteacher. I knew from experience that most adulterous relationships start in the workplace, and usually end in acrimony.

'Shirley Manners,' said a confident voice.

'Mrs Manners, this is Detective Chief Inspector Brock of the Murder Investigation Team at New Scotland Yard.'

'Why on earth are you ringing me?' She sounded guarded, as though she was not alone.

'I need to speak to you with regards to the murder of Denise Barton, Mrs Manners.'

'I don't know anyone of that name. I really think you must have a wrong number.'

'I take it you're not free to talk at the moment,' I said, now convinced that she was in a room with other people.

'I'm at work,' she said.

'In that case, I'd better come and see you at your home in Effingham,' I suggested.

'Er . . . no, that's not a good idea.' Suddenly the confidence diminished a notch or two.

There was a lengthy pause, long enough for me to ask if she was still there.

'Yes, I am. I was just walking out to the grounds. The reception's better outside. Look, I've got the day off tomorrow, and I'm coming up to London to do some shopping in Oxford Street. Perhaps we could meet then. Although I still don't understand why you should want to talk to me.'

'I'm at Belgravia police station,' I said. 'Ask for the Homicide and Major Crime Command offices. I'll see you then.' I had no intention of meeting her in some teashop in Oxford Street.

'Oh!' Shirley Manners obviously didn't like the sound of a police station. Too official, perhaps? 'All right, then,' she said eventually. 'I could be there at about half past eleven.'

'I'll be expecting you,' I said.

'Can't I answer your questions, whatever they are, on the phone?' she asked, making a last-ditch attempt to avoid the nuisance of coming to Belgravia.

'I'm afraid not, Mrs Manners. You see, I may need to take a written statement from you.' That wasn't the reason at all, of course. I liked watching the faces of witnesses so that I could see when they lied, something that could not be detected on the telephone.

I could quite see why Malcolm Warner had been attracted to Shirley Manners. She was a shapely blonde in her mid-twenties, and it came as no surprise when she admitted to being a physical education teacher.

'I'm Detective Chief Inspector Brock, Mrs Manners, and this is Detective Sergeant Carpenter.' I knew, from the experience of others, that it's essential when interviewing a woman to have a female officer present to counter the sort of allegation that some women are prone to make against male police officers. Such allegations, which can range from over-familiarity to indecent assault, are easily made but difficult to disprove. Liz Carpenter's presence was, therefore, a form of insurance. For me.

'Now that I'm here,' said Shirley Manners, 'perhaps you'd tell me what this is all about.'

'Please take a seat, Mrs Manners. Would you like a cup of coffee?'

'Only if it's decaffeinated.'

'I'm afraid I can't guarantee that.'

'In that case, I won't bother.' She made a point of glancing at her wristwatch as if to imply that she had an appointment elsewhere, and fairly soon.

'It's about the murder of Denise Barton, Mrs Manners.'

'I told you on the phone that the name means nothing to me, Chief Inspector.'

It was obvious from the blank expression on the woman's face that she really didn't know anything about the Barton girl or her murder.

'She was Malcolm Warner's fiancée.'

'His *fiancée*?'

I could tell by the shocked look on Shirley Manners's face that this was news to her.

'Yes, Mrs Manners, his fiancée. But more importantly, she was murdered sometime on the night of Saturday the fifteenth of June. Malcolm Warner has made a statement to the effect that he spent that night with you. My job is to confirm his alibi.'

'D'you mean he actually told you that?' Shirley Manners's expression implied that it would be the very last time he spent the night with her. But then came a surprise. 'It's not true. Malcolm Warner is a colleague, and that's all.'

'Am I to understand that you categorically deny having spent the night of Saturday the fifteenth of June with Malcolm Warner?' I wanted to be absolutely certain that was the case.

'I most certainly do.'

'Are you willing to make a written statement to that effect, Mrs Manners?'

'No, I'd rather not have anything written down,' she said, quite adamantly. 'These things often get out and in no time at all people will be writing on social media about there being no smoke without fire.'

'Thank you for coming in, Mrs Manners,' I said. 'It doesn't

look as though you can help us any further.' I sent for one of the uniformed officers to escort her from the building.

She didn't exactly flounce out of the interview room, but she'd clearly been irritated by the whole episode.

'What d'you think, Liz?' I asked, once we'd returned to my office.

'She's lying through her teeth, guv.'

'You think so?' I always relied on a woman detective's intuition when it came to assessing a female witness, and Liz Carpenter was every bit as good as Kate Ebdon.

'Did you notice the way she reacted when you mentioned that Warner had a fiancée? Mind you, she covered it up pretty well. It might just be that she's on the point of separating from Mr Manners, and believed herself to be on a promise of a future with Warner. And then she finds he has – or had – a fiancée and is, therefore, a two-timing bastard.' Liz smiled. 'And I speak from experience, guv'nor, believe me.'

'In that case, it's back to see Warner and rattle the bars of his cage for him.'

We left it until the evening to visit Warner at Cobham again. I could have taken Liz Carpenter with me, but I opted for Kate Ebdon simply because she had been with me on the first two interviews.

'Oh, it's you again.'

Warner's tone and attitude were only just short of belligerent, and I suspected that he had already had an ear-bashing from a furious Shirley Manners.

'When I saw you on Sunday you told us at first that you had spent the evening of Saturday the fifteenth of June playing chess with Justin Lane. When we proved that to be untrue, you then told us that you spent the night with Mrs Shirley Manners.'

'That's right.'

'I interviewed Mrs Manners this morning at Belgravia police station, Mr Warner, and she categorically denied having spent the night with you. She went on to say that you were a colleague and nothing more.'

'She's lying,' said Warner. 'We most certainly did spend the night together.'

'Well, one of you is lying, sport,' said Kate. 'And that means that one of you will most certainly finish up in court charged with wasting police time, or even perverting the course of justice.' She paused to give her next statement effect. 'And perverting the course of justice carries a penalty of life imprisonment.' These days, however, four months is usually the going rate, but Kate didn't mention that.

'For God's sake, it's true, I tell you.' The unworldly Warner had clearly been frightened by Kate's dispassionate statement of the law. 'Just a moment.' He hurried across to a small table and opened a drawer. After a frenzied search of its contents he produced an account with a credit card receipt attached to it and handed it to me. 'That's the hotel Shirley and I stayed at in Guildford on the fifteenth of June.'

'This doesn't prove anything, Mr Warner,' I said, returning the bill. 'You may have stayed there, but it doesn't tell me that Mrs Manners was with you. It just shows accommodation for two people, and that the booking was made by you.'

'If you ask the hotel, they'll tell you. I registered us under our own names.'

'You did *what*?' exclaimed Kate.

'What's wrong with that?' asked Warner, his face a picture of innocence.

'Is Mrs Manners a widow . . . or divorced, perhaps? Or even on the point of divorce?' Kate was struggling to come to terms with Warner's naive approach to adultery.

'No. She's married to someone who works in IT.'

'I wonder if he's hacked into his wife's mobile phone,' speculated Kate, a comment that appeared to discomfit Warner, who had obviously never considered such a possibility.

'What d'you think, Kate?' I asked as we drove away from Warner's Cobham cottage.

'Why on earth would a woman like Shirley Manners risk her marriage for a night in bed with that clown, Harry?'

'I think we may safely assume that that particular affair is over, Kate.'

'If it ever was one in the first place,' said Kate dismissively.

It was only about ten miles from Cobham to Guildford and

we were able to park outside the hotel where Malcolm Warner and Shirley Manners had stayed.

We explained to the receptionist what we wanted, and after she had received the manager's consent to give us the information we required, she confirmed that Mr Malcolm Warner and Mrs Shirley Manners had stayed at the hotel on the night that Denise Barton had been murdered. As a bonus, the receptionist was able to give a good description of Shirley Manners, and to tell us that she and Warner had shared a room.

I phoned Shirley Manners from the car. It was a brief conversation. Once she had recovered from her outrage at learning that instead of passing her off as Mrs Warner, Warner had actually given her name to the hotel, she admitted that she had shared a room – and a bed – with him on the night in question. She also stated that she had been with him for the entire night.

'Well, thank God not all alibis are that difficult to confirm,' I said, once Kate and I were back at Belgravia.

'Are you going to do her for wasting police time, Harry?' Kate asked.

'What, and waste even more police time? It's not worth the trouble, Kate. My one regret,' I continued, 'is that I won't be a fly on the wall to witness Shirley Manners's next meeting with Malcolm Warner.'

'Given that she's a PE teacher, it could get quite violent,' commented Kate.

I arrived home at about eight o'clock and was amazed to find Lydia there. She hadn't mentioned that she was coming over.

'What a surprise,' I said.

'Well, you did give me a key, Harry.' She sounded a little guilty, as though she should have given me warning of a visit.

'For the very simple reason that I wanted you to come and go as you please, Lydia darling. Treat it as if it were your own home.' I took her in my arms and gave her a kiss.

'If you're sure, Harry.' She leaned back against my encircling arms and looked up at me.

'Sure I'm sure. In fact, I'd ask you to move in permanently, but I haven't got a swimming pool.'

She laughed and the tension was eased. 'I've prepared a cold supper, darling. I didn't know what time you'd be in.'

'Great. That'll give me time to have a shower.' I paused. 'Why don't you join me?' I suggested, not thinking for a moment that she would.

Lydia said nothing but, fixing her gaze unwaveringly on my face, she began to unbutton her denim shirt.

An hour later, she turned to look at the bedside clock. 'I suppose we should have our supper,' she said.

'I thought we'd just had it,' I said, and she launched a playful punch at my chest.

It was at half past ten, just as we were thinking of going back to bed, that my mobile rang.

'Can't you ignore it, Harry, just this once?' Lydia implored.

'You know I can't do that, darling.' I picked up the phone. 'Brock.'

Before finishing my conversation with Gavin Creasey, the night-duty incident room manager, I asked him to call out Kate Ebdon and to alert Linda Mitchell.

'I've done that, sir.' Creasey's tired tone of voice implied that he didn't need telling how to do his job.

'Please don't tell me you've got to go out.' Lydia looked disappointed.

'I'm afraid so, darling, and I could be out all night from what they were telling me.'

'Don't your people have any consideration for women like me? Just as I'm in a ready and willing mood, you're snatched away from me.'

'Sorry, darling,' I said. 'I'll see you in the morning.' It was not a very comforting reaction, but my mind was already on what Creasey had just told me.

There was a car waiting for me outside my flat.

'Where to, guv'nor?' asked the driver.

'Richmond Park.'

The park was closed to traffic, but the Kingston Gate had been opened to allow the police vehicles access.

My driver opened his window. 'Where's it all happening, mate?' he asked the policeman who had been posted there to stop rubberneckers. Already, even at this late hour, some had been drawn to the scene by social media.

'A few yards up on the left.' The PC pointed. 'Just before the right-hand turning that leads to Robin Hood Gate.'

'Cheers, mate,' said the driver, and drove the few yards or so to where the centre of police activity was located.

'And you are?' An inspector with a clipboard placed his pen in the 'ready to write' mode and looked at me expectantly.

'DCI Brock, HMCC West.' I'd been tempted on many occasions in the past to say that I was Father Christmas and to ask where the kids' party was being held, but incident officers don't possess the same bizarre sense of humour as CID officers.

The stepping plates did not lead directly from where I was standing but followed a circuitous route so that I approached the canvas structure sheltering the body from the rear.

Jane Mansfield was in a small group talking to Kate Ebdon, Dave Poole and Linda Mitchell, the crime-scene manager, but broke off her conversation to speak to me.

'Looks like the same MO as the last three, guv'nor,' she began. 'Twenty-seven years of age, five foot nine, good figure, long brown hair and naked to the waist. Significantly, her bra was missing, although she did wear one.'

'As you know her age, Jane,' I said, 'I presume you've identified the victim?'

'Yes, guv,' said Dave, joining in the briefing. 'You're not going to like this. She's a Dutch citizen, Danique Vandenberg. Her credit cards and driving licence were still in her bag, along with a five-pound note and some loose change. Oh, and her passport contains details of her next of kin. They live in some place called Apeldoorn,' he added, a hopeful expression on his face.

'Oh, great!' I said. 'Foreign complications are all we need, and in answer to your unasked question, Dave, no, we'll not be going to the Netherlands. Next of kin will be notified via the Dutch Embassy.'

'Oh!' said Dave.

'In the meantime,' I continued, 'we'd better get on with it.' In view of the stark similarity between this evening's victim and the other three I was dealing with, I knew that the DAC would allot this one to me as well.

'Anything yet, Linda?' I said, in the hope that there might be some significant scientific evidence that would enable me to break our evidential impasse and make an arrest. But on the basis of what we had found so far, our murderer had been very careful. Or very lucky.

'There are some deep indentations on the grass. My initial assessment is that the murderer carried the body from a car to where he left it.' Linda Mitchell, looking much brighter than I felt, waved a hand towards the five or six yards of grass between the tent and the road.

'Any chance of identifying the shoes that left those marks, Linda?'

'What, on grass? I'm afraid that's the sort of good fortune that only happens on television, Harry. Nevertheless, I've arranged for casts to be taken, but don't put money on me coming up with anything.'

'D'you want me to do the usual, guv?' asked Kate.

'Yes, please, Kate. As soon as Linda's finished, and as soon as you can assemble the search team.' The search team was a group of specialist officers who would go over the ground, slowly increasing the search area from the body outwards in the hope of finding some tiny piece of evidence that would point me to the woman's killer.

'Has the good Dr Mortlock arrived yet?' I asked of no one in particular.

'No. Pamela's on duty tonight,' said Linda. 'I understand that Henry Mortlock left this morning for a golfing holiday in Japan.'

I crossed to the tent. Inside, Pamela Hatcher was bent over the latest victim. She seemed to spend most of her working day with Seb Mould's team. As a consequence, our paths hadn't crossed for some time. A slender woman of about fifty-two, Pamela wore her long grey hair in a single pigtail, at least when she was working a crime scene or carrying out a post-mortem.

'Hello, Harry. Haven't seen you in a while.'

We exchanged a few pleasantries and Pamela got down to business. 'First signs are that she was manually strangled from the rear, but hypostasis indicates that she was killed elsewhere and then carried here.'

'That's a first for this guy,' I said. 'If it's the same killer. Time of death?'

'I would estimate about seven o'clock this evening, Harry.' But Pamela Hatcher was a cautious forensic pathologist. 'I'll be able to tell you more after the post-mortem.'

'I've been doing some checking, guv,' said Dave, flicking open his pocketbook. 'At this time of year the vehicle gates are closed at nine o'clock each evening, but the pedestrian gates are left open twenty-four-seven.'

'Which means that our killer must've dumped the victim and given himself enough time to get out of the park before the gates were closed. Who found her?'

'A young couple,' said Dave, and gave a sly grin. 'I've taken statements, but they're sitting in the back of that police car if you want to have a chat with them,' he added, pointing. 'The girl's name is Janet Smith. She's eighteen, and her boyfriend John Brown is twenty.'

'Janet and John? Smith and Brown? You're having me on.'

'They produced ID, guv. It's kosher.'

'So, what's the SP, Dave?'

'They parked their car in Queen's Road and came through the pedestrian gate; they eventually admitted that they were intent on a bit of nookie. Privacy, a balmy night, making passionate love under the stars, and just when they thought they'd found the perfect spot under these trees, they came across a dead body.' Dave laughed. 'Quite dampened their ardour, that did.'

'You're a cynical bugger at times, Dave,' I said.

'It's mixing with policemen that does it, guv.'

'Did they see anything of use?'

'No fleeing felon, if that's what you mean,' said Dave. 'I reckon our killer had long gone by the time the Richmond Park Romeo and Juliet turned up on the scene.'

'I might need to talk to them later on, but in the meantime send 'em home.'

THIRTEEN

It was one o'clock in the morning before I got home after wrapping up the crime scene in Richmond Park. Consequently I was in the office an hour later than I usually liked to arrive. I'd not been at my desk longer than five minutes when the DAC walked in.

'Morning, Harry,' he said, settling himself in the only armchair with which my office was equipped. Furnishing is by rank in the Metropolitan Police, and I'd need to go up a few ranks before I qualified for more chairs.

'Good morning, sir.'

'I know it's on HMCC South's patch, but are you willing to take on this Vandenberg murder, Harry?' It was born of a genuine concern, rather than a veiled suggestion that a quadruple murder investigation was beyond my capabilities. If I declined, he would have given the entire caseload to a senior officer with more experience. But I had no intention of giving up now. It had, I suppose, become personal. No detective likes being beaten by a villain, and whatever you might think, a murderer is a villain, just the same as a common or garden robber. Or for that matter, a white-collar employee of a City of London merchant bank engaged in insider trading.

'If you're happy for me to carry on, sir, I'm more than willing,' I said. 'It would probably cause more problems than it solved if I were to hand it over to someone else.'

'I agree, Harry. Ring me if you need anything else: manpower, equipment or a flea in the ear of anyone who gets in your way.'

'Thank you, sir, but I'm all right for the time being.' I knew exactly who he meant when he talked of someone getting in my way, and his next sentence as good as confirmed it.

'Is the commander in?'

'Not yet, sir.'

'When he does turn up, ask him to see me at the Yard. Immediately.'

'Very good, sir.' Something told me that our beloved commander was in for an uncomfortable interview. I'd heard on the grapevine that he'd previously received 'words of advice' about allowing Mrs Commander to dictate that he should only work from ten to six. But if that were the case, it looked as though our commander was even more frightened of his wife than of the DAC. Something of a dilemma.

It was on the stroke of ten, as usual, that the great man arrived. I almost trod on his heels following him into his office.

'Ah, Mr Brock, tell me about this suspicious death you dealt with last night in Richmond Park.'

'Before I do that, sir, I think I should tell you that the DAC was here about an hour ago. He wishes to see you at Commissioner's Office as a matter of urgency.'

'Ah, yes, well. I'll get you to brief me on this suspicious death when I get back.' The commander swept past me and made his way downstairs. He certainly didn't look a happy man, and I thought that awarding him a commendation for good police work was not one of the items on the DAC's agenda.

With the commander out of the way, I could now get on with the job in hand.

Dave parked the car immediately outside the Dutch Embassy in Hyde Park Gate, a turning off Kensington Road, close to the Royal Albert Hall.

There was a Diplomatic Protection Group constable stationed at the gate leading to the embassy's main entrance. He appeared to take our modest Job car and its flagrant disregard of parking regulations as a personal affront. Deliberately deigning not to emerge from the safety of the embassy's grounds, he waited until we had alighted and approached him.

'You can't park there,' he proclaimed importantly.

'Oh, why's that?' asked Dave naively.

'Well, it's diplomatic premises.'

'Yes, I know. It's the Dutch Embassy, and we've got important business with an official.'

'Don't make no difference. You can't park there.'

'I'll bet if it was a police car you'd let it park there,' said Dave.

'Ah, well, that'd be different, see,' said the PC, still not realizing that Dave was winding him up.

'That's all right, then,' said Dave, and produced his warrant card. 'I'm DS Poole, and this officer,' he continued, indicating me, 'is Detective Chief Inspector Brock.'

'Oh, you should've said, Sarge,' muttered the PC.

'I just did,' said Dave.

'You can park inside,' said the PC, suddenly becoming terribly helpful, and opened the gate.

In the entrance hall of the embassy, the attractive young lady at the reception desk smiled. 'How may I help you?' She spoke with an intriguing Dutch accent.

'You speak very good English,' said Dave, ever the flatterer.

'So do you,' replied the receptionist drily.

'I have to inform the next of kin of the death of a Dutch national,' I said before Dave could come up with one of his witty ripostes. 'Is there someone here who can advise me of the procedure?'

'May I say who you are?' The young lady reached for the telephone.

I introduced myself, and gave her brief details of the case with which I was dealing. She made no comment and I assumed that embassy people are trained not to make comments, or to show any emotion.

A few moments later a young man appeared through a door at the back of the entrance hall. He was of medium height and had what is known as a 'round' beard, a sort of extended moustache that encircled his chin. For a moment or two he inspected us through slightly tinted circular lenses. He shook hands and introduced himself, but I couldn't quite grasp his Dutch name, much less remember it.

We followed him into his office and I explained about the murder of Danique Vandenberg.

Like the young lady at the reception desk, his face remained impassive. He carefully noted all the details of the

murder, examined Danique's passport and assured me that
the Apeldoorn police would inform the victim's parents
today. I got the impression that he had dealt with similar
situations before, but mostly traffic accidents rather than
murders, I guessed.

'The parents may wish to come to this country, Chief
Inspector, to escort Miss Vandenberg's body back to Apeldoorn.
Would you wish to see them?'

'If they're willing to be interviewed, yes,' I said. It's always
useful to obtain some background knowledge about a
murder victim, although I doubted that enquiries about friends
or enemies would yield very much as Miss Vandenberg was
a visitor from abroad. I gave the young man one of my cards
and he gave me one of his, promising to call me and arrange
an appointment should Mr and Mrs Vandenberg come to this
country. 'They wouldn't be able to take Miss Vandenberg's
body back to the Netherlands until it's released by the coroner,'
I added.

'Yes, this I know,' said the young man.

Having received a call over the air, Dave and I went straight
from the Netherlands Embassy to Pamela Hatcher's mortuary
examination room.

'I've read all of Henry Mortlock's notes, Harry, and there's
no doubt in my mind that the Vandenberg girl was the victim
of the same killer,' said Pamela. 'Surprised from behind, and
no indication that she struggled against her attacker. The marks
on her neck are almost identical to those on the other three
victims. Incidentally, she wasn't a virgin.'

'At the scene, Pamela, you said that the body was moved
after death.'

'Yes, it was, and that would appear to be the only variation
in the modus operandi. But why that should have happened is
a matter for you rather than me,' she added with a smile.

One way and another, it had been a frustrating morning. The
visit to the Dutch Embassy had been necessary, but in terms
of advancing my investigation it served no useful purpose.
Unless Mr and Mrs Vandenberg knew of a maniac who knew

their daughter – but that wouldn't help with the other three murders.

And Pamela Hatcher's contribution had not been helpful, although that was no criticism of her expertise. If the scientific evidence didn't exist, there was nothing that any of us could do to produce it.

Dave and I had lunch at our favourite Italian restaurant and returned to the office. Linda Mitchell was waiting for us, talking to Kate Ebdon.

'I hope you've got something for me to work on, Linda,' I said as I escorted the two women into my office.

'I'm sorry to say that the casts of the footprints were useless, Harry,' Linda said, 'but I guessed that when I saw them.'

'I'm not surprised. It was too much to hope for. Anything else?'

Linda shook her head. 'I'm sorry, Harry. Nothing.'

'What about you, Kate? Have *you* got any good news for me?'

'The same goes for me, Harry. The search team went over the ground twice, but there was absolutely nothing.'

I shook my head, almost in despair. 'As I said at the scene, this guy is either very clever or very lucky. I suppose I'd better bring the commander up to speed.'

'Shouldn't take long,' said Kate drily.

And she was right.

'You had to go to the Yard this morning, sir, when I was about to brief you on the latest murder.' But having taken the trouble to keep the commander in the loop, I found him in an unusually uncommunicative mood.

'Were you really? I don't remember. I'm sure you're quite capable of getting on with it without any assistance from me, Mr Brock. Perhaps you'd let me know when you've solved these four suspicious deaths.'

'Very good, sir.'

The commander waved a hand of dismissal, but as I reached the door he said, 'By the way, I've decided to arrive at the office at nine o'clock each morning in future. It'll avoid the traffic and will enable me to catch up on the paperwork, which seems to increase every day.'

'Very wise, sir,' I said diplomatically.

'That'll be all, Mr Brock.' And with that, the commander withdrew another of his beloved files from the in-tray.

In my job one gets to be a fairly good assessor of character, and judging by his reaction to my arrival I reckoned he had received a monumental carpeting from the DAC about his keeping of 'gentlemen's hours', in addition to being told not to interfere in my investigation. He certainly couldn't get me out of his office fast enough. His claim that coming to work earlier would avoid traffic was a fallacy, and as for paperwork, he absolutely adored it. If there was a surfeit of it on his desk he had only himself to blame, but in any case he went through it like a hungry mouse devouring a piece of Cheddar cheese.

I was intrigued that our killer had suddenly lighted on a Dutch woman. The only reason that I could think of was that in appearance she was very like the first three victims. But my musing was interrupted by Colin Wilberforce's appearance in my office.

'I've just heard from the police in Apeldoorn, sir. Mr and Mrs Vandenberg will arrive at Heathrow from Schiphol at ten past six this evening.'

'Obviously the Dutch get a move on when the situation demands it, Colin.'

'Indeed, sir. I've arranged for a car to pick them up, and Liz Carpenter will be there to meet them. In the circumstances I thought it best that a woman officer should go. She'll arrange with Border Control for the Vandenbergs to be brought straight through without delay.'

'Thank you, Colin.' As usual, Wilberforce had thought of everything, put it together seamlessly and hadn't sought permission to do so when he knew he didn't need to. As I've said many times, it'll be a bad day for us if he ever thinks of trying for promotion.

'By the way, sir, their full names are Lars and Nina Vandenberg, and Danique was their only daughter.'

Whatever the DAC had said to the commander about the hours he kept, it obviously hadn't made any difference to the time he left the office. Having discovered that he had disappeared on the stroke of six, I decided to entertain the Vandenbergs in the great man's office, commanders being afforded far superior furnishings to those of a mere DCI.

'Mr and Mrs Vandenberg, sir.' The man and woman ushered into the office by Liz Carpenter were probably in their early fifties, given that their daughter had been twenty-seven.

I shook hands with each of them and offered them coffee.

'I'm sorry that you had to come to London in such sad circumstances,' I began.

'Perhaps you could tell us what happened to our daughter, Chief Inspector,' said Lars Vandenberg. Like all the Dutch people I'd met he spoke perfect English.

I explained, as succinctly as possible, the circumstances as we knew them so far, but emphasized that the investigation was still in its early stages. I also told them that their daughter appeared to be the fourth victim of a killer we had yet to catch. It was not a pleasant admission to make, but it was better that they heard it from me than from some speculative article in the British gutter press.

'Why was your daughter in England?' I asked. 'Was it a holiday?'

'Not altogether,' said Nina Vandenberg. 'She was a nurse at a hospital in Apeldoorn, but she was thinking of applying for a post in England. She didn't want to stay here permanently but to get some experience of nursing in another country. She said it would help when it came to being considered for promotion back home.' Danique's mother was quite controlled, and there was no sign of a tear.

'Do you happen to know where she was staying?' I asked.

'She arrived four weeks ago,' said Lars Vandenberg by way of a reply. 'She telephoned from Heathrow Airport to say that she had arrived safely. Her idea was perhaps to stay at a hotel for a few days, and if she was lucky enough to get a post at a hospital in London she would be able to move into the nurses' accommodation. She said she would give it a week, and if she hadn't found anything she would come home. However, she telephoned the following day to say that she had been fortunate to obtain accommodation in a house with other nurses at a place called Richmond, and had an interview at a hospital today.' He shrugged, and looked immeasurably sad. Recovering, he handed me a slip of paper bearing Danique's address. 'You know this place, Chief Inspector?'

'Yes, I do.' I was tempted to say that it was a nice part of Greater London, but in the circumstances decided to say nothing about it. 'Did your daughter have a boyfriend in Holland?' I asked.

'Several. But only one at a time. She was a very attractive girl,' said Nina, and smiled. But I got the impression that the smile was an effort.

We talked for a further half an hour or so, but nothing the Vandenbergs told me was of any assistance in getting me any nearer finding her killer. Not that I expected it would. Danique's parents were as mystified by the whole business as I was. I explained that I would apply to the coroner the next day for the release of her body so that they could take her home to Apeldoorn. In the meantime, I told Liz Carpenter to give them any assistance they needed to find a hotel, and assured them that we were ready if necessary to help ensure the safe return of their daughter's body.

Had I but known that later that evening an event would take place which would enable me to escape the stalemate of the four murders I was investigating, I would have stayed on at the office. Instead, I telephoned Lydia and went home to a decent meal.

When I got in Lydia, wearing a cotton maxi dress that must have cost a fortune, was stretched out on the sofa.

'I decided it was too hot to do anything, so I put together a salad.' Having said that, she stood up and pressed herself against me to give me a lingering kiss.

'Don't overdo it, now,' I cautioned, and was rewarded by another of her playful punches.

After the salad – which, given the hot weather, was the perfect meal – we relaxed over coffee and brandy.

It was at the point where I was about to suggest going to bed when my mobile phone came to life.

'Oh, no,' said Lydia, 'not again.'

'Brock,' I said, and mouthed 'sorry' at Lydia.

When Gavin Creasey, the night-duty incident room manager, had finished telling me the tale, I asked him to get Kate Ebdon to meet me at Kingston police station.

'Already done, guv, and there's a car on its way to you,' said Creasey.

FOURTEEN

'Where to, guv?' asked the driver cheerfully.
'Kingston nick.'
It wasn't far from Surbiton, and I was at Kingston police station in the High Street within minutes.

'I'm DCI Brock,' I said to the civilian manning the front office. 'You have a witness here for me.'

'Indeed, we do, sir. It's a Miss Heather Douglas, and she's in the interview room. I'll show you the way.'

'There's no need. I know where it is. Has DI Ebdon arrived yet?'

'I haven't seen him, sir.'

'DI Ebdon's a woman,' I said. I didn't think she would have got to the station before me. New Malden, where she has a flat, is further away than my place at Surbiton. 'Tell her I'll be in the CID office when she arrives.'

There was a lone detective sergeant in the CID office, doubtless that night's sole crime-fighting force for the large area covered by that particular operational command unit.

'I'm DCI Brock, HMCC,' I said. 'What's the SP, skip?' I didn't have to explain what I was talking about. The fact that I'd mentioned HMCC was good enough.

'It was between nine thirty and ten o'clock this evening, sir. An instant response unit was patrolling Richmond Road when they saw this young woman, er . . .' The sergeant glanced at a note on his desk. 'Miss Heather Douglas, guv, in an apparently distressed state. At first they thought she was drunk; there are several nightclubs in the vicinity and it's not uncommon to find drunken females staggering about, even on a Wednesday. But when the crew of the police vehicle started to talk to her they found that wasn't the case. She told them that a man had attempted to kidnap her.'

'All right, skip, that'll do. I'll get the rest from Miss Douglas, when DI Ebdon arrives.'

'I'm here, guv.' As if on cue, Kate appeared in the doorway of the office. As we made our way to the interview room I told Kate the story so far.

The woman we'd come to interview was about five foot ten in height, quite slender and with long brown hair. She had told the Kingston DS that she was twenty-five years of age.

'I'm Detective Chief Inspector Brock and this is Detective Inspector Ebdon, Miss Douglas. Or would you rather we called you Heather?'

'Yes, please. Miss Douglas sounds so terribly old fashioned. Like someone out of a Jane Austen novel.'

'How are you feeling now?'

'A bit shaky now that it's all over, but I'll recover.' Heather Douglas was dressed in jeans and a T-shirt, but there was a large tear in the jeans that revealed a badly grazed knee. I know some young people wear what are called 'distressed' jeans, which means they've been ripped to pieces simply so that they look the same as every other young person wearing jeans, but this damage appeared to have been the result of an accident.

'Have you had that knee looked at?' I presumed the injury was connected with the incident she was describing.

Heather glanced down. 'No, it'll be all right.'

'I can call the police surgeon to dress it for you, if you wish.'

'No, really, it's only a graze. Anyway, my flatmate's a nurse. She'll do whatever needs to be done.'

I saw that Kate Ebdon was making a note, probably to the effect that the services of the police surgeon had been offered and declined. The police have to be very careful about such things these days. I knew also that she'd ask the same question of the detective sergeant whom Heather had met on her arrival. I hoped, for his sake, that he had made an offer of medical assistance. Kate can get very shirty when it comes to neglect of duty.

'I know you've already told other officers what happened to you, Heather,' I began, 'but perhaps you'd tell us, right from the beginning.'

'I'd been to my health club for a workout and a swim. I

usually go about twice a week, or more often if I can. When I was in the pool I got talking to this guy and he asked me what I was doing for the rest of the evening.'

'Where is this health club?' asked Kate.

'All the details are on there.' Heather Douglas produced her membership card and showed it to Kate.

'What time was this?' asked Kate, once she'd made a note of the health club address and returned the card.

'It must've been about half past eight, I suppose.'

'Have you ever seen this man there before?'

'No.'

'Yes, go on, Heather.'

'I told him I was going to the Talavera. It's a wine bar in Richmond.'

'Yes, I know of it,' I said. So far, it was connected with all the murders I was investigating. 'D'you live in Richmond?'

'Yes, I do.'

Kate handed Heather her pocketbook. 'Just jot down your address in there.'

'Is that where you work? In Richmond, I mean,' I continued.

'No, I work at a London hospital. I'm a microbiologist. I take the train up to town every day, worse luck.'

'What did this man say when you told him where you were going?'

'He offered me a lift, because he said he was going to the Talavera too.' Heather saw my frown. 'Yes, I know. Girls should never accept lifts from guys they don't know, but it was that or get the bus. And he seemed quite a decent sort of chap. Actually, he was quite dishy.' She glanced at Kate, as if seeking understanding.

'So you went with him,' said Kate.

'Yes, but I'll not make a mistake like that again, even if it means waiting hours for a bus.'

'Don't you have a car?'

'Yes, but as I was going for a drink afterwards I thought it wiser to use the bus, and I live within walking distance of the wine bar.'

I found that to be a curious statement. 'If you live within walking distance of the Talavera, why didn't you use your car to go to the health club, return home and then walk to the Talavera?' I asked.

'Oh gosh! I never thought of that.'

I assumed, unfairly perhaps, that maybe microbiologists have tunnel vision.

'Had you ever seen this man in the Talavera before?' I asked.

'No, I hadn't, but to be honest, I don't often go there. I'm not a great drinker. As a matter of fact, I was only going there this evening because my flatmate had suggested we went for a drink.'

'And your flatmate's name?' asked Kate.

'Sarah Newman. She's the nurse I mentioned earlier.' Heather smiled. 'She's a bit of a bossyboots. She'll really go for me when she finds out what happened.'

'When did you realize that this man wasn't just obligingly giving you a lift, Heather?' I asked.

'When it dawned on me that he was driving towards Kingston, away from Richmond. It was just about then that he asked me a creepy question, one that really scared me in the circumstances.'

'Which was?' asked Kate.

'He asked me if I was wearing a bra. Just like that. No preamble or anything.'

'What did you say to that?'

'It suddenly hit me what this guy had got in mind. I thought I ought to humour him if I could, so I told him I *was* wearing one. But that wasn't true – most of the time I don't – and I wasn't wearing one then . . . now,' she added, correcting herself.

'What was his reaction to that?' It was interesting that she should have told us of the question that her assailant had asked. The theft of bras, a factor in all the murders, was information that we'd deliberately not released to the media. Consequently, Heather Douglas couldn't have made up the statement just to plant the idea that she'd almost fallen victim to the notorious murderer we were hunting.

'It took me by surprise, but he reached across, grabbed hold of my breast, and of course he could feel I wasn't wearing one.'

'Did he comment on your lie, Heather?' asked Kate.

'He accused me of lying, so I said that it was in my sports bag and I hadn't bothered to put it on when I'd finished my swim. It wasn't true, but my sports bag was in the boot of his car.'

'Was that it?' asked Kate, teasing out every vestige of Heather's distressing encounter.

'He just smiled and said I should put it on once we arrived.'

'Did he tell you where you and he were going?'

'Not immediately, but after he'd made a grab for my boob I was petrified and thought to myself, Heather my girl, if you don't get the hell out of this car pretty damned quick you'll finish up getting raped or even murdered. Although I'm pretty fit, I'm sure he was more powerful than me. It was then that I asked him where we were going, because it was obvious we weren't going to Richmond.'

'What was his reply to that, Heather?' I asked.

'He said he knew of a nightclub in Kingston that he was certain I'd like. It was then that I decided it was now or never.'

'How did you manage to escape?' asked Kate.

'When we were at the Kingston end of Richmond Road, approaching the railway bridge near Kingston railway station, he was forced to slow right down because of traffic pulling up. I think there are traffic lights there somewhere. I opened the door and rolled out on to the pavement. I tore my jeans, bruised my knee quite badly and grazed it.' Heather made it sound as though the torn jeans were of greater concern to her than her injured knee. 'And I ran, but I had to slow to a walk because my knee was hurting like hell.'

'Didn't he come after you, Heather?' I asked.

'No. The traffic had cleared and cars were piling up behind him, and they all started hooting.'

'What happened next?'

'I was limping along the road when a police car turned up. I think they thought I was drunk, but I told them what had happened. Even so, one of the policemen suggested that I was letting my imagination run away with me.'

'Did he, indeed?' I turned to Kate. 'Make a note that I'll want to see that PC in due course.'

'Didn't you think to phone for help?' Kate asked. 'I presume you've got a mobile.'

'I'd left it at home,' admitted Heather ruefully. 'I hardly ever use it, and I'm always afraid of losing it. But the one time I needed it, I hadn't got it,' she added. 'Anyway, the police were there, so I wouldn't have needed it.'

'Now, are you able to give us descriptions of the man and the car, Heather?' Kate turned over a page in the A4 book in which she'd been making notes.

'The man was—' Heather broke off. 'There's something I should mention. When I decided I was going to bail out I surreptitiously pulled out a few strands of my hair and stuffed them down the back of the front passenger seat as far as I could. I reckoned that if you ever find this guy that might come in useful, because they'll have my DNA on them.'

'Oh, bloody ripper!' exclaimed Kate, lapsing into pure Australian in her enthusiasm. 'What made you think to do that?'

'I'm a scientist, and I know about DNA.'

'Very resourceful of you, Heather,' I murmured, 'but can you describe this man?'

'I'm not very good at describing people, but I'll have a go.' Heather was silent for a moment or two. 'I'd say he was somewhere between thirty and forty, and very well built. I could tell that because I saw him in swimming trunks, remember.' She smiled at the recollection. 'He had dark hair, perhaps dark brown, not black.'

'Did he have a beard or a moustache?' asked Kate, busily writing.

'No, no beard. He might've had a moustache, though. I didn't really notice.'

'How tall was he?'

'A little bit taller than me, and I'm five foot ten.'

'What about the car?' I asked. 'Saloon, sports car, foreign, a Mini?'

'Gosh, I don't really know. It was dark in colour. Maybe black or navy blue or even grey. I didn't pay much attention, and I certainly don't know what make it was. Cars all look the same to me, I'm afraid. I've got a Suzuki, and it wasn't one of those. If only I'd taken the number, but by the time I'd bailed out and started running, he'd driven off. Sorry! I'm not being very helpful, am I?'

'Don't apologize,' I said. 'You've been *very* helpful. I hope there were some roots on the hair you put down the back of the passenger seat; otherwise it won't be much good for analysis.'

'I do know that,' said Heather rather tartly. 'I made sure the follicles were there. There's one thing that really annoys me, though.'

'What's that?'

'I had to leave my sports bag in the car, along with an expensive Speedo swimsuit that I'd only just bought. But worse than that, there was also a pair of Ted Baker trainers in the bag, and they cost me a hundred pounds. And I put them on my credit card, and now I'll have to pay for something I don't have any longer when the account comes in.'

'Your kit might turn up,' said Kate. 'I doubt he'd hang on to any of it, not if he's got any sense.'

'I hope you're right,' said Heather, but she didn't sound convinced.

'One last question, Heather,' I said. 'What was this man's name?'

'I don't know if it was his real name, but he said to call him Guy.'

'Surname?'

'He didn't mention one.'

'Did you tell him your name?'

'Yes. I told him I was Heather, but I didn't give him my surname.'

'Does he know where you live?'

'No, of course not.' But Heather suddenly turned pale. 'Oh my God! My name and address are in my sports bag. It was in case I ever lost it.'

'That's good,' said Kate.

'What's good about it?' asked Heather nervously.

'It means he might come after you at home. And if he does, we'll be waiting to grab him. Incidentally, did you tell him where you worked?'

'No, I didn't.'

'Well, that's something.'

'Excuse us for a moment, Heather,' I said. 'Inspector Ebdon and I have to make the necessary arrangements for your personal protection.'

Kate and I adjourned to the CID office. 'What d'you think, Kate?'

'It's possible, I suppose, that this guy just wanted to take her to a nightclub rather than a wine bar.'

'Bearing in mind that our four murder victims have all had their bras taken, Kate, his question about whether she was wearing one could be quite significant,' I suggested. 'And there's another thing. In appearance, Heather looks similar to our four murder victims in terms of age, hair and build. I don't want to get our hopes up, but it's just possible that this man who calls himself Guy is our killer. So far, he's always gone after women who are similar in appearance.'

'That's what I was thinking, Harry, but there's only one thing that doesn't ring true. If she lives within walking distance of the wine bar she intended going to, why not *drive* to the sports club, leave her car at home when she got back and then walk to the wine bar?'

'You heard what she said when I posed the question to her, Kate. Not everyone thinks that far in advance. She might be a brilliant scientist, but that doesn't necessarily make her think ahead when it comes to her everyday life. If she had thought of the possible consequences she wouldn't have got into a car with a complete stranger just because he looked dishy.'

'Possibly,' said Kate, reluctant to give up on her theory, 'but there's another thing. Harvey and I interviewed a guy in the Talavera wine bar last Thursday. His name was Jason Skinner, and he'd had a fling with Rachel Steele. He was on one of the videos on her phone; it showed her standing with Skinner's arm around her waist.'

'What's the relevance of that? There were a few others too.'

'He belongs to the same health club that Heather was talking about. He's fortyish and has a moustache.'

'I think we'll talk to him.'

'I've still got the video on my mobile,' said Kate. 'We could show it to Heather.'

'Not a good idea, Kate. If we nick this guy, I don't want defence counsel suggesting that she picked him out of a line-up because we'd shown her a video in advance of the ID parade.'

'Yeah, good point,' said Kate. 'But right now, Harry, who are you going to pick to babysit?'

I glanced at my watch. It was now midnight. 'We'll need two officers to be inside her house or flat or whatever it is.'

'Couldn't we get the Uniform Branch at Richmond to do it, Harry?'

'No, it's our job. And I want this guy bang to rights. If he's our four-times murderer, everything's got to be done correctly, right from the start.'

I telephoned the incident room and told Gavin Creasey to get hold of two officers who were to draw firearms and to meet me at Heather Douglas's address as soon as possible.

'That's going to please a couple of our blokes,' said Kate.

'Shouldn't have joined if they can't take a joke,' I said, and with some apprehension I rang the DAC and explained what had happened so far. That could have waited until later this morning, but I needed his authority for firearms to be drawn. Disturbing the commander at midnight was a non-starter; the prospect of being interrogated by Mrs Commander before I was permitted to talk to the great man was definitely not on. Anyway, he'd declared himself uninterested in anything I was doing in connection with the murders.

'Yeah, sure, Harry,' said the DAC. 'Get the forms sent over to my office in the morning and I'll sign them.' I knew he could be trusted not to renege on me, even if the job went disastrously wrong, and sometimes the wrong guy does finish up getting shot by police.

'Thank you, sir.' I knew that the DAC would be all right about it, but I wouldn't have expected otherwise from a real detective.

One of the girls with whom Heather lived was still up when we arrived at the Victorian house they shared in Richmond.

Heather introduced her as Sarah Newman, the nurse whom she was supposed to have met at the Talavera.

'Where the hell did you get to, Heather? I waited in the Talavera for over an hour.' Suddenly her flatmate's bedraggled appearance registered. 'My God! What's happened to you? And who are your friends?'

'We're police officers, Miss Newman,' I said, and explained who we were and why we were there.

'Do call me Sarah, please.' She turned back to her companion. 'I'd better have a look at that knee, Heather. I don't want you getting it infected.'

'What's all the noise about? I was sound asleep. Some of us have to work, you know.' A scantily clad girl, her hair a mess, appeared in the doorway of the sitting room, clearly having just got out of bed. 'Oh, gosh!' she exclaimed as she saw us. 'Is it a party? Shall I go and put some clothes on?'

'No such luck,' said Heather, and told us her other flatmate was Olivia Dee and that she worked as a cabin crew attendant for an airline.

'What's happened? Have we been burgled?'

I left it to Kate to explain while I answered the front door and admitted DS Tom Challis and DC Ray Furness.

'I reckon you were the guys who drew the short straws,' I said.

'If you mean we were the ones daft enough to answer our mobiles, guv'nor, yes,' said Challis with a smile.

I explained what had happened to Heather Douglas and then added, 'There are three attractive girls living here, so I don't want any bloody nonsense, Tom. If this guy escapes there'll be hell to pay. Is that understood?'

'Stand on me, guv'nor,' said Challis, a hurt expression on his face.

But I knew coppers, and I didn't want to learn that one of the officers guarding Heather Douglas was in bed with one of her housemates just when the action began.

'Good. This guy could well be our murderer. So everything's got to be bang to rights, Tom. Got it?'

'Yes, guv, we've got it.' Challis looked slightly offended at the implication.

FIFTEEN

It was almost two o'clock in the morning by the time I'd briefed Heather Douglas and her two housemates about what I proposed to do in respect of their safety. It did cross my mind to tell them that we suspected Heather's attacker of being the man who had murdered four women in this area during the course of the last nine days or so, but eventually I decided against it. If Heather or one of her housemates blabbed it to the media it could well prejudice a trial, assuming that we ever got the murderer in the dock. But I wasn't prepared to take that chance. After all, it would not serve any useful purpose. But that prompted another thought. I advised the women not to talk to any journalist or TV interviewer, because I didn't want Heather's attacker to know that we were planning to catch him.

Finally, I satisfied myself that Challis and Furness knew what to do in the event that Heather's attacker turned up at the house. I didn't want to see the man acquitted because of some legal technicality.

But now I was faced with a problem. Jason Skinner had moved rapidly to the top of my suspect list, mainly because of his membership of the same health club to which Heather belonged, and that the description she had given of the man she had met there was similar. But I was also conscious of the fact that the description would have fitted a lot of other men.

Consequently I didn't think I was justified in paying Skinner a visit at this time of the morning, simply on that flimsy evidence. I determined, therefore, that I would interview him first thing tomorrow morning and hope that, if he was the man I wanted, he would not have found that vital piece of evidence that Heather had pushed down the back of the front passenger seat of his car.

However, just to be on the safe side, I arranged for a discreet

observation to be put in place on his house until then. Heaven
forfend that he got wind of our interest and did a runner,
particularly if it was to a place abroad that created difficulties
about extradition. Which gave me another thought: I got Gavin
Creasey in the incident room to send a message to all ports
and airports. I'd rather briefly detain an innocent man than
allow a guilty one to flee.

As Kate Ebdon had done enough for one day, I sent her
home, and arranged for Dave Poole to meet me at Skinner's
address at eight o'clock, later that morning. But I stayed
on until then. One of the privileges of being a detective
chief inspector and lead investigator is that you work
through the night when duty demands it. And in my welfare
role I tried to ensure that no one else did more hours than
absolutely necessary. Not always easy in the middle of a
murder inquiry.

'How are we going to play this, guv?' Dave yawned and
put his hands in his pockets.

'By ear, Dave.' I rang Skinner's doorbell.

The man who opened the door was probably about forty,
and he had a moustache. If this was the man who had attempted
to abduct Heather Douglas, the description could have fitted.
She reckoned he was between thirty and forty and her doubts
about a moustache could've been explained by the fact that
this man's was almost invisible.

'Jason Skinner?'

'Yes.'

'We're police officers, Mr Skinner,' I said, and introduced
myself and Dave.

'Got a lock problem, have you? Your people often come to
me when they've got something they want opening.'

'Why should they do that?' Dave asked, playing the
innocent. We'd both read Kate Ebdon's statement about her
interview with Skinner at the Talavera wine bar last Thursday.
I had also spoken to her before she went off-duty earlier this
morning just to check whether she had anything to add. We
hadn't forgotten, either, that the girl who was with Skinner
last Thursday had taken advantage of Kate's questioning to

leave the bar hurriedly. I now wondered if some sixth sense had warned her that Skinner was a man to be avoided.

'Well, I'm a locksmith.'

'Oh, I see,' I said. 'No, it's nothing like that. It might be as well if we came in.'

Skinner seemed a little reluctant to admit us, but at the same time it appeared he could find no immediate reason for refusing. We followed him into a sitting room at the front of the house. It was an unremarkable room with just the usual sort of furniture and the obligatory wide-screen television set.

'What do you want, if it's not a lock you want opening?'

'Were you at your health club last evening?' I asked.

Skinner immediately began to look shifty. 'I might've been. Why d'you want to know?'

'A young woman has made a report to police that a man fitting your description attempted to abduct her after promising to take her to the Talavera wine bar in Richmond. We know that's an establishment you frequent.'

'It wasn't me. I wasn't at the health club yesterday.' Skinner actually appeared to be relieved.

'Where were you, then?' asked Dave. 'Yesterday evening in particular.'

'No comment,' said Skinner.

That stupid statement decided it. Suspects don't realize that to say 'No comment' like that immediately makes the police suspicious. Dave glanced at me and I nodded.

'Jason Skinner, I'm arresting you on suspicion of attempting to abduct Heather Douglas, and the theft of a sports bag and the contents thereof,' said Dave, and rattled off the caution.

'It is my intention to search these premises,' I began.

'Oh, you suddenly got a warrant, then?' asked Skinner aggressively.

'You've just been nicked, so we don't need one,' said Dave, 'and I can recite the relevant section of the Police and Criminal Evidence Act for you, if you're interested.'

'I never had anything to do with any girl getting abducted,' protested Skinner. 'So I don't know what you're looking for.'

'Where's your car kept?' I asked.

'In the street.'

'Why?' asked Dave. 'You've got a garage.'

'Er, yeah, well, I keep my van in there. It's got all my equipment in it, and it'd cost an arm and a leg to replace it if it ever got nicked.'

'We'll just have a look, though,' I said. Skinner might've been lying, and the garage might contain a car. On the other hand, Heather Douglas might have been conveyed in a van, some of which are quite modern and comfortable.

Dave led the way and opened the communicating door from the house into the garage. It was then that we discovered a stash of valuables that would have rivalled the stock of even an upmarket pawnbroker.

There was certainly a van in the centre of the garage, but all around the walls were shelves stacked with silverware, antique clocks – one of which was a rather fine gilt brass carriage clock – Royal Worcester vases and candlesticks in abundance. In a large wooden box Dave discovered a quantity of jewellery; in another he found a number of credit cards.

'What's in that?' asked Dave, pointing to a locked steel cabinet on the back wall of the garage.

'No comment,' said Skinner.

'Look, sport, you can either open it for me or I'll have it taken apart with a thermal lance.'

'No comment,' said Skinner again.

'On second thoughts,' said Dave, as he spotted a crowbar on the bench, 'I think we can manage without a thermal lance.' Finding an appropriate gap where the door met the cabinet, Dave inserted the crowbar and forced it open. 'Well, well, well!' he said, gazing at row upon row of keys, each of which was labelled. Some bore details of private addresses, while others clearly related to doors at the health club of which Skinner was a member.

'I'll get on to the local nick, Dave,' I said. 'They can deal with all this stolen property. Should keep them occupied for a few months.'

We didn't have long to wait. Twenty minutes later a couple of CID officers arrived from Twickenham police station.

'Thanks very much, guv'nor,' said a detective sergeant once I'd explained the situation. 'It's not every day we get a percher as good as this guy's looking. Mind you,' he added gloomily, 'half the losers of this property won't want to know. They'll have had the pay-out from the insurance company and they've probably spent it already.' He looked around at some of the stolen property. 'Personally, I wouldn't want any of it back.'

'Don't bail him, skip,' I said, once the sergeant had finished his little whinge about the fickleness of losers. 'I may want to put him up for an ID parade. Apart from being a professional thief, right now he's a suspect in an abduction case. Possibly even murder. Which reminds me: if you come across a collection of bras, let me know straight away.'

The local DS gave me a strange look, but then said, 'Don't worry, guv, we'll hang on to him.'

'Put him back in the house, but don't take him to the nick just yet, skip,' I said. 'Just in case we find what we're looking for.'

The DS told his DC to remove Skinner to the sitting room, but he stayed here.

'What's the story behind that, then, Dave?' I asked, pointing at the rows of keys. I turned to the Twickenham DS. 'You'd better listen to this theory of Dave's, skip.'

'I'll put money on them being duplicate keys for all the houses where he's replaced locks,' said Dave, 'and it looks as though he fitted the locks at the health club as well.'

'Are you thinking what I'm thinking, Dave?'

'I reckon so, guv,' said Dave thoughtfully. 'He's been nicking gear from the health club. He could let himself out to the car park by a back door and put anything he'd nicked in his car. Those credit cards were probably knocked off from the changing rooms. Secondly, as the computer at the club will have shown him to be there all the time, he could have left and returned without anyone knowing, and come up with the perfect alibi. And the same would apply when it came to a burglary. Once again, he could slip out of the health club, do the job and return.'

'But why is he hanging on to all that stolen gear, Dave? It's asking for trouble.'

'Two possible reasons. Firstly, he's an overconfident bastard

who thinks he can outwit the Old Bill, or secondly, he can't
find a fence who's willing to take that sort of gear off him. I
only had a quick glance, but I'd think that a lot of it would
be easily traceable, despite what our friend from Twickenham
here just said, and a fence's not going to touch anything
that hot.'

'My view as well, Dave,' I said, 'but d'you still fancy him
for these toppings?'

'They could be down to him,' replied Dave. 'I think what
we've found here confirms that he wasn't at the health club.
If he had been, he'd have wanted to let himself out the back
way instead of leaving through the front with Heather.
Then he could have returned after he topped her – because
I think that was the abductor's intention – and the computer
would have shown that he was there all the time. There again,
the attempted abduction might not have anything to do with
him, but that doesn't rule him out of the murders.'

'But why did the abductor ask Heather whether she was
wearing a bra? That wasn't coincidence, surely.'

'A lecherous male's curiosity, perhaps. Anyway, we'll have
a look at his van.' Dave turned his attention to Skinner's van
which, despite what he'd said about not wanting the contents
stolen, was unlocked. Donning a protective glove, he ran his
hand down the back of the front passenger seat. He glanced
at me and shook his head. If Skinner was the abductor, he had
removed Heather Douglas's hair. Disappointing though it was,
I had to admit that Skinner might not be the man we wanted.

We returned to the sitting room, where a handcuffed
Skinner was being guarded by the other CID officer from
Twickenham.

'You said you kept your car in the street, Skinner,' said
Dave. 'Where is it, and what's the index number?' And when
Skinner appeared hesitant Dave added, 'We can break into it
if you'd prefer, and the cost of repairs would be down to you.'

I never knew whether Dave was right when he came up
with statements like that, but he sounded so convincing
that Skinner believed him. And I very nearly did too, but
Dave's not had as many dealings with the Directorate of
Professional Standards as I have.

Skinner handed his car keys to Dave and gave him the number of a green Subaru.

Minutes later, Dave returned and again shook his head.

For the next two days, round the clock, a pair of police officers remained in the Victorian house occupied by the three women. The officers guarding them enjoyed the variation from the usual run-of-the-mill police duty, as did the officer who drove Heather Douglas to work each day. However, for the three women the initial feeling of security, and the novelty, wore off very quickly.

On the Saturday morning, Detective Sergeant Challis phoned me from Richmond.

'Everything all right, Tom?' I asked.

'Not to put too fine a point on it, guv'nor, and in the nicest possible way, Heather and the other two girls want us out of the house. They reckon that us being there is ruining their social life.'

'I can understand that,' I said, 'and perhaps as the kidnapper hasn't turned up already, he won't come at all. Have you explained the risks involved if they choose not to have you there, Tom?'

'Yes, guv, and I explained to Heather that she'd be obliged to sign a form of indemnity.'

'I don't think we need a form of indemnity this time, Tom. Withdraw the protection detail.' I was not happy about Heather Douglas's decision, but we couldn't force her to have our people in her house against her will. Having visited the street where she and her fellow residents lived, I knew that any attempt at an observation would stick out like a sore thumb, and our wanted man would disappear like a rat up a drainpipe. 'One other thing, Tom . . .'

'Yes, guv?'

'Tell her that she can call the incident room at any time of the day or night if she has any fears. Or if this guy does turn up, tell her or one of her housemates to dial nine-nine-nine.' It was not an outcome that I would have wanted, having the Uniform Branch arresting someone who might turn out to be the murderer of four women, but there was no alternative.

It seemed to me, as I sat considering the matter on that Saturday morning, that we had reached deadlock again. But deadlocks are meant to be broken, and it's not always the police who do the breaking.

However, we still had to search Danique Vandenberg's flat. I shouted for Dave, and decided to take Nicola Chance with us once again.

'This flat is far too expensive for a nurse,' I said, gazing around the plush Richmond apartment that Danique Vandenberg had lived in, albeit for only four weeks. Although not in the same block as the one occupied by Rachel Steele at the time of her murder it was similar in appointment, and probably incurred a maintenance tariff that would certainly be beyond my income.

'Perhaps her father was paying the rent, guv'nor,' volunteered Nicola. 'Nurses are grossly underpaid and they'd never be able to rent a place like this,' she said, agreeing with what I'd said when we arrived.

'Give Liz Carpenter a call, Dave,' I said, 'and ask her if she found out what Lars Vandenberg did for a living. I think she had quite a long chat with him on the way back from the airport.'

Dave had trouble getting a signal and had to go outside the building to make his call. Some minutes later he returned. 'According to Liz, Lars Vandenberg was a bit ambivalent about what he did, and didn't actually say much beyond the single word "business".'

'I wonder why. Dave, get on to Colin Wilberforce and ask him to have a word with the police in Apeldoorn to see if they can shed any light on this guy.'

I let Nicola start by having a look around the bedroom and the en suite bathroom. 'It looks similar to before, guv,' she said when she returned to the sitting room.

'Go on.'

'Very expensive perfume in the bathroom. High-end cosmetics on the dressing table and a wardrobe full of pricey clothes. I had a look at some of the labels and they don't come cheap.' Nicola paused. 'In another section of the wardrobe there is a load of fancy gear: thongs, peekaboo bras, suspender belts and black nylons. And some very sexy dresses, what there is of them. They're so skimpy it'd be hardly worth putting them on at all. There's the usual couple of canes, too.'

'So she's on the game. Not a nurse at all.'

'Looks like it,' said Nicola.

'Thongs, suspender belts and the rest of it,' I said.

'It's all that men ever want, guv,' said Nicola. 'They've got one-track minds and no imagination,' she added crushingly.

'Yes, you're probably right.' I should have kept my mouth shut, having remembered too late that Nicola had a tendency to speak her mind. 'However, that makes three, to our knowledge,' I said. 'Rachel Steele was a prostitute, and so was Lisa Hastings. I think we'll need to look deeper into Denise Barton's background. Thinking about her, she was almost too good to be true. Tennis club, lover of Gilbert and Sullivan operettas and working with a respectable online business in Richmond.' As it turned out, events overtook this necessity and we didn't have to bother.

The three of us spent the next hour poking around in the apartment, but nothing of any importance came to light in terms of pointing to Danique Vandenberg's killer. The fact that she was a prostitute made life much more difficult. It could have been any one of her clients, and God knows how many there were of those. The common factor was the likelihood of the murderer being the same in each case, and that might make life easier.

Dave's phone rang, and he was forced to go outside again to take the call. 'You're not going to believe this, guv,' he said when he returned. 'Lars Vandenberg is the owner of a licensed brothel in Apeldoorn.'

'A *licensed* brothel?'

'Apparently prostitution is allowed in the Netherlands, guv, provided it's properly run and licensed. According to the Apeldoorn police this establishment is called . . .' Dave paused to examine the note he'd made, '. . . it's called *Het Passie Huis*, which translates as The Passion House.'

'And the Vandenbergs have returned to Apeldoorn,' I said. 'Not that I think Lars Vandenberg would have admitted employing his own daughter. If he did.'

'She probably saw it as paying better than nursing,' said Dave.

'I doubt if she ever was a nurse,' I said. 'I can't imagine that even a licensed brothel owner would admit that his daughter was a prostitute.'

'I'll bet he did employ her,' said Dave. 'In my book, he's a two-timing, lying bastard.'

'There were the usual bank and credit card statements, with one or two large unexplained deposits to her bank,' said Nicola, 'but I don't think we have to look very far for a reason now we know what she was up to.'

'Back to the office, then,' I said. 'I doubt we'll gather anything else of interest here.'

I spent the rest of Saturday immersed in paperwork, but deciding it was high time that I took Lydia out for a meal, I picked up the phone and tapped out her number.

'Why don't I come over and cook for you, darling?' said Lydia.

'I thought that a meal out would be a change for you,' I said.

'I'd rather we had dinner at your place.' She paused. 'Or mine. You could have a dip in my heated swimming pool.'

'Much as I'd love to come to Esher, Lydia, I'd rather stay closer to Richmond.' Reluctantly, I explained the reason.

'I quite understand, Harry. Another time perhaps. I could come to your place.'

'I hope you don't get fed up with me always rushing off on some job.' I couldn't understand her acceptance of my uncertain lifestyle, and the frequent cancellations of social engagements because of it.

'It'll take more than that to get rid of me, Harry darling. What time would suit you?'

'About eight? Or is that too late?'

'That'll be fine,' said Lydia. 'I'll see you then, darling.'

At about three o'clock I was preparing to leave the office when Dave came in.

'There's a PC outside, sir. He was the one who picked up

Heather Douglas the night she was abducted. He was the guy who made some smart remark.'

'Oh, yes, I remember, Dave. Bring him in.'

I knew his sort the moment he stepped into my office. Swaggering and full of himself.

'I understand you want to see me, sir,' said the PC.

'I'm told that you were the officer who found Miss Heather Douglas in a distressed state in Richmond Road, Kingston, on Wednesday the nineteenth of this month. Am I right?'

'Yes, sir.' The PC was now looking a little twitchy, and probably wondering what was coming next.

'Sergeant Poole, perhaps you would read the appropriate part of Miss Douglas's statement.'

'Yes, sir. "I was limping along the road when a police car turned up. I think they thought I was drunk, but I told them what had happened. Even so, one of the policemen suggested that I was letting my imagination run away with me".' Dave put the statement on my desk and sat back.

'Have you any comment to make about that?' I asked the PC.

'Well, sir, we get a lot of drunks about that time of night, even on a Wednesday, and I thought she might've been one of them.'

'I see. Turning to the matter of this young lady's injured knee – did you offer her medical assistance?'

'I didn't know she'd hurt her knee, sir.'

'Did you bother to ask if she was injured?'

'Well, I, er . . .'

'This young woman had just been the victim of an abduction, Constable,' I said. 'A serious crime that can attract a sentence of life imprisonment. I think your conduct was far from professional, if not cavalier, and I shall refer this entire matter to your chief superintendent. That's all.'

A much-chastened PC left my office, but I cannot abide sloppy police work, particularly when dealing with a matter as serious as an abduction.

I got home at around seven o'clock that evening. It had been a day or two since Gladys Gurney had been in and put everything to rights. But since then I'd managed to do a lot of untidying that had to be rectified before Lydia arrived.

At twenty minutes past seven my mobile played its ominous little tune, the one that told me when the incident room was calling.

'Yeah, Brock.'

'It's Don Keegan, guv'nor,' said the night-duty sergeant. Keegan was the man who occasionally stood in either for Gavin Creasey or Colin Wilberforce, the regular incident room managers.

'What is it, Don?'

'There's been a sighting of the man who attempted to abduct Heather Douglas, guv.'

'Tell me more.'

'She decided to go to the Talavera wine bar this evening to celebrate her freedom from us and one of her housemates, a girl called Olivia Dee, went with her. She's an air hostess, apparently.'

'Yes, I know all that, Don. Cut to the chase, there's a good chap.'

'She saw this guy in the wine bar, guv. She was absolutely certain it was the man who tried to kidnap her last Wednesday. Fortunately, he didn't see her, so she and Miss Dee beat a hasty retreat to the street and called me. I alerted the local nick, gave them the SP and asked them to send a car. Silent approach, of course.'

'And by the time they got there, the bird had flown.'

'How did you know that, guv?'

'Because I've been at this game for a long time, Don, and that's what always happens. Where's Miss Douglas now?'

'She went home, and I've sent Tom Challis and Liz Carpenter down there to babysit.'

I debated cancelling my evening with Lydia, but decided that there was very little I could do apart from interfere in a situation that a couple of sergeants could deal with quite capably.

'Get in touch with Tom Challis or Liz Carpenter, Don, and ask one of them to get as full a description as possible, as quickly as possible, circulate it around the team and put it on the PNC. You never know, someone might pull a name out of their memory. But Heather must be talked into not going out without a police escort until we've captured this guy.'

Lydia arrived on the stroke of eight, carrying a bag that doubt-less contained this evening's dinner. I immediately offered to pay, but just as quickly she refused.

'This doesn't seem right, somehow, Lydia,' I said. 'I started by inviting you out to dinner and you finish up paying for it.'

'You can make it up to me when you've got some guaranteed time off,' said Lydia. 'In the meantime, I must get the dinner under way.'

Needless to say, Lydia produced a magnificent meal, and afterwards we relaxed with a brandy.

'I suppose you're allowed to take a holiday occasionally, are you?' Lydia asked suddenly.

'As a matter of fact, I was thinking of taking a few days off once this present case is wrapped up,' I said. 'Why d'you ask?'

'Perhaps we could have a holiday together somewhere,' suggested Lydia hesitantly.

I had a feeling that my idea of a holiday, limited as it was by income, would be somewhat different from that usually enjoyed by Lydia. I could imagine that she and her late husband had enjoyed lengthy vacations in some exotic, sun-drenched paradise. And I'm not talking about a package holiday on the Costa Brava either. But I was in no position to offer an opinion. Shortly after my marriage to Helga, when I was a constable, she and I had spent a week in Brighton with our young son Robert. But I'd not been on holiday since then. The boy's death was the start of the breakdown between Helga and me, and our life never seemed quite the same after he was drowned.

'A cruise?' I suggested impishly, knowing Lydia's dislike of boats, but I was surprised.

'Sounds a wonderful idea. As long as it's not a very small boat where you're the captain and I'm your first mate,' said Lydia, and laughed.

'Sailing's not my scene,' I said, 'but aren't you averse to flying?'

Lydia pouted. 'I'd prefer not to. It's not a fear of flying, but I absolutely hate crowded airports and the inevitable delays. The idea of a cruise with nothing to do but laze around sounds like a very good idea.'

'Maybe,' I said, wishing I hadn't got into this discussion. 'It wouldn't be like one of those films where the detective on a cruise gets called in by the captain to solve the murder of a passenger. That's pure fiction.'

Lydia stayed the night, and although I was tempted to go into the office, I decided against it. Kate Ebdon was the duty inspector and I knew that she would get in touch with me if anything arose that needed my attention. Furthermore, I knew that the Talavera wine bar was closed on Sunday evenings.

Consequently, Lydia and I lazed around on Sunday morning, reading newspapers. She produced a cold lunch and eventually went home at about four o'clock, having failed to persuade me to go with her to Esher to try out her swimming pool.

She didn't mention a holiday again, for which I was grateful. I'm not really a holiday sort of person.

SIXTEEN

On the Monday morning, I held a briefing in the incident room. The murder of Rachel Steele, two weeks ago, had been the start of this inquiry, and since then most members of the team had become familiar with the Talavera wine bar in Richmond. It was there that Heather Douglas was convinced she had seen her attacker.

'We have a description of the man who abducted Heather,' I began, pointing to the whiteboard that I had insisted should be installed. My theory was that officers visiting the incident room were more likely to look at the latest information posted on it than to ask Colin Wilberforce, a computer-orientated officer if ever there was one, what was new. Wilberforce had afforded me a frown of disapproval. 'But,' I continued, 'as was to be expected, that description fits quite a few of the men who are known to frequent the Talavera.' I had considered asking Heather to return to the wine bar in the company of two of our officers, but decided against it. If our suspect caught sight of Heather, he'd likely turn and run.

'Do we set up an observation on the wine bar to try and catch this alleged abductor, guv?' asked DC Ray Furness.

'I don't think we can continue to call him an *alleged* abductor, Ray,' I said. 'In my view, he became an abductor the moment he deviated from the route between the health club and Richmond. But that apart, I can't see what good an observation would be if Heather wasn't with the obo team all the time.' I paused and looked around the crowded incident room. 'And if any of you lecherous male coppers think you're going to spend a few hours in the back of an obo van with the gorgeous Heather Douglas, forget it.' And that, as I expected, produced a laugh.

'Can I put my two penn'orth in, guv?' asked DI Brad Naylor.

'What's on your mind, Brad?' I asked.

'D'you think we could persuade Heather Douglas to change

her appearance so that she wouldn't be recognized by the guy who kidnapped her? Then we could put her into the Talavera with one of our blokes, one who's not been there before, and if our friendly neighbourhood abductor turns up we could have a team standing by waiting to house him.'

I glanced across at Kate Ebdon. 'Kate, you're a woman—' I began.

'Oh, you've noticed, guv,' said Kate.

'Yeah, all right, all right.' Once the laughter had subsided, I continued. 'D'you think you could persuade Heather to go along with Brad's idea? Particularly if we explained that we might catch a multiple killer.'

'Is that wise?' asked Kate. 'It might frighten her to the extent that she refuses to take part.'

'I think it's only fair to tell her the whole story.' Since thinking over my original reason for not telling her or her housemates, I'd changed my mind.

'She's made of sterner stuff than we seem to be giving her credit for, guv,' said Tom Challis, a comment that rather surprised me. I think it also surprised Challis that he'd mentioned it.

'I reckon I could alter her appearance so that even her own mother wouldn't recognize her,' said Kate. 'It's worth giving it a shot, anyway. I'll catch her this evening when she gets in from work.'

'Hello, Inspector.' Heather Douglas was clearly surprised to see Kate Ebdon seated in an armchair in the sitting room that she shared with the other girls in the house. DS Challis was reclining in another chair, talking to Sarah Newman, the nurse. 'What brings you here? Have you caught him?'

'No, Heather, but we hope to arrest him with your assistance. If you're willing to help, that is.'

'Of course.'

'I'd better tell you the whole story before you agree.' Kate Ebdon knew that what she was about to tell Heather Douglas might scare her to the extent that she refused to take part in the plan that Brad Naylor had put forward. But, as we'd discussed at the conference that morning, she was duty-bound to explain about everything that had happened so far. 'We have reason to believe that the man who abducted you last Wednesday is someone we want to talk to about four murders.'

'Gosh! You mean the murders that have been in all the papers?' Heather tried to make light of that uncompromising statement, and that she might have been murdered by the man who abducted her. She folded her arms and gripped her upper arms tightly with her hands. Kate knew from that classic body language that Heather was terrified at the prospect of helping the police to find this man, but after a second or two of obvious introspection, she made a decision. 'I'll do it,' she said, unfolding her arms. The grim determination was quite apparent on her face. 'After all, it might save another girl from going through the ordeal I suffered.' She paused for a moment. 'Or even getting murdered.'

Tom Challis smiled. He'd said Heather was made of sterner stuff.

'Good girl,' said Kate, and turned to the practicalities of the plan. 'The first thing for you to do is to dye your hair blonde.'

'Oh, no!' It seemed that Heather found this proposition more alarming than setting out to find a murderer.

'Why not? It'll look great,' said Olivia Dee, the air hostess who was Heather's fellow resident. 'It's time you had a change anyway.'

'All right,' said Heather reluctantly, 'but I'm not cutting it.'

'There's no need for that,' said Kate. 'Put your hair up instead of wearing it long as you do now. I'm sure Olivia will give you a hand.' Kate had noticed the first time she'd met her that the long-haired Olivia had been wearing her hair in a French roll. And that was probably how she wore it when she was on duty.

'Sure. It'll look great,' said Olivia again.

'There you are, then,' said Kate. 'A different outfit, and you'll look like another woman. The plan is that you'll go to the Talavera every night with Tom Challis. We're just hoping that our man is an habitué, and that you identify him. A team of officers led by a detective inspector will be right outside the wine bar. They'll wait until the suspect leaves and they'll follow him to his house. The rest is down to us.'

'Sounds easy,' said Heather.

'Not necessarily,' said Kate. 'I've known even the easiest of operations go wrong.' She didn't immediately realize that what she'd said might alarm Heather.

'Whatever else happens, I can assure you that *you* won't be in any danger,' said Challis, having registered the brief frisson of concern on the girl's face.

'That's right,' added Kate hurriedly. 'What Tom says is dinkum. You won't be in any danger at all.'

'When d'you want me to start, Inspector?' asked Heather.

'Can you get your hair dyed by tomorrow, and get some suitable alternative clothing?'

Heather looked doubtful, but Olivia Dee said, 'Don't worry about that. We'll get her ready so that even you won't recognize her.'

'In the meantime, I'll arrange to have your house guard put back on. Although you said that the suspect didn't recognize you, you can't be sure. Tom will stay here until the reinforcements arrive, and then he'll pick you up tomorrow.'

Challis followed Kate out to the street. 'That was a bloody silly thing to say to Heather about this sort of operation sometimes going wrong. You scared the daylights out of her.'

Kate bridled at Challis's attitude. 'I'd remind you you're talking to an inspector, *Sergeant.*'

'OK, so you scared the daylights out of her, *ma'am,*' said Challis, emphasizing the honorific.

'Sorry, Tom. I'm a bit tired.'

'Aren't we all, ma'am.' Going back into the house, Challis slammed the door, leaving Kate on the pavement swearing to herself for having lost her temper unnecessarily with a trusted colleague.

Detective Sergeant Tom Challis arrived at Heather Douglas's house at seven thirty the next evening. Steve Harvey and Nicola Chance were already there, having relieved the day shift an hour and a half previously.

'If we don't find Heather's attacker this evening, Nicola,' said Challis, 'you and Steve are here for the night.'

'Thanks a bundle, skip,' said Nicola.

A few moments later, a woman entered the room. Slender, and a couple of inches under six foot tall, she was wearing white jeans, a black T-shirt and stylish trainers, and her blonde hair was fashioned into an immaculate ponytail. Large, round, black-rimmed spectacles finished off the picture of an elegant but informally dressed girl.

Tom Challis stared at this vision for some seconds before realizing that it was Heather Douglas. 'Good grief!' he exclaimed. 'I didn't recognize you, Heather. You've done a brilliant job of disguise.'

'You can thank Olivia, Tom. She's very good at this sort of thing.'

'So it seems, but I didn't realize you wore glasses.'

'I don't,' said Heather. 'They've got plain glass in them, but Inspector Ebdon seemed to think it would be a good idea. Pretty cool, eh?'

'And I thought you were going to put your hair up.'

'Olivia and I decided that would be too formal for going to a wine bar with a fellah.' Heather chuckled, nestled up close to Challis and took his arm. 'Shall we go out on the town, darling?'

'I think changing your whole appearance has changed your character too.' Challis had a sudden fear that he'd got a wayward girl on his hands, and that could easily foul up the operation.

'Great, isn't it? I can do what I like and no one will know it's me.'

'That's what's worrying me,' said Challis, earnestly hoping that she wouldn't bring herself to notice in the Talavera by some scatterbrain showing off.

As Heather Douglas entered the Talavera wine bar, the attention of the clientele was immediately riveted upon her, and Challis wondered whether her striking appearance might prove to be counterproductive. The purpose of her being there was to discreetly identify her attacker, not to make a spectacle of herself.

However, she later told Challis that there were people there who knew her extremely well, but who hadn't greeted her in their usual effusive way. 'And that,' she said in conclusion, 'included a guy I had a brief fling with six months ago.'

Heather was without a current boyfriend and took full advantage of having Tom to take her out, courtesy of the Metropolitan Police. It was a situation that she used to her advantage, becoming coquettish and from time to time leaning across to kiss Tom on the cheek, secure in the knowledge that he couldn't object without revealing that they weren't an 'item'.

They stayed in the wine bar for a couple of hours, but Heather was unable to spot her attacker. At ten o'clock, Challis escorted her back to her house.

The second evening of the police operation was blisteringly hot, with temperatures only a degree or so below ninety Fahrenheit. Heather, proclaiming that a woman could not wear the same outfit two nights running, appeared in a pair of denim shorts and a white T-shirt. Challis groaned.

'What's wrong, Tom? Don't you like my shorts?' Heather pushed out a suntanned leg.

'I've no objection at all,' he said, 'but I don't want you to be too noticeable. It might blow the whole operation.'

'I think you worry too much, Tom,' said Heather, seizing his arm and steering him towards the front door.

The Talavera was not so crowded this evening, many of the habitués having chosen a nearby pub, preferring the cooler air of its beer garden to the stifling atmosphere of the wine bar. Naturally enough, Heather received several admiring glances, but after a glass or two of Chablis, and in Challis's case just one small glass of Merlot, she told Challis that her attacker was not there.

Challis gave it a while longer, but at a quarter past ten he decided that their suspect was unlikely to show up. He called DI Naylor on his mobile and told him that he was abandoning the observation for that night. Having escorted Heather back to her house, he received another lingering kiss. This time she invited him in, but Challis wisely refused, suspecting what she might have in mind; mixing duty with pleasure was a sure way to attract the eagle eyes of the Department of Professional Standards. Particularly in a case as important as this one.

Regrettably, the following night, Thursday, proved to be a washout too, and Challis was beginning to wonder whether Heather Douglas had been mistaken in her conviction that she had seen her attacker in the Talavera.

On Friday morning, Challis came into my office.

'Have you got a moment, guv?' he asked.

'Sure. Sit down. What's on your mind?'

'We don't seem to be getting anywhere with this obo at the Talavera, guv.'

'It could take time, Tom,' I said, 'And given the time of year, the suspect might've decided to go on holiday.'

'I take your point, guv, but that's not all,' continued Challis. 'Each evening, Heather is wearing an increasingly provocative outfit. In fact, it's as if, in her mind, the whole thing is some sort of fantasy charade.'

'Never mind what she's wearing, Tom. Is there any danger of her being recognized by this guy who abducted her?'

'No, sir, none at all.' And Challis explained about the man with whom Heather had had an affair not recognizing her; this was also the case with several other people who frequented the Talavera who, she said, knew her well.

'If this guy's going to show at all, Tom, I reckon tonight or tomorrow. Fridays and Saturdays are the days when people unwind. If we draw a blank, come and see me on Monday morning and we'll have to rethink the plan. I thought it was too good to hope that something like this could solve the case. We've got plenty of scientific evidence to convict the murderer. All we've got to do is find the bloody man.'

Challis collected Heather Douglas at five minutes past six on Friday evening. The temperature had cooled slightly, and to Challis's relief she was more soberly attired in a pair of designer jeans and a Breton sweater.

'How much longer are we going to keep this up, Tom?' she asked once they were seated with a glass of wine at one of the 'ledges' that dominated the large room.

'Mr Brock's going to review the situation on Monday

morning,' said Tom. 'If your guy hasn't turned up by then, we'll
have to come up with a different plan.'

'I don't think you'll have to do that, Tom, darling,' said
Heather, laying a hand on Challis's arm. 'He's just come in.'

Challis shot a quick glance in the direction that Heather
was looking. 'The guy in khaki chinos and a red and white
check shirt?'

'That's him.'

'Are you certain?'

'When you've spent nearly an hour in a car with a guy
asking you intimate questions about your underwear, and trying
to work out how to escape, you remember what he looks like.'

'All right, all right,' said Challis impatiently. 'I don't need
a lecture. You're absolutely certain he's the guy?'

'I'm absolutely certain he's the guy,' repeated Heather
slowly.

'Don't look at him again, Heather. I want you to walk out
of here naturally. Just outside there's a green van. It's one of
our nondescript observation vans. As soon as the guy inside
sees you approaching, he'll open the back door. Get in as
quickly as you can. He'll tell you what to do next.'

Heather sauntered across the room and paused briefly at the
door to wave to Challis. Challis swore under his breath.

Outside, Dave Poole, who was one of the detectives in the
van, almost dragged her inside. 'This is Detective Inspector
Naylor, Heather,' he said, indicating the other man in the vehicle.

'Hi! I'm Brad Naylor, Heather. I want you to keep a careful
watch out of the window of this van. You'll be able to see
him, but he can't see you. It's one-way glass.' The DI told her
to pay close attention and didn't tell her that Challis would
call him on his mobile once the suspect started to move.

Half an hour later, the man in the khaki chinos and the red
and white check shirt emerged from the Talavera. Naylor
received a call from Challis seconds later.

Naylor broadcast the man's description to the detectives
positioned in the street nearby. 'And don't bloody well lose
him,' he added.

'We won't lose him, Brad,' said Kate Ebdon. 'I know him.'

SEVENTEEN

I received the call from Dave Poole just as the surveillance team began to follow the suspect. I could hardly believe that the man Heather Douglas had identified was the murderer of four women. Nevertheless, I told Dave to arrange for one of Linda Mitchell's scenes-of-crime officers to join us. If we found the few strands of hair that Heather Douglas claimed to have put down the back of the front passenger seat of her abductor's car, I didn't want any foul-ups that might prejudice the trial. And if this guy did turn out to be the killer, everything had to be lawyer-proof from the word go.

I agreed to meet my team near the suspect's house and rang for a car to get me to Richmond as quickly as possible. DI Naylor and Dave Poole were waiting at the end of the road when I arrived.

Just getting out of a van I recognized as an evidence recovery vehicle was a guy I'd seen before. 'Hello, Mr Brock,' he said. 'We met a few years ago.'

'I thought I recognized you,' I said. 'Remind me.'

'Trevor King. I'm one of Linda Mitchell's guys. I helped your chaps dig up a garage floor belonging to a man who'd murdered his wife.'

'Oh, yes, I do remember that,' I said, but it was the nasal intonation that fixed him in my mind. I turned next to Naylor. 'What's the SP, Brad?'

'We've got the suspect holed up inside, guv,' said Naylor, looking rather pleased with himself.

'And he's no idea that he was followed here?'

'No, sir,' put in Dave Poole, contriving to look hurt at the insinuation that things hadn't gone according to plan.

'And you've got the search warrant?'

'Yes, sir.' Dave was calling me 'sir' again, as he always does when he thinks I've made a stupid comment or asked an unnecessary question, but I had to be sure.

'Where's Heather Douglas?'

'Tom Challis has taken her home, guv,' said Naylor.

'Right, then, let's do it.' I walked up the path and rang the bell by the front door.

'Yes?' But before the man could say anything more, Brad Naylor and Dave Poole had pushed past him uninvited, and were now standing behind him ready to seize his arms if he suddenly decided to cut up rough. 'Heh, what the hell's going on?' he demanded, somewhat alarmed at this incursion. He knew by now that we were the police, having recognized Dave from his previous encounter with him and Kate Ebdon at Richmond police station. He was tall and well built, testifying to hours spent in a gym. His muscular physique suggested that he was also sickeningly good at tennis and could handle a cricket bat with panache.

'Max Roper, I have a warrant to search these premises.'

At that point, a woman appeared behind him. 'What on earth is happening, darling?' She turned to Dave Poole. 'I know you, don't I?' she said accusingly.

'Good evening, Miss Preston,' Dave said. 'Or is it Mrs Roper now?'

Sophie Preston ignored him and tossed her head. It was a rather amateurish gesture.

'Where's your car, Mr Roper?' I asked.

'In the garage. Isn't that where you usually keep a car?' Roper's reply was almost dripping with sarcasm, but I'd seen this sort of behaviour before, and to me it often indicated guilty knowledge, a cover for nervousness bordering on panic. And he'd have been even more nervous if he'd known what we were looking for.

'Lead the way, then.' We left Sophie Preston in the living room.

'I really don't know what you hope to find,' said Roper, almost sneering. Apparently still confident of the outcome of a search of the garage, he did as he was asked.

'Come with me, Inspector,' I said to Kate, 'and bring Trevor.'

Kate, Trevor and I followed Roper along the hall and through the connecting door to the garage.

'There it is, but I don't know what you hope to find,'

said Roper yet again, but this time there was a hint of nervousness.

'We'll let you know when we've found it,' said Kate, and held out a hand. 'Key, please.'

It was obvious that Roper was under the impression that we wouldn't find anything in his car that would connect him to any crime, and he handed over the key to a black BMW without further comment.

Kate released the locks and turned to the forensic practitioner. 'See what you can find down the back of the front passenger seat, Trevor.'

Roper appeared surprised at this request, but Trevor King just nodded; Dave had briefed him beforehand.

Donning a pair of protective gloves, Trevor pushed his hand down the crack between the cushion and the back of the seat. Seconds later he produced a few strands of long brown hair, placed them carefully in an evidence bag and labelled it.

'Complete with follicles, Mr Brock,' said Trevor, a triumphantly broad smile on his face. 'That should be enough.'

Max Roper's expression was a mixture of concern and perplexity, but once again he resorted to irony. 'Is this some sort of conjuring trick?' he asked. 'The reverse of planting evidence, which is what you guys usually do.'

'No, Mr Roper,' said Kate. 'If the DNA matches, that hair will belong to the young woman who was abducted on the nineteenth of June, a week ago last Wednesday.'

'Balls!' exclaimed Roper, and gave a nervous laugh. 'That hair will be Sophie's.'

'The lab will soon tell us,' said Trevor King mildly, his nasal delivery making him sound for all the world like a downtrodden Dickensian clerk. 'I'll need to take a DNA sample from this gentleman's fiancée for elimination purposes, Mr Brock.'

'Of course,' I said.

'And then there are these,' said Kate, emerging from the car. In her gloved hand she held a number of bras.

'Now that's what I call interesting,' I said lightly, in a desperate attempt to keep my voice level and not to display any jubilation. 'How many have you got, Kate?'

'Four, sir.'

'Bag each one separately, please, Miss Ebdon,' said Trevor King, 'although they may have been cross-contaminated already.'

'What on earth is a collection of bras doing in your glove compartment, Mr Roper?' I enquired, and chuckled, as though sharing a man's joke with him.

'It was back when we were driving through Spain this year, Chief Inspector.' Roper laughed too. 'When Sophie got too hot, her bra always finished up in the glove compartment.'

A likely story, I thought. From what I recall of the four dead women, the bras were likely to be different sizes anyway, and Kate Ebdon confirmed it.

'I checked the sizes as I bagged them,' she said. 'They were thirty-four B, thirty-four C, thirty-six B and thirty-two D.'

We all returned to the sitting room.

'We found this in a sort of storeroom, guv'nor,' said Brad Naylor, holding up a sports bag. 'It has a label bearing the name of Heather Douglas and the young lady's address. Inside is a good quality Speedo swimsuit and a pair of Ted Baker trainers that must be worth at least a hundred notes.'

This damning evidence, coupled with the fact that we'd found the lengths of hair in exactly the place where Heather Douglas said she'd put them, was good enough for me to detain Roper, at least for the abduction. Murder charges would have to await the results of scientific examination and comparison.

'Max Roper,' I said, 'I am arresting you on suspicion of kidnapping Heather Douglas on or about Wednesday the nineteenth of June this year. You are not obliged to say anything, but it may harm your defence if you do not mention now something you later rely on in court. Anything you do say will be given in evidence.'

'I've never heard of anyone called Heather Douglas,' said Roper airily. 'I haven't a clue what you're talking about.'

Dave slowly repeated what Roper had said and wrote it in his pocketbook.

'I suppose she was going to be another of your trophies, was she, Max?' said Sophie Preston mildly.

'Oh, shut up, you stupid cow,' snapped Roper, now clearly worried.

Sophie Preston leaped from her chair like an avenging tigress, her face distorted with anger, and for a moment I thought she was going to strike her fiancé. 'I've forgiven you once too often, Max,' she said, standing very close to him. 'From now on you're on your own. What's more, I'm not coming back, and this time I mean it.' Once again, she tore off her engagement ring and threw it at Roper. 'I'm going upstairs to pack.'

'Not yet, Miss Preston. Inspector Ebdon has a question to ask you.'

Kate held up the four transparent bags containing the bras that she had found in the glove compartment of Sophie's fiancé's car. 'Mr Roper stated that when you and he were motoring through Spain earlier this year, Miss Preston, you sometimes got so hot that you'd take off your bra and leave it in the glove compartment. Do you agree with that?'

'No, I don't. And we've not been to Spain. At least I haven't. Ever!' Sophie Preston burst out laughing. 'Apart from which, I don't wear a bra,' she said. 'I don't have to.' And then she added the final condemnation. 'Anyway, I prefer to use my own car. I've never been in Max's car because he's such a bloody awful driver.'

'Miss Preston, would you make a statement to the effect that you've not been to Spain in Mr Roper's car and, further-more, that you have never travelled in it at any time?' I asked. 'And that therefore you have never left a bra in the glove compartment?'

'Of course.'

'It won't be of any use,' snarled Roper. 'She's my fiancée and she can't give evidence against me. It's the law.'

Oh, I do love amateur lawyers. 'Only if you were married, Mr Roper, and not always then,' I said. 'But certainly not if you're only engaged.'

'Supposing we were to get married before the trial?' enquired Roper hopefully and glanced at Sophie. But his sudden self-serving volte-face left his erstwhile fiancée unimpressed.

'Huh!' snorted Sophie. 'In your dreams, Max.'

'I think Miss Preston's answered your question,' said Dave

mildly. 'In any case, you'll probably be remanded in custody, so you won't have much opportunity to get married. Even less to enjoy a honeymoon.'

'You said just now that you were going to pack, Miss Preston,' I said. 'Where were you thinking of going?'

Sophie Preston paused for quite a few seconds before replying, but eventually she said, 'Tony Miles told me that there's always a bed at his place should I need it.'

'And presumably he'll be in it, waiting.' Roper gave a cynical laugh that was almost a snarl. 'And it won't be the first time, will it, you slut?'

With a commendable show of restraint, Sophie Preston completely ignored Max's bitter comment and turned to me. 'I'll go upstairs and pack now, if you've finished with me, Mr Brock.'

'Before you go, Miss Preston, Inspector Ebdon will take a DNA sample, and the statement from you about the underwear found in Mr Roper's car and the other things you mentioned just now, and then you're free to do whatever you want.' I knew that when a couple broke up, even when her relationship with Roper was as volatile as it seemed to have been, a change of mind at a later stage could not be ruled out. Love is a strange phenomenon, and I'd seen it happen on more than one occasion when a careless detective had rushed an investigation only to finish up with egg on his face. The last thing we needed at the Old Bailey was for Sophie Preston to deny that she had disclaimed ownership of the four bras. To have her immediate reaction to the contrary, and to have it in writing, would guard against any change of heart. The fact that each of the four bras was a different size would give the prosecuting counsel something with which to amuse the jury. I didn't think Sophie Preston would risk it, but it's always safer to make sure. 'But I'd be grateful if you'd keep us informed of your whereabouts. You may be called to give evidence at Mr Roper's trial.'

'I wouldn't miss it for all the tea in China,' said Sophie maliciously.

At the police station in London Road, Twickenham, I charged Roper with abducting Heather Douglas and the theft of her sports bag. That would do for a start, but I explained to the custody sergeant that Roper was also strongly suspected of the murder of four women and might interfere with witnesses. I therefore required the prisoner to be kept in custody until his appearance at court the following morning.

It was close to midnight by the time Dave and I returned to Belgravia. Brad Naylor had remained at Richmond, overseeing a thorough search of Roper's house for any further evidence.

I dictated an urgent email for Linda Mitchell, explaining that Max Roper was in custody charged with abduction and theft. The important job, as far as Linda was concerned, was to start connecting Roper with the scientific evidence that had been recovered from the scenes of the four murders.

One of the few advantages of having the Crown Prosecution Service, and there aren't many, was the advice, albeit extremely cautious and cost-driven, they would give about what charges to prefer and when to prefer them. The last thing we needed was a soft district judge who would release our man on bail. We could offer all manner of objections – flight risk, interference with witnesses, creating false alibis – but it would be the district judge who made the decision. And some have been known to make wrong decisions.

Fortunately, our CPS adviser was prepared to offer advice late on a Friday evening without complaining. Wonders will never cease. This splendid lawyer – and I don't often say that of lawyers – advised me not to charge Roper with the four murders yet, but that he would seek a remand in police custody in order that we could question him about them. He also suggested that Roper should be transferred to a central London police station and taken before the district judge at Westminster Magistrates Court.

And that is exactly what happened. The central London police station we asked for and got was Belgravia. Very handy, being just downstairs from our offices.

On Saturday morning, our CPS man made a successful application to the district judge to remand Roper into police custody in order that he might be questioned about serious matters unconnected with the charge before the court.

*   *   *

We now had a maximum of three days, after which we must either charge our suspect with murder or release him to a remand prison, providing, of course, that the district judge didn't release him on bail. Immediately on our return from court, and with Dave Poole beside me, I began to question Roper about the murders of Rachel Steele, Lisa Hastings, Denise Barton and the young Dutch woman, Danique Vandenberg.

When we mentioned that three of the four victims had been prostitutes, he said that he'd never paid for sex in his life. To have found three prostitutes who didn't charge for their services was unbelievable, but he dismissed the allegations with a cynical laugh and maintained his denial until we broke for a midday meal. It was then that we had a stroke of luck.

I'd returned to the incident room just as Colin Wilberforce put down the phone.

'Sir, Miss Sophie Preston is downstairs and wishes to speak to you. She said that she has information that may be of assistance.'

As Dave and I entered the interview room, Sophie Preston handed me a photograph. 'Her name's Margaret Hall.' There was no preamble, no explanation, at least not yet. Just a name and a photograph of a slender young woman, probably under thirty years of age, with long brown hair. 'Remind you of anyone?' she asked.

She did remind me of someone. She reminded me of the woman seated in front of me but also, more ominously, of the four murder victims.

'I suppose she looks a bit like you,' I said cautiously, not wishing to commit myself any farther. 'Who is she?'

'As I said, her name's Margaret Hall, known as Maggie, and she was Max's girlfriend. In fact, she was more than that. They were engaged, but come the day of the wedding, Maggie didn't turn up at the registry office.'

'How do you know all this, Miss Preston?' asked Dave.

'Maggie's brother-in-law told me. He said that if I was going to marry Max, I ought to know.' Sophie laughed, but it was more cynical than humorous. 'I don't know whether it was malicious or friendly. But he said that he thought I ought to know,' she said again. 'It seems that Maggie worked in London as a computer operator in a bank, but when she wasn't on duty – she worked shifts apparently – she would go home to Berkhamsted in Hertfordshire and spend the nights in the bed of a man she'd been having an affair with for ages. Her brother-in-law described her as a two-timing bitch.'

'I don't see how this helps me, Miss Preston,' I said.

'I'm coming to that. The next her sister heard of her was a letter from Australia, in which she said that she'd emigrated there the day before her wedding was due to take place. And she also admitted going there with the guy she slept with whenever she went home to Berkhamsted. She said something about the two of them making a new life "down under".'

'This is all very interesting, but—'

'I haven't finished yet,' said Sophie, somewhat tersely. 'According to Mike—'

'Who is Mike?' asked Dave, as he struggled to keep his notetaking up to date.

'Maggie's brother-in-law,' said Sophie, with a sigh of exasperation. 'He's Maggie's sister's husband,' she continued, as though explaining it all to a couple of dimbos. 'According to Mike, Maggie never wore a bra, and one of the first questions that Max asked me when we first met, eight weeks ago, was whether I wore one. When I said I didn't, he immediately started taking me out for expensive dinners and even treated me to a luxury weekend in Paris. His obsession with bras was almost frightening. It was as if he was paranoid about it, and Mike reckoned that Maggie running off like that affected Max's mind, because he never seemed the same after that.'

'Do you know the date of this wedding when Max was supposed to marry Maggie?'

'Not exactly, but I think it was a matter of a week or so before Max and I met.'

'You say that you met Max Roper about eight weeks ago, Miss Preston. So you became engaged almost immediately.'

'You could say he swept me off my feet,' said Sophie, 'but then I found out that he was a womanizer who didn't care how much he embarrassed me, even in public. That video of him all over that woman in the Talavera—' She suddenly stopped. 'Oh, God!' she exclaimed. And I could see that she was, at last, putting two and two together. Then she recovered. 'I broke off the engagement three times altogether, apart from when he was arrested, but each time, like a fool, I went back to him. He was so contrite, but it didn't last long.'

I wasn't sure whether Sophie Preston was being vindictive or whether she had belatedly believed she could help Roper out of his present trouble. The four murders had found their way first into the more lurid newspapers, and were picked up later by the respectable organs of the national press. Sophie hadn't been told that we suspected Roper of those killings, although she must've guessed; she seemed bright enough to have worked it out, especially when she thought back to the video of Roper with Rachel Steele. However, no mention had been made in the media of the fact that, in each case, the murderer had removed his victim's bra.

'I require you to make a statement encompassing what you have just told us, Miss Preston.'

'Willingly,' said Sophie.

'And we'd like the full name and address of Maggie Hall's brother-in-law. We'll need to take a statement from him.'

'I'm not sure he'd want to appear in court,' said Sophie.

'He won't have an option,' said Dave, 'once a subpoena is issued.'

EIGHTEEN

We started again at just after two o'clock. Max Roper maintained his disdainful attitude, presumably believing that he could talk his way out of whatever accusations were put to him by two thick coppers. After all, he was a manager in human resources, and he could see right through the lame excuses employees came up with for covering absence or wanting time off. Oh, yes, the old 'sick mother-in-law in Cornwall' excuse to cover a holiday on the Costa Brava or wherever. He could write a book about the stupidity of the human race, and it would take more than this pair opposite him to get a confession out of him.

What Roper didn't know, however, was that Dave and I had discussed our afternoon strategy over lunch.

'Where were you during the evening of Monday the tenth of June?' I asked, kicking off the renewed interview with a question I'd asked before lunch. This was not forgetfulness on my part, but a technique to discover whether the answer was the same as Roper had given previously. It's really quite surprising how many guilty people trip up over a question as simple as that.

'I've already told you. I was with my fiancée.' Roper examined his fingernails, as though he was finding the entire conversation insufferably boring.

'But you told Detective Inspector Ebdon and me,' said Dave, 'that you'd had a row with your fiancée, that you'd gone to your local pub and, to use your exact words, "got pissed". So, which was it?'

'I can't remember. You're confusing me.'

'And what were you doing during the evening of Wednesday, the twelfth of June?' I asked. Kate and Dave had interviewed Roper at Richmond police station that evening, but the interview had ended at eight thirty. He would, therefore, have had adequate time to commit the murder of Lisa Hastings, whose body was found on Ham Common, a mere three miles from Richmond police station.

'The same.'

'What exactly *were* you doing that evening, then?'

'I stayed in and watched TV with Sophie.'

Dave made a big thing of thumbing back through the book in which he'd recorded details of their conversation. 'That was the evening you were interviewed by DI Ebdon and me at Richmond police station. After you'd crawled about in the gutter to find the engagement ring that Sophie had thrown at you.'

'Oh, yes,' said Roper lamely. 'I'd forgotten. I must've been confusing that with another evening.'

'You seem to be confused about all sorts of things, Mr Roper,' commented Dave drily.

'How well did you know Lisa Hastings?' I asked.

'Who?'

'She was the girl whom I suggest you murdered on the evening of the twelfth of June.' Dave pointed a menacing pencil at Roper.

'How could I have done? I was being given the third degree by you at Richmond nick,' sneered Roper, staring at Dave. 'And the woman policeman who was with you.'

I glanced at Dave and nodded. It was time to spring the surprise.

Dave took a copy of the photograph of Maggie Hall that Sophie Preston had given us and dropped it casually on the table between him and Roper.

'For the benefit of the recording, I am showing Max Roper a photograph of his former fiancée, Margaret Hall, also known as Maggie Hall.'

Roper shot forward, his face white. 'Where the hell did you get that from?' he demanded. His face was working and he looked like a man on the verge of losing his reason.

Dave parried question with question. 'Did Maggie wear a bra, Roper?'

'What in God's name has that got to do with anything?'

'Please answer the question,' said Dave mildly.

It seemed that Dave's refusal to be riled by Roper's outburst and his constant sneering condescension disconcerted him more than if Dave had banged the table or even leaned across and shouted in his face. But Dave was a good interrogator and knew that to bully a suspect would finish up with him telling his inquisitor what he *thought* he wanted to hear, rather than telling the truth.

'Frankly, I don't see that questions about her underwear—' began Roper.

'Maggie Hall *didn't* wear a bra, did she, Mr Roper? And whenever she had a day off from the bank she spent it in the bed of a virile multiple-times-a-night stud in Berkhamsted, but I suppose even you couldn't compete with that sort of stamina.' Dave's tone of voice was one of curiosity coupled with a little banter, rather than one seeking a confession to four murders. 'And that's why you took the bra from each of the women you'd murdered, each one of whom was very similar in appearance to that woman.' Dave gestured at the photograph on the table between them. 'It was a strange way of exacting revenge on Maggie just because she'd stood you up at the registry office and preferred another man's bed to yours, but understandable in the circumstances. It must really have hurt your pride, standing there looking like a complete prat with a stupid grin on your face and a carnation stuck in your buttonhole but no bride. I'll bet all the guests who couldn't wait to get their lips around a free glass of champagne were sniggering behind their hands. Especially the girls, eh? "Oh dear, poor old Max. What a loser." Can't you just hear them saying it? And then down the pub that night, they'd be laughing like drains at you in bed all by yourself.' Dave shook his head. 'But *she* wasn't alone in bed that same night, was she? She had her Hertfordshire stallion in bed with her in Australia.'

Suddenly Roper snapped. 'Yes, damn you,' he yelled. 'Of course I killed those bitches. They're all the same, trying to get as much as they can out of a man and giving nothing back. That'll give those sniggering bastards something to think about. It'll put a stop to their snide remarks on social media about me being stood up.'

And that simple statement put an end to any further

questions. That was the law. Unless, of course, there was any ambiguity or danger to others in his statement, in which case I was permitted to ask questions about anything I thought needed clarification. But what Roper had said was incapable of misinterpretation.

'Max Roper,' I said, 'I'm charging you with the murders of Rachel Steele, Lisa Hastings, Denise Barton and Danique Vandenberg on divers dates between the tenth of June and the eighteenth of June this year.' I followed this up with the usual caution. 'Detective Sergeant Poole will now take a written statement from you.' I expected Roper to refuse to put his confession into writing, as was his right, but he acquiesced.

I had time to reflect, while Dave was taking the statement, how so very often the slightest remark by an interrogating police officer will bring forth an admission of guilt. It's not easy to define, and may be something as simple as a comment that unwittingly damages an individual's ego. I'm pretty sure that Dave's jibe about Roper being laughed at by his wedding guests was enough to produce a confession. It was, I suppose, Roper's way of restoring his ego – by acquiring a reputation for having murdered four women. None of his friends was that good.

In this enlightened age, when the perpetrator of a crime seems to merit more consideration than the victim, murderers have been known to be granted bail. Fortunately, the district judge at Westminster Magistrates Court flew in the face of political correctness and on Monday morning remanded Roper in custody to appear at the Old Bailey on the following Friday, the fifth of July. The Old Bailey judge remanded Roper in custody for a month, and that gave us a bit of breathing space while we composed the lengthy report that would form the basis of brief to counsel.

'You look remarkably pleased with yourself, Harry darling,' said Lydia when I arrived on that same Monday evening.

Although Lydia Maxwell and I had known each other for almost a year, it was the first time I'd visited her house in Esher, next door to my old friends Bill and Charlotte Hunter. But now that Max Roper was in custody, charged with the four murders that had occupied my mind for nigh on three weeks, I felt that I could afford to relax. Briefly. And when Lydia had invited me to dinner at Esher, I jumped at the opportunity.

'I think we've got our murderer at last,' I said, relaxing into one of the armchairs in Lydia's large living room. The French windows were wide open, but it had no effect on reducing the humidity. If anything, it made it worse.

'You only *think* you have?' Lydia smiled and raised a quizzical eyebrow.

'I shan't be convinced until a guilty verdict is delivered,' I said. 'An English jury is a fickle creature. Taken individually, its members are usually quite rational. But when twelve members of the human race are gathered together in the name of justice, there's no telling what they might decide, even if they're intelligent enough to have understood what's been going on.'

Lydia laughed. 'There must be a word to describe a combination of philosophy and cynicism, which is what you seem to possess.'

'There is,' I said. 'It's called honesty.'

'Anyway, enough of your so-called *honesty*, darling. D'you fancy trying out my swimming pool before we have dinner?'

'I didn't bring my swimming trunks with me,' I said.

'So?' said Lydia.

The trial of Max Roper opened at the Old Bailey on Monday the twenty-ninth of July. We were now in the hands of the lawyers and the aforementioned fickle jury.

It came as no surprise that Roper should have pleaded guilty to manslaughter by reason of diminished responsibility, his counsel presumably having explained that it would improve his chances of a lesser sentence. He was duty-bound to mention that if the plea failed, Roper would be sent down for four life sentences. But I doubt that that prospect would have made any difference to Roper's mindset.

The plea regarding 'diminished responsibility' is, to say the least, confused and stacked full of case law. I don't even begin to understand it, but I don't have to. That's why we have lawyers.

As the case progressed, prosecuting and defence counsel

each called their own psychiatric expert witnesses, managing to elicit from them views about the state of Roper's mental health that suited their particular intention with regard to the hoped-for verdict.

The defence's psychiatrist's theory was that the simplest incident can push an otherwise sane man to sudden and inexplicable psychotic behaviour. He went on to develop this argument by suggesting that in this case, when a woman who Roper thought loved him reneged on their wedding at the last minute, it constituted such an incident. Particularly when he learned that the woman had been unfaithful to him for the entire period of their betrothal.

After days of esoteric argument between opposing counsel, the judge delivered a long but amazingly lucid summing up, leaving the jury in no doubt about the decisions facing them.

It took the six men and six women of the jury a total of about ten hours to reach a verdict. To my surprise, and to the obvious surprise of a few others in the courtroom, they returned a verdict of guilty of manslaughter by virtue of diminished responsibility. The jury had clearly opted to believe the argument put forward by Roper's psychiatrist.

The judge made a hospital order subject to periodic psychiatric review.

Although that statement was greeted with a maniacal laugh from Max Roper, I think he was as sane as the rest of us, but the case demonstrated just how an expert witness, spouting psychiatric gobbledegook, coupled with a silver-tongued barrister, can convince a jury that the argument they put forward is the only tenable one.

On the other hand, one could argue that a sane man was unlikely to murder four women in the space of three weeks just to take revenge on a woman who'd left his self-perceived macho image in tatters.

But the job of police officers is to put the accused person, together with the evidence, before the court. The rest is up to them.

A couple of months after the case against Roper was over, Detective Sergeant Tom Challis appeared in the incident room with Heather Douglas. Those officers who had been in on the disguise plan to catch Roper were surprised that she had kept her hair blonde. But in view of what Challis said next, it was apparent that she had done so to please him.

'I thought you all ought to know,' he announced, 'that Heather and I are getting married next week, and you're all invited to the wedding.'

This announcement was greeted by a barrage of comments which generally took the form of advice for Heather, such as suggesting she shouldn't do it. For the most part, it consisted of warnings against marrying a copper. Challis and Heather not only took the badinage in good part but seemed to enjoy it. Which just went to show that she was probably suited to take on that most difficult of roles, that of a copper's wife, full of cancelled social engagements, and the dread of opening the door one day to find a senior officer and the force chaplain on the doorstep with sombre expressions on their faces.